BEFORE YOU GO

CLARE SWATMAN

LARGE
PRINT

First published in Great Britain 2017
by
Macmillan
an imprint of Pan Macmillan

First Isis Edition
published 2017
by arrangement with
Pan Macmillan

ISBN 978–1–78541–440–4 (hb)
ISBN 978–1–78541–446–6 (pb)

Published by
F. A. Thorpe (Publishing)
Anstey, Leicestershire

Set by Words & Graphics Ltd.
Anstey, Leicestershire
Printed and bound in Great Britain by
T. J. International Ltd., Padstow, Cornwall

This book is printed on acid-free paper

For Tom, Jack and Harry

Prologue

29 June 2013

It's a hot day, the bright sunshine in stark contrast to the sombre mood. Zoe's face is pale, expressionless, as she climbs out of the black car and makes her way unsteadily towards the low brick building in front of her. Her mother Sandra hurries to catch up, and grips her daughter protectively by the elbow.

A huddle of people, their shadows shortened by the midday sun, stand to the right of the doors. Zoe can't tell who they are, as the bright light has turned them into nothing more than silhouettes, but one or two are smoking, blowing uneven puffs into the warm summer air. They watch as Zoe approaches, and one gives a tight smile in greeting. Zoe doesn't notice.

Inside, mother and daughter make their way stiffly towards the front row. Zoe's mother-in-law Susan is already there. Her eyes are red and puffy, despite the carefully applied make-up, and she manages a weak smile as they sit down next to her. Instinctively Zoe reaches out and grabs her hand and clutches it tightly on the seat between them.

Behind them they can hear the shuffles and sniffs and murmurs of the other mourners as they move to take their seats. But it's what's in front of them that holds all their attention: Ed's coffin, sitting proudly on a table at the front of the room. Zoe stares at the innocuous wooden box and finds it impossible to believe that the body of her husband, so strong, so vibrant, so alive, is actually contained in there. It's totally unreal.

It's totally unfair.

It had been hot the day he died too. Zoe had been rushing round the flat, as always, throwing things into her bag: laptop, diary, apple, mobile, Diet Coke, book, iPad.

"Put any more in that and you're going to need a packhorse to get it to work," Ed had mumbled through his toothbrush. A line of toothpaste had dribbled down his chin and plopped onto the floorboards.

She rolled her eyes.

"For God's sake, Ed," she said, feeling her temper rising. She'd known she was overreacting, that he was only trying to lighten the mood, but she couldn't help herself. She stomped into the bathroom, unrolled a length of toilet paper and bent down to mop the dribbled toothpaste off the floor. As she rubbed, her nail caught on a floorboard and ripped.

"Fuck's sake," she muttered, feeling the anger rise in her throat like bile. She stood up and stomped back into the bathroom, yanked the bathroom cabinet open and rummaged around for the nail scissors. She was late, Ed was pissing her off, and she just needed to get

2

out of the flat. Scissors located, she clipped the hanging nail, threw them back in the cabinet and slammed the door.

Marching out of the bathroom, she could see Ed skulking in the living room trying to stay out of her way. She couldn't blame him. She was always angry these days, an unexplained rage that bubbled beneath the surface, ready to explode at any moment. But knowing it was there didn't mean she could keep it in; it was the hormones, she knew. Always the bloody hormones.

She yanked the cupboard door open and reached for her sandals. As she stuck her head into the wardrobe she heard Ed's muffled voice saying something from the other room.

"What?" she snapped, tilting her head to hear him better. He appeared at the door, clipping his cycling helmet to his head.

"I'm going to work. See you later."

"Bye." Brief, curt. She wasn't in the mood for a conversation, and Ed knew it. He turned and left. Seconds later the door slammed and she heard rattling as he unlocked his bike then pedalled away. Her heart did a little flip of regret but she ignored it and turned back to the wardrobe.

And that was the last time she'd seen him alive.

It wasn't until later that she'd heard the news. She'd been in a meeting all morning, and when she came out, her boss Olive was waiting at her desk, her face ashen.

"Olive? Is everything OK?" Zoe said.

Olive said nothing for a few seconds, and Zoe started to feel worried. Had she made a mistake with something? Was she in serious trouble?

"Come with me," Olive said. Her voice was gentle and soothing rather than harsh and angry, which made Zoe even more confused. They walked back into the meeting room Zoe had just left and Olive closed the door behind her.

"Sit down," she said, gesturing to the chair next to her, taking one herself. "Please."

Zoe pulled the chair out and perched on the edge of it nervously. Her hands had started to shake.

"Zoe, I don't know how to tell you this," Olive said, without preamble. "There's been an accident. It's Ed. He was hit by a bus."

She stopped and Zoe held her breath, wanting Olive to say the next words quickly, to get them over with; yet not wanting to hear them, not really, not out loud.

A gentle knock on the door broke the terrible silence and Zoe almost jumped out of her seat. Olive rushed to open it. Zoe turned too, and as she did, her world fell apart.

Two police officers stood in the doorway. They were asking for her.

A strangled sob escaped her mouth instead of words. She tried to stand up but her legs wouldn't support her and she fell back onto the chair. Her hands shook and as the female police officer came into the room Zoe looked up at Olive, her eyes begging her to tell her there had been a terrible, awful mistake. But Olive couldn't meet her gaze.

Zoe stared at the police officer's shoes. They were polished to such a shine that the glare from the strip lights overhead was reflected back brightly from their toes. She thought about this woman getting ready for work that morning, standing in her kitchen, buffing her shoes to a shine, thinking about the day ahead. Had she imagined that later that day she'd have to tell someone their husband had died?

She continued to say nothing, gazing at the floor.

"Zoe?" a voice said.

She looked up. Three faces were looking at her, waiting for her to say something.

"I . . . I . . ." The words wouldn't come out. "Where is he?" she finally croaked.

Relieved finally to have something to say, the male police officer stepped forward a foot. "He was taken to the Royal Free," he said. "I'm so sorry, but he . . . there was nothing the doctors could do." He paused. "We can take you there if you like?"

Numb, Zoe nodded and stood up. Olive raced towards her, eager to have something useful to do.

"Let's go and get your stuff, love," she said, taking Zoe by the elbow and steering her to the door.

At her desk Zoe bent to pick her bag off the floor, scooped her cardigan from the back of her chair, and scanned the desk to make sure she'd left nothing behind.

Then she and Olive followed the officers as they led her out of the office and Olive helped her into the waiting police car. The street was oddly quiet. In the back of her mind she knew she had to let people know what was happening, so as the car rumbled quietly towards the hospital she'd tapped in a familiar number. Jane first. Her best friend.

"Hey," she said, picking up after the first ring. Her voice was light and bright, and it sounded so incongruous Zoe gasped.

"Zo, what's wrong?"

"Ed . . ." Her voice cracked and she struggled to get the words out. "It's Ed. He's . . . there's been an accident and . . ." She couldn't finish. She couldn't say the word. She didn't need to.

"Fuck, Zo, where are you? I'm coming."

"Royal Free." Her voice was barely more than a whisper.

"I'm on my way."

As she ended the call they pulled up outside the hospital. No time to ring anyone else. The sun was low behind the brown brick building, giving it a strangely Gothic feel silhouetted against the bright sky. She climbed out of the car. Her legs shook and she stumbled and the female police officer — she wished she could remember her name — took her elbow to steady her. They walked together towards the doors and as they closed behind her Zoe felt as though she was being swallowed into hell.

She was led to a bank of chairs in a small room tucked away in the depths of the hospital. As she waited she stared blindly at the posters on the wall for bereavement counselling and depression, reading the words but not taking them in. The effort of keeping her mind empty was taking all the strength she had. Then she heard a familiar voice and looked up and there was Jane, who ran towards her across the tiny room and then their arms were wrapped tightly round each other and Zoe was sobbing: huge, jerking, body-wracking sobs that felt as though they were going to break her in two.

"He — he's dead," she gulped through thick, snotty tears.

"Oh Zoe, Zoe, Zoe," Jane said as she held her dearest friend and rubbed her back firmly. They stayed like that until Zoe's sobs subsided, then they sat, holding hands.

"I was so horrible to him this morning," Zoe said as her breath began to even out. "He couldn't even look at me. He hated me, Jane."

"Zoe, Ed would never have hated you. He adored you, and he knew you loved him. Please don't think like that."

"But I was so angry with him and he hadn't done anything wrong. I didn't even say goodbye and now he's gone and I can never tell him how much I love him. It's too late. What the hell am I going to do?"

Before Jane could answer, the doctor was there and they were being led to where Ed was, to identify his body. Zoe listened in a daze as doctors explained Ed had been hit by a bus, that he'd stood no chance, that he'd been dead on arrival at hospital. The words "massive brain trauma" and "nothing we could do" drifted in and out of her head but she couldn't bear to think of Ed in pain, hurting. All she could think was why. Why did she let him leave the house without telling him she loved him? If she'd delayed his departure even a few moments by giving him a hug, he'd be alive now, and they could sort things out; she was sure they could. If she'd driven him to work instead of letting him cycle — she hated him cycling, she was always terrified he was going to get knocked off and hurt . . .

But now it was too late. Ed was dead.

Oh my God, Ed was dead.

Numbly, she was led to Ed's bedside. Despite his injuries — they'd cleaned him up as best they could but there were still traces of blood on his face and down his chest — it was her Ed lying there, and the urge to reach out and touch him, hold him and tell him everything would be OK, was overwhelming. But she knew she couldn't. Instead she turned and walked away, Jane holding her up by the shoulders.

The next few hours were a blur. She remembers people bringing her tea, giving her comforting hugs, the whoosh and whir of trolleys passing by the relatives' room where she sat waiting. Then Ed's mum Susan had arrived and the two women had held each other, united by a grief that threatened to overwhelm them both.

And now here they are again. It's only ten days later, and it still hurts so much Zoe can barely believe she's still breathing.

A sob wracks through her chest and escapes her mouth and she clamps her hand over it, tries to compose herself. Her mum squeezes her other hand more tightly.

And then the ceremony starts.

8

Zoe sits dry-eyed as the celebrant begins, speaking soft, gentle words about her husband.

And then it's Zoe's turn. She's not sure she can go through with it, but she's promised Susan, and, as she steps onto the podium holding the half-screwed up piece of paper in her hand and looks out at the sea of faces, all these people who loved Ed, who love her, she knows she has to say something. She steps up to the microphone.

"I'd written some words down here that I wanted to say but now I'm not sure they're quite right." Her voice cracks slightly and Sandra moves to comfort her but Zoe gives a tiny shake of her head and takes a deep, shuddery breath. "For the last fifteen years Ed has been my world. He's meant everything to me and the truth is, the thought of carrying on in a world without him feels like walking across a vast, open desert with no sign of water. It feels like a half-life already, and he's only just gone. And I know everyone says that time heals, but I don't think I want it to. I don't want the memory of him, of what we had together, to fade. I want to hold it in my mind forever, to keep me going through the dark days I know are going to come."

She pauses, looks down at her hands clasped tightly on the podium in front of her, her knuckles white.

"I'll always wish there were things I'd said and things I hadn't, and I'll always wish I could have a chance to change some of the things I did on the day he died and in the months and years before that. But I can't and so instead I'll try to carry the happy times with me, and try to forget the bad —"

She stops again, looks up and catches Jane's eye. Her friend's face is pale, drawn, a faded version of her usual self.

"I hope you can all do the same. Remember Ed with love. I'm glad you're all here. I'm not sure I could do it without you. Thank you —" And then her voice breaks, the tears start and she hurries back to her seat and to her mother's arms.

The celebrant carries on but Zoe can hardly take the words in. Then it's the end of the ceremony, and as the curtain is drawn round the coffin, Ed's favourite song, "Under My Thumb" by the Rolling Stones, starts up. "No!" Zoe cries out, then turns her head away, buries her face in her hands and lets the tears flow freely. And when she looks up again, Ed is gone.

16 August 2013

Standing by the window, Zoe rubs her head and watches the rain run in rivers down the grimy glass, dragging her mood down with it. The pummelling of the rain on the window sounds like a distant drumbeat mirroring the hammering of her heart, and she can't tell where the raindrops end and where her tears begin.

Outside she sees the blurry garden; it's been less than two months but she's already let it get overgrown, out of control. The roses in their pot sag under their own weight; dozens of weeds and several thistles stand proud in a small patch of soil; the decking is slick with moss and rain. She closes her eyes briefly and sees Ed hunched over, carefully planting, pruning, weeding. This tiny patch of garden was his pride and joy; it was one of the reasons they bought the flat in the first place. She should be looking after it properly but she hasn't been able to go out there yet, even the thought of seeing it without Ed pressing heavily on her heart.

She shoves her hand deep into the pocket of her cardigan and feels the foil packet there. She glances at her watch. It's only been two hours since she took the last one and they make her feel a bit wobbly. But she really needs it. It's an antidepressant; she's depressed. It's a no-brainer. She pops it into her mouth quickly and swallows it down dry, making her gag.

Turning away from the window, she walks into the kitchen and unlocks the back door. The key won't cooperate and she fumbles a little. Then finally it turns with a click and she yanks the door towards her and steps outside. The rain's so heavy her hair is almost immediately plastered to her face, but she hardly notices. She crunches across the gravel and steps up onto the decking; she leans forward and yanks a thistle out, oblivious to the prickles piercing her skin. She throws it onto the floor angrily then turns and pulls up another, does the same. The anger is raging through her now and she pulls out weed after weed, not seeing what she's doing. Plants go flying, petals are ripped from flowers; she is taking out her rage on the place that Ed loved the most. It's not making her feel any better, but she can't seem to stop.

The rain continues to pummel her head, making her clothes cling to her cool skin, but she's not cold: she feels nothing. Finally, when there's nothing left to pull up, she turns and steps over the pile of damp, soggy leaves she's created, water dripping from her eyebrows, her lips, her cheeks. She places her foot on the decking and makes a move to go back inside, but her foot slips out from under her, not making proper contact with the wet, slippery ground, and kicks out in front of her instead. She loses her balance and her body tips backwards as though in slow motion; her arms windmill, trying to grasp for something, anything, to stop her falling. But there's nothing but air and she feels her stomach leap into her throat as she falls backwards onto the wet ground. She thinks she screams but she can't be sure as her head smashes into a ceramic pot, bounces up and falls back to hit the ground with a sickening thud. The pain is intense, but over quickly as she loses consciousness and everything goes black.

CHAPTER
ONE

18 September 1993

From the moment I wake up, my eyes still firmly closed, I know something has changed. While my mind struggles to pin down what it might be, a crazy thought flits through it: maybe this has all been a terrible nightmare, and Ed isn't dead after all. Then I remember all over again and my stomach contracts, my muscles tighten and I feel as though the delicate string keeping me tethered to the earth, to my life, is in danger of breaking forever.

So what, then, is so different about today?

I can tell even with my eyes still closed that the room is flooded with light, which is odd for a start. I like my room dark. Could I just have forgotten to shut my blackout blinds last night? Maybe. But it definitely feels like more than that.

And then something drifts into my mind. It's not clear, but there's a vague memory there, lurking in the shadows trying to elude me. I was in the garden. It was raining and I was pulling up weeds, wildly; I remember that. But then I can't remember much else. There's just a blank space dotted with the occasional clear image: falling, a pain in my head, roses, Jane's face, bright strip lights ... and then nothing.

Could I be in hospital? Perhaps that's it. I fell, hit my head and now I'm here, in a hospital bed, safe.

It makes sense, but somehow I don't think that's what's so different about today either.

I keep my eyes shut a minute longer and listen carefully to the sounds around me. I can hear a radiator banging as though the heating has just come on. I can make out the distant rumble of a radio and noises like someone clattering around in a kitchen, the hum of an electric shower, someone whistling. It's familiar, and yet not quite, and it certainly doesn't sound like a hospital.

Finally, I try to open my eyes and a blurry world slowly swims into focus. I can make out a white ceiling, covered with the same swirls and semicircles as the ceiling in my childhood bedroom. Odd, I haven't seen that pattern for years. There's even a small pink mark just the same as the one I made on my bedroom ceiling at home when I'd thrown a lipstick at my sister and missed. I shake my head, confused by the memory. The grey lampshade hanging from the middle is familiar too, tugging at my mind like a child pulling at my coat, desperate for my attention, desperate for the memory to fall into place.

I flick my eyes to the right. There's a chest of drawers there, pine, with stickers covering it and a mirror on top, surrounded by bulbs. It's empty of toiletries, but it's still so familiar.

I sit bolt upright in bed, my heart pounding. I can hardly catch my breath.

I'm scared to look round any more, but I have to. Twisting my head I see the pine wardrobe that I knew I'd see, one door open, a row of empty coat hangers inside. In front of it sits a black suitcase, and a cardboard box with *Zoe's stuff!* scrawled on it in black marker pen, and a smiley face sticking out its tongue. On top of that is a wine box with *Threshers* printed on it, stuck down with white tape with the word *Warning* repeating all the way along it in bright red letters. I know without looking that it's packed with my precious CDs, all lovingly sorted the night before.

I move my eyes around the room. An empty hook on the back of the door where a dressing gown would normally be; my old CD player on the floor, wrapped in bubble wrap; a desk stripped of papers and pens, just one lonely pot with a couple of blunt pencils and a marker pen sticking out of the top. It's my old bedroom, and it looks exactly as it did on the day I left for university.

My heart's still hammering and I take a few deep breaths, trying to calm it down. This is nothing to worry about, it's just a dream. Your mind is playing tricks. Go back to sleep and when you wake up everything will be back to normal, whatever normal is.

I settle my head back down on the pillow and close my eyes. But I can't resist, and when I peek again, nothing has changed.

What the hell is going on?

I yank my duvet off and swing my legs over the side of the bed and pad cautiously towards the mirror. It's about waist height, and I can already see my short pyjamas and vest top reflected back at me as I approach — pyjamas I haven't worn for about eighteen years. I'm not sure I'm ready for what I'm about to see, but I sit down carefully on the edge of the stool anyway, and peer into the mirror.

I gasp. Not because it's awful. It's *me*. But it's not the thirty-eight-year-old me, with dark circles and fine lines under my eyes and a deep V etched into my forehead, that I'm used to seeing. It's an eighteen-year-old me, with flushed cheeks and no lines — and black make-up smudged under my eyes that makes me look like Alice Cooper. My hair is dyed a strange reddy-purple colour and sticks out all around my head like a halo. Hand shaking, I reach up and pat it down, then squint at my reflection and pull a face. My forehead doesn't wrinkle and pucker like it usually does, but stays smooth and strangely springy.

I laugh out loud. The sound is unexpected and makes me jump. It's a sound I've not heard for a while. But it seems appropriate because this is utterly ridiculous.

How can this be happening?

I consider going back to bed, burying my head under the pillow and pretending none of this is happening. But I'm curious. Terrified and confused, but curious to see what might happen too. Because the truth is I know this is more than just a dream. I don't know how I know, but I can just tell. It feels — real. It feels as though I'm really here, however insane that might sound.

I'm clueless as to what to do next, though. What *do* you do when you wake up in your old life? Is there an instruction leaflet, a set of rules to follow? And how long will it be until it ends and I'm back in real life again? A day, a week, a month? Forever? I shudder at the thought.

I stand up. There's a pile of clothes dumped at the end of my bed, crumpled from being kicked in my sleep. I clearly remember having spent ages choosing what to wear today, for my first day at university. I was moving to Newcastle and I'd been so excited. Scared too, but mostly excited.

"I can't wait to get out of here," I'd told my best friend Amy. But it was all bravado. The truth was I loved my home in Doncaster with Mum and Dad and my little sister Becky. I moaned, of course. But I knew Mum and Dad loved me and it was all I'd ever known. Moving to Newcastle, where I knew no one, was going to be a huge change. It was hard to believe I was ever that scared little girl.

I step out of my pyjama shorts and slip on the clothes from the end of the bed: a pair of black-and-white-striped tights; a fitted black dress, short; and a scruffy, oversized cardigan. I look down at myself. Weirdly, it feels pretty good.

I flick my eyes over to the bedside table. I'm looking for my mobile and I tut (I wonder whether I'm tutting in my sleep too and smile at how funny I'd look if there was anyone there to see me). This is 1993. I didn't have a mobile in 1993. Nobody did, apart from businessmen with their enormous clumsy bricks attached to the sides of their heads. Instead, my clock radio shines the time back at me: 08.10.

I head downstairs to see what's going on.

I remember Mum once telling me that when I left to go to university she'd cried for three solid days. I'd never believed her. She wasn't much of a crier, my mum, always too busy looking after everyone to have time to be self-indulgent. It just seemed so unlikely.

But when I get downstairs and peek through the crack in the kitchen door, I watch Mum for a minute before she knows I'm there. She looks so young, her hair no longer grey but a deep, dark brown. She's slimmer too, and is wearing a blouse instead of the endless M&S sweaters she prefers these days. She looks so pretty. I'd forgotten she'd ever looked like that. A voice on the radio drones on in the background. Mum slowly takes dishes and pots out of the dishwasher with one hand, and in the other she clutches a tissue which she dabs round her eyes every now and then. My heart surges with love for her.

Then Becky comes crashing down the stairs and breaks the spell.

"What are you standing there for?" she says. I stare at her, unable to reply. Now, when I see Becky, I'm always shocked at how grown-up she looks. At four years younger than me, I've always thought of her as my baby sister, and seeing her as a proper grown-up throws me every time. This, right here, is the Becky I always picture in my mind.

Plus, of course, this proves something else too: Becky can see me, which somehow means this whole thing is real.

Without waiting for an answer, Becky barges past me and into the kitchen. "Mu-um, where's my hockey kit?" she whines.

Mum straightens up. "Over there, love," she says, pointing to a neatly ironed pile of clothes on the worktop. Bless her, she's got the patience of a saint.

Mum then notices me and smiles weakly.

"Hello, sweetheart, all ready, are we?"

So Mum can see me too, then. Right. I take a deep breath and smile at her falteringly. Normally I'd have said something flippant like, "Yeah, I can't wait to get out of here." But having seen how upset she was a minute ago, I don't have the heart. "Yep, everything's packed," I say, noticing Mum's puffy eyes for the first time. I step forward and give her a hug. She seems surprised and it takes her a few seconds to respond. But as I breathe in the scent of her lily of the valley soap, I feel a pang of nostalgia for how simple life used to be. If only it were still like this. If only all I had to think about was leaving home, what I wanted for breakfast, and making new friends.

I pull away and notice a frown briefly cross Mum's face. She's probably wondering why I was hugging her. The teenage me didn't behave like that — she was far too busy worrying about herself to notice Mum was feeling sad, far more likely to ignore her completely and

20

mess up her nice clean kitchen than stop and hug her because she looked upset.

Behaving like a teenager is going to be tough. I'm just not that person any more. But I'm going to have to try.

I step away and fill the kettle with water.

"Tea?" I say to the room.

"Yes please, love."

"Yeah," grunts Becky, who's standing by the cereal cupboard shovelling Cheerios into her mouth from the box like she hasn't been fed for a month.

I flick the switch then put the teabags into the cups before sitting down heavily at the table while I wait for the water to boil.

"Where's Dad?" I'm dying to see him again.

"Oh, he's just popped out for a paper." She makes quotation marks in the air with her fingers. We all know that when Dad pops out "for a paper" it means he's having a sneaky fag. He comes back reeking of it, and there's always a telltale fag-packet bulge in the pocket of his shirt, but we all pretend we don't know, and he pretends we don't know either. I don't know why we bother. I roll my eyes and watch Mum flitting around the kitchen. She pulls open drawers, wipes imaginary stains from the worktop, bends and picks up Cheerios that had landed at Becky's feet.

"Don't clear up after her, she's more than capable." I nod at the trail of Cheerios that Becky's leaving behind her like Hansel and Gretel.

"Shut up." Becky looks furious.

"It's all right, love, I don't mind. I'm cleaning anyway."

"But —" I stop myself. I can't bear to see Mum being treated like a servant, but I'm fully aware I used to do exactly the same myself, so I bite my tongue. Instead I stand and fill the cups with water, adding milk to each one as well as sweetener for mum, one sugar for Becky, just the milk for me.

"Do you want some breakfast, love?"

My head aches, and I rub it gently.

"No thanks. I think I'm going to take my tea upstairs and finish getting ready."

"OK. See you in a bit. But don't be too long, your dad wants to get on the road."

I nod and head upstairs, placing my tea gently on the floor next to my bed. Then I lie back down again. I need a moment to think.

I don't know how much of this day I'm going to see again, but it is strange knowing what's going to happen next. In a couple of hours, Mum, Dad and I will bundle my few belongings into the car, wave goodbye to Becky, who's being allowed to stay at home so she can go to hockey practice and meet her friends for lunch in town, then I'll arrive in Newcastle, my heart hammering with terror as we drive through the unfamiliar streets. When we arrive at my house we'll unload the car, and then I'll be left all on my own, for the first time in my life, just me and my new housemates.

And that's when it hits me like a train, so hard I'm winded and can hardly breathe. I can't believe it's taken me this long to remember.

22

This day — the real one, at least — was the very first time I ever laid eyes on Ed. My Ed, who I've been grieving for endlessly over the last two months, whose death has left me broken and lost and angry.

I roll over onto my side and clutch my stomach, my breath coming in gulps.

Could this mean . . . I hardly dare even form the thought . . .

Could this possibly mean that, after two months of grieving for him, of feeling as though my heart has been ripped from my chest; of dreaming about being able to touch the stubble on his chin, push the hair from his eyes, wrap my arms round his tanned neck and hold his body against mine, I'm going to get the chance to see him again?

I feel faint with the possibility.

I can hardly believe it, and yet I can hardly wait.

The rhythm of the car must have sent me to sleep because when I open my eyes we've stopped and Dad has switched off the engine, and just for a moment, as Mum turns to smile at me from the passenger seat, I'm back in 1993 and everything's OK, and I smile back.

And then I remember and the breath is knocked from me once again.

"You OK, love, you've gone awfully pale?"

I sit up straight, wipe the dribble from the corner of my mouth and nod.

"Yeah, just fell asleep, sorry."

Dad tuts. "Makes a change."

"John, leave her alone."

"What? — she's a teenager, it's what they do." Dad nods his head towards the window. "Look, it's your new home."

I peer out of the window to check out the little house where I'll be living for the next year. It's as familiar as my own face and despite myself it makes me smile.

The tatty door of the terraced house is open, and we climb out of the car as a familiar middle-aged woman comes bundling out of the house and walks down the path to meet us.

"Hello . . . er?" she says, holding out her hand to Dad and smiling warmly.

"John," says Dad, shaking her hand firmly. "John Morgan. And this is my wife, Sandra."

They shake hands and then she turns to me. "So you must be Zoe," she says, shaking my hand too. "I'm Jane's mum, Cara. It's lovely to meet you."

"Hello," I mumble, trying not to let on that I already know who she is.

We take my stuff inside and dump it in the first room we come to.

"I'll find the kettle," Mum says, ripping the tape from one of the boxes.

"No need, I've already made a pot," says Cara, directing us all into the kitchen.

While Mum and Dad chat to Cara I sneak upstairs to have a look around before anyone else arrives. But when I come to the second bedroom, I gasp. There, with her back to me as she hangs her jeans neatly in the wardrobe, blonde hair swinging in a high ponytail, is someone very familiar. She turns to see who's there,

24

and her exceptionally young, pretty face breaks into a huge smile.

"Hiya, I'm Jane. You must be Zoe. Come in and sit down. Oh, if you can find a space." She pushes a pile of clothes to one side to make some room for me, and I sit and try to think about what to say to someone I know as well as I know myself, who I'm meant to be meeting for the first time. God, I wish there *was* an instruction manual — it would make things much easier.

"It's nice to meet you at last," I say, perching precariously on the edge of her single bed.

"You too. I was hoping you'd arrive first."

Good, this is how it should go. No one else is meant to be here yet. I look round her room and smile. "So, it looks like we're the only two girls. I wonder when the others will get here?"

She shrugs. "God knows, but let's hope they're not axe murderers." She winks and I grin at her and for a moment the knot in my stomach loosens. This is Jane, my best friend for about twenty years. There's nothing to worry about here. "What were their names again, the boys?"

"Rob, Simon and Ed." I answer too quickly, my voice cracking slightly on the last name, and Jane's smile falters briefly.

But seconds later her smile returns full beam. "I wonder whether we'll snog any of them? You know, a house romance that goes tits-up and ends up being awkward all year? There's got to be one, hasn't there? I think it's the law."

My face flames. "Yeah, bound to."

Undeterred by my lack of enthusiasm, she squeezes onto the bed next to me and carries on. "So I know I sound like a walking cliché, but what are you studying? I'm studying drama. Mum and Dad wanted me to take a 'proper' course, but I'm not clever enough. Anyway, I reckon it'll be fun."

"French and marketing." It sounds deadly dull and I feel the need to elaborate. "I thought it would be useful to have a language and, you know, something I can actually do as a job too." I shrug.

"Ooh, the girl has ambitions. I like it." She picks a jumper off the pile and starts to fold it. "So, what else? What about music, films, hobbies? Boyfriends? Are you secretly a lesbian karate champion with a penchant for jazz?"

"Ha, if only I were that interesting," I laugh. "Nah, I'm quite boring really. I'm a bit of a rock chick —" I glance down at my clothes to prove the point — "and a bit of a swot, and my favourite film is *Back to the Future* because I think it would be awesome to travel back in time —" I stop, realizing the significance of my words. "And no. No boyfriend. Or girlfriend." There have been boyfriends, of course, but it feels wrong to talk about them. "You?" I add weakly.

"Not much to report, to be honest. Mum and Dad would say I've had a bit of a misspent youth, drinking in the park and not doing nearly enough work for my A levels, but it's OK because I'm here now and they can both be proud." She rolls her eyes. "I had a boyfriend, Rich, but he's gone to Plymouth and I told him there was no point in trying to stay together so I don't suppose I'll ever see him again. Anyway, it gives me a chance to meet some nice, sexy rugby player while I'm here, doesn't it?" She grins wickedly, but before I have a chance to answer we hear heavy footsteps coming up the stairs.

My body tenses, even though I'm sure it's not Ed. Seconds later a head appears round the door, a handsome face topped by a mop of floppy dark hair.

It's Rob, and at the sight of him the tension seeps from my body.

"Can anyone join in, or is this girls only?" he says, as the rest of his body follows his head into the room.

"Come in," Jane says. "Which one are you, then?"

Rob grins. "I'm Rob," he says. "The handsome one."

I smile. Rob *is* handsome — but he's also a total ladies' man and will have slept with half the freshers before the end of the month. Plus, he's no Ed.

"Nice to meet you, handsome one," I say instead. He flops onto the edge of the bed beside me, stretching his feet out in front of him.

As Jane and Rob get to know each other, I look round the room, at the black spots in the corner where the damp has taken over, at the squares of darker paint and greasy Blu-Tack circles where past posters have left their marks, and think about how surreal today has become.

For whatever reason, I've woken up in 1993, back in my eighteen-year-old life. Whether it's just for one day or for much longer I have no idea, and right now I don't care because all I can think about is one thing: Ed. If this day goes as it did the first time round — and it has so far, so I have no reason to believe that it won't — then I'll be meeting Ed soon. It won't be my Ed as I know him now. It will be the Ed I first met, the young, sexy, slightly arrogant Ed who I liked but didn't fall head over heels in love with at that moment: there was no lightning bolt, no spark of electricity shooting across the room. There was just me and a boy, meeting for the first time, with a whole world of possibilities ahead of us.

This time, it's going to be hard — almost impossible — to behave as though I've never met him before. I've loved him and hated him intensely; I've held him and comforted him and fought with him and lost him and grieved for him, and with all that in my mind, how am I supposed to get through this? I have no idea.

"What do you think?" With a start I'm brought back to now to see Jane and Rob looking at me expectantly, waiting for an answer.

"Sorry, I was miles away. What did you say?" I hope neither of them notices the wobble in my voice.

"Shall we find the local?" Rob says. "Have a quick pint before the others get here?"

"Good idea." I need some Dutch courage to get me through the next few hours. A drink is just what I need. I stand quickly. "I'll just put my stuff in my room before Mum and Dad leave."

We traipse down the stairs to say our goodbyes as Dad ferries my bags and boxes into the room next to Jane's.

"Take care, love." Mum hugs me tightly and I feel tears welling in my eyes again. "Make sure you ring me, and come home to see us soon."

"Not too soon, though, I'm turning your room into a B & B." Dad smirks as he gives me a quick hug, then I wave as they drive off down the road, leaving me to my new life. I can do this. I can live the student life again. It's only one day, after all — and it might just be the day I've been hoping for since I lost Ed.

"Right, let's go," I say, taking a deep breath and pasting a smile on my face, and the three of us march down the path for the short walk to our local.

As we push through the swing door I'm surprised by the pang of nostalgia. It's a long time since I've been here, and the memories come flooding back. I can picture Ed at the pool table, deep lines etching his forehead as he concentrates on potting the black, a pint balanced on the table edge, half drunk. I remember Jane getting so drunk she fell off her chair and curled up for a nap in the corner. I can almost hear Blind Melon's "No Rain" on the jukebox we used to play, pumping in endless coins to hear our favourite tunes. And despite the utter ridiculousness of the situation and the apprehension I'm feeling at what's to come, a sudden warmth washes over me as I settle at the table to spend the afternoon with these people — my oldest friends, who I've only just met.

Three hours later we're back at the house. Simon has arrived and after a quick introduction we get on with the job of claiming kitchen cupboards and sharing a cheap bottle of wine we picked up at the offie on the way home. It tastes like paint stripper but it's blurring the edges of my anxiety.

Outside it's starting to get dark and I know what this means. Ed will be here soon. I feel the knot in my chest tighten.

I haven't exactly accepted the fact that I'll never see Ed again, but somewhere deep down I know it's true, and I'm terrified that his face is already starting to blur in my memory, however desperately I try to hold it there. I can see the outline of his face, almost trace it with my fingertips. But I can't picture the shape of his eyes, the exact rise and fall of his nose or the angle of the cupid's bow in his lips, and it's been driving me mad. I'm not sure I can handle being in front of all these people when I see him again. How do I look at him, without reaching out to touch him or worse, throwing myself at him? How can I possibly do that?

The hands on the cheap plastic clock above the sink tick monotonously on; the tap drip, drip, drips endlessly into the sink. I can feel my hands start to sweat and my head feels fuzzy. Voices murmur in the periphery, but I'm blocking it all out, focusing instead on the in and out, in and out of my breath, the rise and fall of my chest and the steady, insistent thump of my heart. I just want to get this over and done with.

And then, as if in answer to my prayers, there's a loud knock on the door, and before anyone has a chance to open it, the kitchen door bursts open and there's Ed, a huge smile lighting up his handsome face.

The blood rushes to my head and I think I might pass out.

Around me there's a frantic wave of activity as everyone leaps up to greet him, but I stay stock-still, my eyes trained on the air just to the side of his head, too scared to look directly at him. But I have to eventually, and when I force my eyes to see him properly, I feel as though I've been punched in the guts. Oh God. It's him, he's really here.

I stand and move slowly round to the back of the chair, gripping hold of it tightly in the hope it will hold me up. And then I look at him again, trying to drink in every inch of him. His dark hair flops over his bright blue eyes, and he keeps pushing it out of the way with his hand, a gesture so familiar it hurts. He looks so young, and I can't believe that when we met for the real first time I wasn't in love with him at all.

Now, I feel as though my heart has been ripped out and is being dangled in front of the whole room for all my friends to see. I'm in love with this man yet my heart is breaking, because he's gone and I know this might be my only chance to see him again. Yet I can't tell him how I feel.

At least, I can't with words. But surely he'll know, the moment he looks in my eyes, surely he'll see everything we've shared together since this moment? Surely there's no way he *can't* see the bond we have? I need to make this moment count, because this could be the only chance I get.

So I take a deep breath, wipe my hand on my dress and hold it out as I step forward, trying to stop it shaking. "I'm Zoe," I say. "Lovely to meet you."

And as he takes my hand in his, everything around me explodes.

"Lovely to meet you too," he says, the deep timbre of his voice vibrating straight through to my heart. I grip his hand a moment longer than necessary and I feel the warmth seeping into my skin. He feels it, I know he does, and I look deep into his eyes. But then the spell is broken by another knock and he gently tugs his hand away and turns to where a face is peering round the door.

Ed's face lights up and he wraps his arm protectively round the newcomer's shoulders and pulls her towards him, his eyes full of love. She's tall and graceful, her short hair stylish and her eyes warm. It's clear she adores Ed, and that the feeling is mutual.

"Everyone, this is Mum. Mum, this is everyone." He sweeps his arm majestically round the room and we all murmur our hellos. But all I can think about is the day I stood by Susan's side at Ed's funeral, watching as the curtain closed round his coffin and we held each other up, locked in grief.

"Mum wanted to make sure I got here without getting lost, didn't you, Mum?"

Susan dips her head and smiles apologetically. "Yes, sorry to be the embarrassing mum, but you know. Got to make sure my little boy's OK."

She grins as Ed groans, but I know he's secretly thrilled she's here. At this moment in time she's the only woman in the world he loves.

"But she's not staying long, are you, Mum?"

"No, don't worry, I won't cramp your style." She peers at the bottle of wine on the table. "Anyway, I'm not sure my stomach's strong enough to drink that."

Ed rolls his eyes and she grins, the same impish grin he has when he thinks he's being funny. "Sorry, I'd better get going before he kills me." She hitches her handbag up onto her shoulder and moves to give Ed a kiss, and my stomach contracts with envy. I'd give anything to kiss him right now.

But I'm learning; I'll just have to wait.

"Lovely to meet you all," Susan says, then the pair of them leave the room as he sees her out. I will my heart to slow down as the conversation around me returns to normal. Just another day for everyone else, albeit an exciting one full of new people. What would they think if they knew what I was going through?

"Are you all right? You've gone really pale." Jane's face wrinkles in concern as she sucks deeply on her cigarette. I smile weakly, pushing the smoke out of my face.

"I'm fine. Just a bit drunk, I think."

"Ha, we've hardly got started; you need to get some stamina, girl!" Holding her cigarette in her mouth she walks to the sink and rinses out a mug, fills it with water and brings it back to the table. "Here, drink this."

I take the mug, hoping she doesn't notice my hand shaking, and down the whole thing in one.

"Better?"

I nod. "Thanks."

"Good. Right, more wine." She slugs some of the warm, cheap plonk into my glass and grins.

Ed comes back, rummaging around in his backpack. I watch, knowing what he's going to produce, and then he pulls out a bottle of vodka. "Right, anyone for a proper drink?"

A chorus of "yeah!" goes up and I groan. I want to make this moment count and if I'm drunk I won't remember any of it. But I don't want to look like a party pooper either, on the first day these people have met me.

Glasses are filled — there's no ice but someone's found a bottle of Diet Coke — and are being handed round. I take one and hold it to my lips, watching the faces of my friends round the table, trying not to stare at the face of the man I love more than anyone else in the world.

"Cheers." Ed raises his glass and looks at me, and I feel as though his eyes are looking inside me, not just at me, and my face burns. I hold my glass up and clink it against his and finally he looks away. My heart is beating so fast it feels as though I'm going to spin off my chair.

The rest of the evening passes in a blur of drinking and laughing and talking, and eventually, late into the night, it's time to go to bed. I don't want to go; I have no idea what's going to happen tomorrow, whether I'll ever see Ed again or whether this was just a one-off, and I really don't want to sleep, in case. But I'm tired and I'm drunk, and I know I have no choice. However long I stay awake, this day can't last forever.

34

"Night," Ed says as we reach the top of the stairs.

"Night, sweetheart."

"Blimey, bit forward."

I cringe, and hide my red cheeks behind my hair. "Sorry, just a bit drunk. Goodnight, Edward Williams. It's been lovely to meet you." I hold my hand out and he grabs it, gently shaking it up and down. His touch makes me shiver.

"It's been an absolute pleasure to meet you too, Zoe Morgan."

Then he lets go, shuts his door behind him, and is gone.

CHAPTER
TWO

22 July 1994

The first few seconds of being awake have passed, the agony of remembering everything has settled into its usual constant aching hum rather than the initial scream of anguish as I lie with my eyes tightly shut.

But the memory of seeing Ed again yesterday, and of his touch, has also stayed with me, and I'm desperate to see if it's happened again, if I'm back in the past. So I take a deep breath and open my eyes, sit up, and look around. The first thing I see at the end of my double bed is a very young Jane, curled up like a baby, fast asleep. She's still dressed, and her hair is matted and stuck to her face. Ignoring her, I look round the room. It's my bedroom in the second year at university. It's the bedroom I unpacked my things in "yesterday", and I can see the posters that I'd stuck up on the wall: Pop Will Eat Itself, Soundgarden, Red Hot Chili Peppers. There's a huge pile of clothes on a chair in the corner, and CDs scattered all over the floor next to my stereo. The rest of the CD cases are stacked neatly in their tower.

I feel a little bit dizzy.

Is this another day? It certainly seems that way. But why?

I take a few deep breaths and sit a moment longer, trying to work out what to do next. I don't have a clue what's going on, or what day I'm somehow "reliving", but I'm pretty sure I'll find out soon enough. I swing my legs down the side of the bed, careful not to wake up Jane. The carpet's rough under my feet and dust floats in the air, caught in the light streaming through the paper-thin curtains. I step over the pile of CDs, careful not to slip on one, and pull open the wardrobe door. There's a mirror hanging on the back of it and, trying not to think about it too much, I take a look at myself.

My hair's long and knotted, dyed a dark, dark brown, almost black. It hangs over my shoulders and halfway down my upper arms. My eyes are ringed with black make-up and silver glitter, and my skin looks white and smooth, like porcelain. Not a hint of a wrinkle here, despite evidence of a heavy night the night before. I'm wearing an oversized black T-shirt and my slim white legs poke out of the bottom. There's a bruise on my shin, small but deep purple, ringed with yellow. I've no idea how I got it. My nose has a silver ring in it, and four silver studs creep up my left ear. I smile. I loved my piercings. I miss them. I kind of miss dressing like this.

I creep downstairs and pick my way through the ashtrays and empty cans littering the living-room floor and turn on the TV. I press the teletext button and am surprised to find it actually works, the old-fashioned letters scrolling across the page like tickertape. Finally, after a few minutes of searching through the slow-loading pages, I find what I'm looking for.

The date: 22 July 1994.

I frown, rewinding wildly through my memories, trying to place the date. Why this day? Was it important? Does it involve Ed?

And then I realize. How could I have forgotten?

It's a few days after Ed and I had our first kiss. Which can only mean one thing.

It's the day he broke my heart.

My legs go weak beneath me and I sit down quickly on the edge of the grubby sofa before I fall. I remember it as clearly as if it were yesterday, and I can't quite believe I'm going to have to live through it all over again.

The kiss had been unexpected, but amazing. As the year had gone by I'd been surprised how much my feelings for Ed had grown. I'd found myself watching him all the time: as he talked to people, as he ate his breakfast, as he dozed on the sofa. And slowly, I realized I saw him as more than just a friend. I really fancied him. I had no idea whether he felt the same way, but still I harboured dreams of kissing him before the year was out. By the time we had a house party, a week or so before we all went home for the summer and started boring jobs, I'd been running out of hope that anything would ever happen between us.

"When do you start?" Simon had asked at the party; he had a few weeks of work experience lined up at his dad's law firm and was keen to make sure we'd got ourselves sorted too.

"First week back home," I said. I had a holiday job in the pub round the corner from my parents' house.

"What about you?" I said to Simon. "You starting straight away too?"

"Yeah," he said. "And I've got to wear a suit."

I laughed out loud. Simon lived in rarely washed combat trousers, scuffed boots and faded band T-shirts.

"What?" he said, pretending to be hurt. "I think I'll look quite handsome." He stuck his chin in the air and adjusted an imaginary tie before passing me a spliff.

"Yes, I'm sure you will." I took a drag and blew the smoke into the air. "You'll have trouble concentrating on work with all those women queuing at your desk."

"That's what I'm hoping." He winked and I laughed again. "What're you up to, Eddie?"

Ed shrugged. "Not sure. I'm going back to Mum's; I'll look for something then. I quite fancy a bit of gardening, get outside in the sunshine, use my hands. Might play a few gigs in the locals too." He flashed me a look. "Or not."

"All right for some, eh?" Simon said. "Wish I could just goof around playing guitar all summer and Mummy would look after me."

"Yeah, it's a tough life but someone's got to do it." Ed laughed along but I could see the hurt in his eyes. He knew the boys all thought he was a mummy's boy, but I knew differently. Ed and his dad hadn't been close even while his dad was still alive, and it had been just Ed and his mum for years.

"You'll find something." I leaned over and passed him the end of the spliff and our fingers brushed. I shivered and snatched my hand away, but I could see Ed watching me from the corner of my eye and I felt uncomfortable. I stood up and walked into the kitchen, my legs feeling wobbly. I stood by the sink for a moment, trying to sober up, the bassline of "Insane in the Brain" by Cypress Hill thumping through the floor.

"Hey."

With a start I turned to find Ed standing behind me, and my heart did a little flip. Without looking away, he hauled himself up onto the worktop and sat studying me carefully.

"So, how're you feeling about being at home all summer?"

I shrugged. "OK. You know." I felt awkward beneath his gaze and turned to fiddle with something on the counter. "You?"

Ed didn't answer. Instead he said, "Will you miss me?" His voice was teasing and I wasn't sure whether he was flirting with me, or just being Ed. I turned back to face him.

"Nah, course not." My face was growing hot, threatening to give me away, but I held his gaze, daring him to look away. He jumped down from the counter and stood less than a metre away from me. "Oh, that's a shame."

"Is it?"

He nodded, a smile playing on his lips. "It is. Because I think I'm going to miss you, Zoe."

Scared that the wine was making me read too much into his words, I stayed silent, waiting. The deep blue of his eyes was sparkling, teasing. "Right. Good."

"Is that it? Good?" He went to move towards me and stumbled a little. "Oops," he grinned. "Think I've drunk a bit too much." He reached me and stood, hardly an inch between us, looking down at me. "That's not why I'm saying it, though, because of the beer. I really will miss you."

Then, very slowly, he brought his head down and gently touched his lips to mine. I felt as though I'd been lit up, and I responded hungrily. He brought his arms around me and pulled my head closer, deepening the kiss. Finally, he pulled away.

"I guess this is OK, then?" he said.

I nodded. "More than OK."

He moved to kiss me again.

"Hey, hey, hey!" A voice interrupted us and Ed pulled away quickly. "What's all this, then?"

Rob was standing in the kitchen doorway, swaying slightly, looking rather too pleased to have caught us in the act. I grinned happily.

But Ed didn't look so pleased. "Nothing," he mumbled, taking a couple of steps further back. "I was just saying goodbye."

"Yeah, looked like it." Rob grinned. "I only came to get some more beers. Want one?"

"Please."

They took their beers from the fridge and turned to me.

"Zoe?" Rob held a drink out.

"No, thanks." My head was spinning and I was trying to work out what had just happened. Had Ed dismissed me, or was he embarrassed we'd been caught? I tried to catch his eye but he wouldn't look at me, and my face flamed. Whatever his intentions, I couldn't help feeling furious with him. I turned and walked out, back to the party, and poured myself another glass of warm wine from the bottle on the floor.

Ed had been funny with me ever since, acting as though nothing had happened, and I'd decided to go along with it. I didn't know what his problem was but I wasn't going to ask him. He could tell me.

Now, I'm back in the day a week or so later, the last day of term, that I'd hated the first time round, wondering what the point is of reliving it all again. There *has* to be a reason, otherwise why am I here? Have I been given a second chance so I can do something differently?

I gasp, the breath knocked from me.

That's it! I've got to try to change something today, see if I can make a difference. Maybe it's like the butterfly effect — one small change somewhere along the way can create a huge, all-consuming change to someone's life miles — or years — away. Which could mean that even one tiny change today could be significant enough to stop Ed being taken from me.

I have no idea if it will work, but I do know it's got to be worth a go.

It's five in the afternoon; the sun is high and hot in the sky and I tilt my face up towards it as I sip from a can of Coke, enjoying the warmth on my face.

Jane sits beside me, her legs jumping up and down impatiently, puffing on a fag.

"Come on, I need to get home for a shower, I stink."

"Ah, just a few more minutes," I beg.

"Go on, then," she says, and I know without even looking at her she's rolling her eyes.

"Thanks. And don't do that."

"What?"

"Roll your eyes."

"Ha, sorry." I know her better than I know myself sometimes — and vice versa. It's hardly surprising, considering we see each other every day and tell each other everything. It gives me a pang of regret to think about it. In 2013, I still adore her, but I know I've let our friendship slide, and at this precise moment in time I can't for the life of me think why I would do that.

I sip my drink and turn to her. "I love this, you know."

"Love what?"

"This. The fact we can sit here together in silence, and it feels OK."

She smiles. "Me too. Even if you do make me stay here against my will."

"Oh, I give up." I jump to my feet, my head spinning a little. I've been trying to avoid going back to the house because I know Ed's going to be there and I'm not ready to see him yet. I'm nervous and I need to compose myself.

Jane and I have been hanging out today, avoiding lectures and drinking cheap, flat cider in the student union. Now we're out for some fresh air but it's just made my head feel even fuzzier. I grab her shoulder to steady myself.

"Careful," she says, holding me upright and stubbing out her cigarette on the pavement. Then she grins. "Oops, think we might have had too much cider." Then she lets out a delicate burp. I shriek with laughter. "You pig!"

We link arms and start walking, unsteadily, towards home. It's been lovely spending the day with her, although as I got more and more drunk it got harder and harder not to tell her what was going on. What I was going through was so weird and so inexplicable and so, well, huge, that it felt totally wrong to be holding it back from her.

But now, as we stroll home arm in arm, I'm glad I did. We've had a perfect day and I don't want anything to ruin that. Jane's always been there for me, throughout all the heartache of the last few years, but I knew I'd shut her out, unable to cope with her kindness. Today has felt like a tonic, like we've got our friendship back and, although I know it probably won't change anything in the future, it feels bloody great.

I blink back tears and before I know it we've walked the two miles back to our house. We've both sobered up a bit and as Jane slides the key into the lock I feel myself tensing up.

Jane notices. "You need to talk to him, you know."

"I know, I know. But what if he doesn't want to talk to me? What if I've read it all wrong and the kiss was just a drunken mistake he's trying to forget?"

"Or how about this? What if he's just embarrassed? You know, the cliché house romance, and he doesn't know how to handle it any better than you do? Maybe you just need to talk to each other."

I shake my head. "No, no way. He kissed me, and he said he was going to miss me. None of it was me. Now it's up to him to come and tell me why he's refusing to talk to me."

Jane looks at me for a moment, then shrugs. "I've said my piece; I won't nag you again. But you know what I think you should do, and it's not nothing."

I nod, my face set. We fall silent as Jane opens the door and flicks on the light. Voices drift from the living room and I can make out laughter and the gentle hum of the TV. The walk down the hallway seems longer than usual. Finally, we arrive at the living room and push the door open. I have to stop myself from crying out.

There, curled up on the sofa, is Ed. Next to him, snuggled into the crook of his arm with a smug look of satisfaction on her face, is — actually, what the hell *is* her name? She had such a big impact on my life that day I can't believe I've forgotten, but somehow it's escaped me. I call her Big Tits, for want of anything better.

Rob's sitting on the other sofa, sprawled out with an open can of beer next to him, chatting to Ed.

But it's Ed I can't take my eyes off. My Ed, holding another woman, holding a woman who's not me, just days after that kiss. I'd thought of nothing else and here he is, not caring. I feel as though I've been kicked in the stomach, and as my head spins I grab the back of the sofa to steady myself. Of course it's ridiculous. I knew this was coming. But that doesn't make it any easier.

Last time I'd sat down and spent the evening pretending I hadn't noticed, and then taken myself off early to bed for a cry.

This time, though, it's going to be different. I'm going to try something, see where it takes me. It might sound crazy, the thought that one little thing now, in 1994, might have the potential to prevent someone dying in 2013, but if not, what's the point of all this?

I sit down and wait, biding my time. Ed still refuses to look at me. The conversation flows, but I hardly hear a word. I'm waiting for my moment.

Finally, Ed stands. "Just going for a wee."

He walks out of the room. I wait a few seconds then stand too. Jane catches my eye, tips her head quizzically, but I just shake my head and walk out of the room casually. I feel ridiculous, hanging around in the kitchen waiting for the flush of the loo. But when it comes I walk down the corridor and pass the toilet door just as Ed comes out. He bumps into me and our shoulders collide.

"Oh, sorry." He looks at the carpet and turns to walk away.

46

"Ed." My voice is firm and he stops, his eyebrows raised in question.

"Zoe."

My heart is pounding so hard I can feel it right through my body to the ends of my fingertips, into my toes. I force my breathing under control.

"Ed, you can't ignore me forever, you know. Are you going to tell me why you're pretending you didn't kiss me?"

Ed looks shocked. He should do, he put me through hell. I don't let him off easily, though, and wait for him to speak, my head spinning with the thrill of doing something so totally out of character.

"I'm not pretending, I'm . . ." He stops, and looks down at his shoes. Then he raises his head and looks me in the eye. "I'm sorry, Zoe, I don't really know what I'm doing. I do really like you, but it's just . . ." He trails off again, and he looks so guilty I start to soften.

"Oh Ed, I just want to know why you've been avoiding me since — well, since you kissed me."

"I'm sorry. I really am. I know I've been an arse. I just didn't want to make a big thing of it, you know, with the others. I didn't want them to know anything was going on."

"But is it? Going on, I mean." My voice is softer now, and Ed smiles.

"Well no, I suppose not. But I would like it to."

"Really?" My heart almost leaps out of my chest.

Ed nods. "I think so. Just — I'm not sure now is the right time."

My heart plummets again and I struggle to control the wobble in my voice. "Because of her?" I jab my thumb in the direction of the living room.

"Amy?" He has the decency to look guilty.

"Yes, Amy."

"Oh God no, not because of her. I mean, she's OK and everything but — well, she's just a friend, really. A girl from uni. It's not because of her, no. It's . . ."

I wait for him to continue.

"It's just not the right time, Zo. I'm sorry. I really am."

I look down at my shoes, trying to blink back the tears. I don't know why I feel so sad this time, knowing we get together in the end anyway. It just feels so hard to hear those words come from his mouth. I want to tell him that it's never the right time and that life is too short to put things off, to waste time being apart. But I can't, and I know that a nineteen-year-old man won't listen to a word of it anyway. Why would he? And so I just take a deep breath, then slowly let it out.

"Me too, Ed. I'm really sorry too. But I get it."

"You do?"

I nod, and we stand there for a moment, unsure how to be with each other. The air between us is so thick with unspoken words, it's almost alive.

Finally, he takes a step towards me. We're less than an inch apart and I can feel the heat from his body as he hesitates for a moment. I raise my arms and place my hands on his chest, feel his heartbeat beneath his thin T-shirt, his warm skin.

Then he snakes his arms round my waist and pulls me towards him, kissing me deeply. My heart is in my throat and my legs are shaking with relief as I kiss him back, even though I don't know what this means. Then he pulls away and I look up at him.

"I've at least got to get rid of Amy, this isn't fair."

I nod.

"Give me half an hour, then I'll be back, I promise. I think we need to talk some more."

He walks away and leaves me in the hallway. Seconds pass as I stand there, dithering.

"What the hell are you up to, you little minx?"

Jane's laughing as she walks towards me, her hands on her hips. "Ed's trying to get rid of poor old Amy, and now I find you standing here looking like the cat that got the cream. What's going on. Have you two — you know?"

I tell her what just happened and she looks at me appraisingly. "Well, well, well," she grins. "Never saw that one coming."

"Me neither. And I don't have a clue where it's taking us, either."

She cocks her head to one side, studies me. "So what's happening now?"

"I'm not sure. What should I do?"

"Do? You should go to his room and wait for him, you big dork." She grins mischievously. "I'll make sure he knows where to find you."

"Really? Don't you think that's a bit — forward? Especially given what he's just said."

"Maybe, but who cares? He likes you, you like him; nobody's asking you to get married. Just go and have a bit of fun."

"OK." I pause, unsure.

"Go on, then." Jane pushes me gently towards the stairs. "Go and wait for him. And Zo? Good luck."

I grin, then turn and walk up the stairs, the blood rushing in my ears. I can't believe what I've just done, what I'm doing. But whether it changes anything or not, at least I get a chance to be with Ed. Who knows whether I'll get another one. I've got to grab it while I can.

Pushing open Ed's door, I feel like a naughty schoolgirl. I've been in his room before but only with everyone else, never alone, and I feel like an intruder. I *am* an intruder. I close the door behind me and let my eyes wander round the room. His bed is roughly made, the duvet wrinkled and creased. His guitar sits in the corner in its case, and I smile. The first time he ever played to us was the day I realized how much I liked him. Who doesn't like a man who plays the guitar? It's a shame he let it slide later, as life took over. There are three or four plants by the window, and a mini watering can.

A few photos are stuck haphazardly to the wall next to his bed and, curious, I move closer to have a better look. There's one of him and his mum smiling happily at the camera, his arm slung protectively round her shoulders. It looks as though it was taken at home but I can't make out any details. The next one is Ed and four other boys, all half-naked and tanned and holding drinks up to the camera. It must have been the holiday he had before he started uni, but I don't remember ever having seen this picture before. I recognize only one other boy, his friend Jake, who I met a handful of times in the village when we went home to visit his mum. The rest are strangers. There's a black-and-white photograph which I recognize as the precious picture of his grandparents. He missed them desperately and he always had this photo somewhere in the house. There are a couple more photos lying on the desk next to the bed and I can't help picking one of them up. It's a picture of Ed and a girl I don't recognize, their arms around each other, smiling happily. She's very pretty but young and he only looks about fifteen. We talked about exes over the years and I wonder which one she is. I feel a pang of jealousy and feel ridiculous. This is in the past right now, in 1994, let alone in 2013. Her photo's been taken off the wall, the Blu-Tack still on the back, dumped unceremoniously on the desk with papers and wrappers and pens. What on earth have I got to feel jealous about?

I move to his bookshelf and see some familiar books there, books that are in my house even now. There aren't many, just a handful: *The Catcher in the Rye*, *The Hitchhiker's Guide to the Galaxy*, a couple of detective novels, a book on gardening and a history of the First World War. There are also a few guitar books, with songs he was teaching himself to play.

I feel guilty for snooping round his room, even though I know more about him than anyone else in the world, so I take a detective novel from the shelf and sit on the bed, cross-legged, to wait for him.

But it's hard to concentrate on the words: I'm too busy wondering whether I'm doing the right thing. Should I be letting nature take its course and not trying to change anything? I don't really know what I'm trying to achieve: I only know that I don't have much power; this is all I seem to have, so I'm going to use it.

Straining my ears, I try to hear what's going on downstairs. Have the others noticed I'm missing? The minutes drag by and there's no sign of Ed, and I start to wonder whether he's going to come up. But then finally I hear voices and the sound of the front door closing, then footsteps coming softly up the stairs. As they reach the top I start to feel dizzy, in case it's not him, or he's changed his mind, or is angry with me.

But when he comes through the door his face is plastered with a grin, his eyes twinkling mischievously, and he shuts the door firmly behind him and jumps on the bed next to me, pushing me off balance.

"I wondered if I'd find you in here. Had a good look around?"

My face flushes. "A bit." I gesture at the wall. "Nice photos."

He glances up, nods distractedly.

"Fancy some music?" He jumps up and picks a CD off the floor, shoves it in the CD player. Seconds later the sound of the Rolling Stones' "Under My Thumb" comes gently from the speakers and it hits me like a train.

"I love this song," he says.

"Me too." My voice comes out in a whisper. All I can think about is the moment the curtain closed round his coffin and I feel as though I'm going to be sick. I look away and hope he doesn't notice the pain etched on my face.

He sits back on the bed next to me, and stretches himself out, arms behind his head, looking up at the ceiling. I lie down next to him, nothing but our hips touching, and stare at the ceiling too, listening to the music. Finally the song comes to an end and a new one starts, and I can think about something else.

"So, what's happening here?" Ed's the first to speak.

I shrug. "No idea."

He struggles to raise himself up on his elbow and turns towards me, his face looming over mine.

"Ed, look, when you kissed me last week —"

"You kissed me as well, as I remember it."

"Shush a minute. You know what I mean. You kissed me, and it was great."

"Is that all? Great? Not amazing? Earth-shattering?"

"Ed, stop interrupting."

"Sorry."

"OK, it was more than great. But that's not the point. The point is that since then you've been horrible —"

"Bit harsh."

"True, though. You've hardly spoken to me, most of the time you won't even look at me. I know you said you're not ready for anything but we're going home for six weeks now, and I'd like to know where we stand. If anywhere. Life's too short to play games." The significance of the words are lost on him.

Ed studies me, his face serious. "You're right, and I'm sorry. I have been avoiding you, because I thought it would be easier."

"Easier?"

He looks guilty. "You know, we've got this house again next year, we're all going to be living in each other's pockets, and if we start something and it goes wrong, it's going to be a nightmare."

"So you're refusing to be with me in case it goes wrong? Always look on the bright side, right?"

"I know it sounds crap, I do. But Zo, we're only nineteen, I reckon we should just chill a bit, see what happens."

I wait, let his words sink in.

"So you're saying you like me but you don't want to be with me?"

Ed squirms. "Yeah, I think so. I'm sorry, Zo, I really am. I just want to enjoy myself. You know . . ."

I nod miserably.

Ed lies back down and we stay like that for a few minutes, listening to Mick Jagger's voice filling the room. I think about what Ed's just said and I know I have to listen to him. Nothing has really changed because we weren't together right now the first time round either. I had to spend the next couple of years admiring him from afar and trying not to think about the other girls he brought home from time to time. It looks as though that's going to happen again and I'm going to have to let it and hope that we end up together anyway, just like last time. Otherwise, who knows what might happen? I'm too scared to push it any more.

I haul myself up to a sitting position and swing my legs onto the floor to stand. Ed squints up at me quizzically. "You going?"

I nod.

"OK. Listen, Zo, I am sorry, you know. Truly."

"I know. Me too."

Then I kiss him briefly on the cheek, walk out of his room and into my own and lie down on my bed, staring at my own ceiling. And then I let myself go, the sobs wracking my body until I fall into a fitful, restless sleep.

CHAPTER
THREE

18 February 1999

I'm still half asleep when a sound shatters my peace and I sit up, my heart thumping wildly. It's the radio, and the Spice Girls' "Stop" is blaring round the room.

I lean over and fumble around in the almost-dark, trying to find the source of the racket before it wakes anyone else up. Finally, I smack the top of the alarm with the heel of my hand. The silence is an instant relief.

I fall back on the pillow, and for a second I feel happy before the pain floods in again as I remember Ed is dead. But then I sit up, heart pounding as I remember "yesterday"; I'd tried to change things and I'm dying to find out if I succeeded.

I look round, trying to work out where — and when — I am. The only light comes from some slats of weak sunlight filtering through a wooden blind hanging at the window. It's familiar, yet a sense of nostalgia tugs at me. I'm in a single bed and the room is small with just a wardrobe and a chair in the corner and nothing else. As always, a pile of clothes is slung over the back of the chair. There's a collage of photos pinned onto the wall above it. I can't make them out from here but I know what's in every single one of them.

I know this room well: it's the room in the first flat I rented in London after university. Jane had moved down with me and we'd scraped together all the money we could find for the deposit on this place. It was tiny — bijou, as the letting agent described it. There was this room, Jane's room, which was even smaller if that was possible, a small lounge-cum-dining-room-cum-kitchen and a cupboard that passed for a bathroom. But it didn't matter to us that there was barely more than standing space for two. It was our first flat together in London, and we loved it.

Now my heart is hammering with the same excitement I felt yesterday. Nothing's changed as far as I can tell — there's no sign of Ed, no clue he's been here — but I've been given another chance. Maybe I will see Ed again today.

With a knot of anxiety deep in my belly I pull the duvet back and climb out of bed. It's colder in the room than I expected and I shiver, pulling the duvet round my shoulders as I stand. There's no mirror so I walk over to the chair — about two steps — and rummage around for something to wear. A pair of tight tartan trousers and a black polo neck fall out. I sniff them. They seem fairly clean so I yank them on and walk to the bathroom. It's locked and I can hear the shower running behind the door and Jane humming tunelessly, so I go into the kitchen instead and flick the kettle on.

There's a bag hanging from the back of a chair and even though I recognize it as mine I still feel guilty when I open it up and have a peek inside, as though I'm raiding someone else's private things. I'm not sure what I'm hoping to find, but it would be good to have even a tiny clue about what I'm meant to be doing today. There's a small diary inside and, amazingly, it's marked by a ribbon.

"Thursday, 18 February 1999." I'm not a hundred per cent sure that's today or whether it was yesterday but at least I know roughly when I am. Underneath the date some words are scribbled in my terrible handwriting.

8p.m., Andy. The Bull?

My heart sinks. Andy. The boy I'd been out with for a few half-hearted dates and then never seen again. If I've arranged a date with him then it really looks as though yesterday changed nothing.

I reach over and flick the radio on. "Give It Away" by the Red Hot Chili Peppers fills the room and despite myself I smile. It's funny how music can bring memories flooding back more lucidly than anything else. The first thing that comes to my mind when I hear this song is dancing at my favourite indie club at university with Ed and all my friends.

The song comes to an end and I listen carefully for any mention of the date. In the bathroom I can hear Jane shuffling around and I know it won't be long before she comes out and I have to pretend everything is normal. Finally, the DJ announces the news.

"Here is the news for Thursday, 18 February," he says.

My heart sinks. It *is* Thursday, which means I'm meant to be meeting Andy tonight. I'm not sure I can face that. It's not just the thought that I might have to kiss someone who isn't Ed after all these years, although that is a worry, of course. It's more that I'm not sure how I can pretend to feel anything for anyone else when my heart is still broken, when I'm still missing Ed. When I still love him with all my heart. How am I meant to get on with things and pretend that it isn't happening?

But I'll deal with that later. For now I've got enough to contend with, keeping Jane from getting suspicious and working out where and when I have to be at work.

At that moment the bathroom door swings open and Jane's face appears round the side.

"Morning," she grins. "You making coffee?"

"Yes, I just . . ." I gesture to the cooling kettle and smile. "Sorry, I got distracted. I'll make one now."

"Thanks, Zo." She looks at the clock on the oven. "Aren't you going to be late?"

I glance at the clock too. It's 7.50. I'm not sure what to say. Late for *what?*

"Er, I suppose so."

Jane's face furrows. "Zo, you OK?"

"Yes, yes, course. Fine," I mumble. "It's just . . . I can't remember what time I'm meant to be at work today."

She looks at me for a second, a look of confusion flitting across her face before clearing. "Haven't you got an interview with Madeline before work today, for the junior job? Have I got the wrong day?"

It only takes a second for the memories to whizz around like a fruit machine and slot into the right place, but it feels as though I'm standing there under Jane's confused gaze for ages before my brain unscrambles the information. Of course! For the first few months in London I'd been working for a charity on a work placement. It was unpaid so I'd had to work behind a bar in the evenings to pay the rent. Now, finally, my boss Madeline had decided I was ready and when a job as a junior copywriter had come up, she'd asked me to apply for it. I'd been excited and nervous about this day for ages. No wonder Jane thought I'd gone mad.

"Bugger, of course," I say, jumping up. I run into the bathroom and close the door behind me. I'm not sure exactly what time I need to be there, but everyone else starts about 9.30 so I'm guessing 9.00. Including the walk to the station, it takes me about forty minutes to get from my flat in Tufnell Park to Camden where my office is, and that's on a good day, if the buses and Tubes are kind. That gives me about half an hour to get showered, dressed, and work out what on earth I'm going to say in this interview.

I've got no time to lose.

In the end I'm at the office five minutes early. I'm hot and sweaty and I've got a blister forming on my toe from the cheap high heels I'm not used to wearing, but I'm here and, I hope, on time. Even though I haven't been here for fourteen years the building is still familiar. It's a 1960s monstrosity on a busy corner. The windows are always filthy, the floors are stained with years of unidentifiable spillages, the lift rarely works and the heavy door makes a loud creaking sound as I push it open. It seems strange, after all this time, that the details haven't faded. It's funny, what the mind chooses to remember.

I reach the top of the stairs — it's three flights up but there's no way I'm risking the lift. Then I take a deep breath and walk towards Madeline's office and knock on the door.

"Come in!" calls a sunny voice from the other side. I'm glad it was Madeline I had to deal with today. She's lovely, and the sort of person who disproves the theory that you have to be a bitch to get to the top. She never has a bad word to say about anyone and although she never raises her voice and is never rude to anyone, she always gets what she wants. She's earned the respect of everyone who works for her.

"Hi, Madeline," I say, holding out my hand to shake hers.

"Oh, don't be silly, there's no need to be so formal," she says, gesturing for me to sit in the chair opposite her. I sink onto the hard plastic and sit, stiff-backed.

"Don't look so nervous, Zoe, you know as well as I do that this is only a formality. You've been doing this job for the last few months and you're great at it. I'm confident you can do it, I just really want to know if there's anything you want to ask me about it?"

I feel my body relaxing as she speaks, and I wrack my brains for something to ask her, but my mind's a blank.

"Er, I don't think so," I mumble, stupidly.

"Don't you even want to know how much we're going to pay you?" she grins, wickedly.

I smile back. "Yes, I suppose that would help."

"Well, it's not much to start with, I'm afraid, but I'm hoping it will soon go up. How does a starting salary of £18,000 sound, with an increase after three months if all goes well?"

I nod. "That sounds great," I say. "Thank you."

"Right," she says, clapping her hands. "Well then, that's that. Are you on board?"

"Of course, that would be brilliant, thank you."

I'm aware I sound like a bumbling idiot but at this point I don't care. I'm just relieved to have got through it without slipping up.

I stand to shake her hand but instead she comes round the desk and pulls me into a hug. Her soft hair brushes my cheek and she smells of a musky perfume that still makes me think of her when I smell it. "Well done, Zoe, I think you're going to be brilliant." I pull away, trying to blink back the tears. It's all thanks to the faith Madeline put in me today that I've got as far as I have in my career. I have her to thank for a lot. I brush away a tear before she notices.

"Right, let's get to work then," she says, grinning. "I'll let everyone know you're the new girl later."

"Thank you, Madeline," I say, opening her office door and walking to my desk. The office is still deserted and I fire my computer up. It's one of the original iMacs, all round and sleek and see through. Mine's purple, but there are oranges and blues and greens dotted all round the office. At the time it must have looked cutting-edge but now, to my 2013 eyes, it looks cutely retro.

I leave the computer warming up while I go and make myself a cup of tea. I look out of the grubby window for a few minutes, watching the cars inch slowly through the heavy traffic along Camden Road, and wonder where Ed is right at this minute. The thought makes my head reel. Because the fact is, somewhere out there, among the jumble of buildings and people and cars, is Ed, alive, getting on with his life, not knowing the love, happiness and heartache that his future is going to bring.

I grab the windowsill to steady myself as a memory floats into my mind. It must have been about eighteen months before this day: our last day of university, and the last time I'd seen him. We'd got through to the end of the four years at university sharing a house, and I'd learned just to bury any feelings I had for him. He never had a girlfriend for more than a month and, although it broke my heart seeing him with other girls, I learned to close my heart to it, smother my feelings and stay friends with him. Friends, I decided, was better than nothing.

When we left university we all agreed — and meant it — that we'd see each other all the time. The trouble was, life got in the way. I'd had to move back home to Doncaster for a few months to earn some money. Living with Mum and Dad and Becky again had been fine, but I longed to make the move I'd always planned down to London.

Finally, a year ago, in March 1998, Jane and I had scraped together enough cash to make the move, and although we were skint, we loved every minute of it.

There was just one thing that had bothered me. I hadn't heard from any of the boys since we'd left the house. In my heart I'd expected it from Rob and Simon — I knew what boys were like about keeping in touch, at the best of times — but the radio silence from Ed had been harder to deal with. Not having him in my life should have been easier, should have given my heart the chance to get over him and move on. And to some extent it had. But the truth was, I missed him. I missed his laugh, I missed his face and most of all I missed the way he teased me mercilessly.

"Just ring his mum, find out where he is," Jane said when I told her how I was feeling. But there was no way I was doing that. I'd just have to hope that fate would bring us together again.

"Fate?" Jane rolled her eyes. "You make your own fate. Just ring him and stop being so lame."

But I just couldn't bring myself to do it, and so it's now eighteen months since I last spoke to him, and I still have no idea where he is.

Except, I realize with a jolt, I do know exactly where he is. And I know exactly when I'm going to speak to him next. I glance at the clock. In just a few hours, if all goes the same as it did last time.

My heart leaps with excitement. But at the same time I feel a crushing sense of disappointment deep in my chest. Because if I'm right it means that, despite my best efforts to make a difference this time, nothing has changed at all; things are still exactly as they always were. Ed and I are still not together; at least, not yet.

I turn to open the fridge and pull some milk out. I sniff it. It seems OK and I splash some into my tea, squeeze the teabag out and go back to my desk. A girl I used to sit next to has arrived. As I walk across the office I try desperately to think of her name.

"Morning," I mumble, sitting down at my computer, hoping she won't drag me into conversation.

"Hi, Zoe," she says. "You OK?"

"Yeah, good, thanks." Then I remember to be polite. "You?"

"Yeah, great. Bit of a late one, though, I need coffee." She grins. "Want one?"

"No, I'm fine, thanks." I hold up my cup sheepishly. "Sorry." She grins, leaps up then mercifully disappears into the kitchen, giving me the chance to work out what I'm meant to be doing today.

The morning passes surprisingly quickly. I find what I've been working on, Madeline announces my new position, and everyone congratulates me. I make polite small talk without engaging in anything too deep and meaningful. And then it's lunchtime. I need a sandwich but I'm also waiting hopefully for the phone to ring. I sit drumming my fingers impatiently on the desk.

And then it peals out and I almost fall off my chair. I pick it up, my hand shaking.

"Hello?"

"Hello, could you tell me who I need to speak to about water coolers, please?" The voice is deep and familiar and it sends a warm buzz down my spine. I try to stay polite, make the conversation seem normal.

"I'm afraid you need to speak to Lizzie, the secretary, but she's not here at the moment." My voice is wobbly but he doesn't seem to notice.

"Do you know when she'll be back?"

"Ed, is that you?"

He pauses, clearly suspicious.

"Ye-eees?"

"Ed, it's Zoe. Morgan," I add, just in case.

"Oh my God, it's you!" he says. He sounds happy, at least. "I can't believe it!"

"Me neither. How are you?"

"I'm good, really good," he says, and I can picture him, nodding his head as he speaks. "How about you? How have you been?"

"Great. I just got a new job today."

"That's brilliant!"

"Thanks, I'm really chuffed." I stop, not sure what to say next. The silence stretches, waiting to be filled, and I'm sure he can hear my heart hammering from the other end of the phone line.

"Where are you?"

"London. Brixton," he adds. "What about you?"

"Camden right now. I live in Tufnell Park, though. With Jane."

66

"Do you now? Gosh, last time I saw her she was snogging the face off anything that moved."

"Jane never did that!"

"She did do that. Oh, except not with me." He pauses, embarrassed. "Surprised she didn't snog you, to be honest."

"Cheeky sod. No, Jane's great, we love our flat. It's fun living together and we love living in London too, even though it took us a while to get down here; but now it's great and . . ." I stop, aware I'm rambling, but trying to fill the silence.

"Sounds terrific." Ed pauses and when he speaks again his voice sounds unsteady, unsure of himself for the first time. "I was thinking, maybe we could meet up? Go for a drink?"

Static crackles down the line and I can hear him breathing. The silence stretches out and I feel a throbbing at my temple.

"When?"

"Um, maybe, I'm sure you're not free, but, well, how about tonight?"

I smile. He sounds terrified, so I answer quickly. "That would be nice."

"Nice?"

"Yes, nice. What's wrong with nice?"

"Well, it's just a bit —" he pauses — "tame."

"Well, OK then, that would be lovely. Smashing. Brilliant. Better?"

"Yes, much."

"Good. So, er, where do you want to go?"

"Soho any good?"

"Perfect. How about seven?"

"Seven it is. Meet you at the Shakespeare's Head, at the top of Carnaby Street."

"OK, great. See you later." And before he can change his mind I put the phone down, my pulse racing. It was so good to talk to him that I feel like a teenager again, giddy with excitement and possibility. I still have no idea what's going on but it seems clear I'm reliving days that involve Ed, or more specifically me and Ed: the day we met, seeing him with someone else after our first kiss — I never have any idea whether this will be the last day I get to see him, and so I have to make the most of it. There's got to be something I can change.

The rest of the day crawls by. The hands on the clock above the door hardly seem to move all afternoon and each minute feels longer than an hour. I read the same thing 300 times and still can't make sense of it. I chat mindlessly to Anna — the girl next to me, whose name I finally remembered when someone called it across the office — about what she's doing that weekend with her boyfriend. Something involving Hoxton and an art exhibition, but I'm not really listening. All I can think about is meeting up with Ed later.

At last, after what seems like days on end strung together, the clock struggles round to six and it's time to leave.

It won't take me an hour to get to Oxford Circus, so on the dot of six I pick up my bag from the floor and practically run into the office toilets. They're grim. A bare bulb gives out a harsh overhead light, the mirrors are splattered with black marks, some of the tiles on the wall are chipped and there's always an unpleasant smell that seems determined to battle its way through the overpowering air freshener that the cleaner squirts round the room every time she leaves. But tonight I don't care. I don't notice at all.

I rummage in my bag and find my lip gloss, mascara and hairbrush. It's not much but it'll have to do. I glance in the mirror and as I pull the brush through my hair I realize this is the first time today I've had a chance to look at myself properly. My hair is still very dark but it's not as long as before and the shorter style makes my face look rounder and even younger, which probably wasn't the effect I was going for at twenty-four. It's straightish with a hint of frizz and I have a memory of blow-drying my hair in the days before straighteners and feel a pang of sympathy for the old me. My hair has always been unruly. It never looked sleek apart from when I went to the hairdressers, and I wish I had my straighteners with me right now to give it the once-over.

I apply one more slick of lip gloss — pointlessly, because it will all be gone by the time I get there — and turn to leave. I walk the familiar route past Sainsbury's, past the string of tatty shops, their wares spilling out onto the pavement: mops, buckets, plastic boxes, tea towels, saucepans, shoehorns, all vying for attention. The icy wind has picked up and it feels very wintry all of a sudden, the heels I threw on this morning in preparation for my interview doing a terrible job of keeping my feet warm. Scraps of paper whip around in the wind, and a homeless man sitting in a shop doorway pulls his blackened blanket tighter around his shoulders. The weak sun has disappeared now and dark clouds are gathering. "It looks like snow," my mum would have said.

I carry on walking, head down, to the Tube station, the wind whipping my hair round my face. By the time I get there a few spots of rain have started and I must look like I've been dragged through a hedge backwards. But I don't care, because all I can think about is seeing Ed.

I go down the escalator in a dream, staring blindly at the posters lining the wall. I step off and stand on the platform, people walking round me and behind me, and I hardly notice any of them. The wind in the tunnel picks up, indicating the arrival of the next train, and when the doors slide open I step on and stand in a tiny space between bodies, holding on tightly to the overhead bar, swaying gently with the movement of the train. I try to empty my mind.

The train pulls into Tottenham Court Road and I step off. I still have twenty minutes until I'm meeting Ed, so despite the weather I decide to walk the rest of the way, through the backstreets of Soho. I wind through the streets, my hair whipping wildly and my mind racing just as fast. As I approach the beautiful black-and-white Liberty building at the top of Carnaby Street, the familiar place where we often used to meet for after-work drinks, I feel my heart rate picking up, and I take some deep breaths. I slow down, aware I'm a few minutes early, not wanting to seem too keen. After all, as I have to keep reminding myself, he doesn't know what happens next. He doesn't know that we fall in love. He doesn't know, yet, that I like to read my book in the bath, or that I'm like a bear with a sore head in the morning until I've had two cups of tea; he's never seen me naked; he's never seen me sobbing my heart out while he holds me tightly, trying to calm me down. He knows none of this and yet I know it all and more, so I have to be careful.

I'm waiting, staring into the crowds, when I spot Ed, his distinctive amble as he slowly makes his way up Carnaby Street towards the sign that spans the top of the car-less road. He looks so handsome and so young in his jeans with a rip at the knee and his hair flopping over his eyes, and my heart squeezes a little tighter as it surges with love.

My Ed.

And then he's there in front of me and his face breaks into a wide smile as he sees me, and it's as though the sun has come out.

"Hi, gorgeous," he says, hugging me tightly.

I hug him back, not wanting to let go, but eventually I do.

I keep my voice steady. "Hey, you." I smile, and look him up and down. "Look at you, all grown up."

He rolls his eyes. "God, I don't know about that." He doesn't say any more and I think I see a hint of sadness behind his eyes which clears almost immediately.

"So, where shall we go?" I say. "I need to warm up a bit."

"Let's go in here for a drink first, then we can decide." He takes me by the hand and drags me towards the Shakespeare's Head. His hand feels warm in mine, and so right.

We run into the darkness of the pub and stop, giggling as we push the bar door open. I scan the room and spot a free table in the corner and make a dash for it, trying to hide my disappointment at him letting go of my hand.

"Right, what do you want?" I dump my bag under the table and start to head for the bar.

"Don't be daft, I'll get these. What'll it be?"

"Are you sure? It's pretty expensive in here . . ." I tail off.

"Of course. I think I can afford to buy you a drink."

"Yes, sorry, sorry. I didn't mean —" I pause, take a breath, reminding myself that Ed doesn't know he's always so skint that it's usually me who pays for drinks — and everything else — these days. "I'll have gin and slimline, please. Lime, not lemon."

"Coming right up." He does a little bow and heads to the bar.

Alone for a few minutes, I take some deep breaths to steady my nerves. I feel so overwhelmed at seeing Ed again, but he has no idea how happy it makes me feel. To him I'm just a friend he had a snog with a few years ago, whereas to me, he means everything. And everything I've lost.

I watch him at the bar as he waits to be served. His face is caught in a spotlight and it's so familiar I can hardly believe I'd started to forget its beautiful details. Long lashes frame his deep-blue eyes, and there are yet to be lines creasing the corners. They'll come later. I touch my own smooth skin in wonder. Stubble covers his chin and cheeks, a couple of days' growth, and the light picks out his sharp cheekbones. There are shadows under his eyes and he looks tired, and a small frown creases his forehead. Then it's his turn to order and he leans forward across the bar, his lips breaking into a smile, and my heart leaps. And then I can't resist. My eyes travel down to his bum, barely discernible under his loose-fitting jeans, trying to make out its contours, remembering how I used to grip those bum cheeks when we were — God, Zoe, stop it! My face flushes at where my thoughts were heading, and I tear my eyes away, trying to calm myself.

Ed walks back towards the table, a gin and tonic in one hand, a glass of red wine in the other.

"Not beer these days?" I nod at the drinks as he places them on the table to cover up my embarrassment. I feel as though I've been caught out doing something really naughty.

"Nah, never really liked it anyway. Red wine, though, is the dog's bollocks."

"Charming." I grin and he smiles as he takes a sip. I feel nervous, which is ridiculous. This is *Ed*, who I've known for years, shared a bed with, shared my life with. How can I be shy with him?

"So, what's new with you, then?" he says.

"What, since I last saw you? Well, I moved down here, obviously, and as I said, me and Jane got a flat together."

"Ha, yeah, bet that's fun."

"It is, actually, although it's the size of a postage stamp. Not quite like the house we had before, at uni. But it's great to be living with Jane. And I work at a charity, in the marketing department, and I just got a new job today."

"Oh yes!" he says. "I forgot. We should be drinking champagne, celebrate a bit."

"God no, my budget doesn't run to that." I stop, hoping I haven't insulted him by implying he couldn't afford it either. Since when did it get this complicated to talk to Ed? Well, since you haven't been a couple for fourteen years, you idiot.

"Well, it sounds like you've done brilliantly," he says. "But then who'd have ever doubted it, Miss I-Got-My-Homework-Done-Before-We-Went-Out Morgan?"

It's said with a smile and I can't take offence. He's right, I did work hard. I was probably a right pain in the arse. "Yeah, thanks. What about you, what are you up to these days?"

"Not much. After uni I went travelling for six months — a cliché, I know, but I didn't know what else to do. I lived with Mum for a few months after that but, much as I love her, she drives me mad, always trying to do everything for me, so I came to London to seek my fortune. Now I live alone in a tiny studio flat in Clapham with a bed like rice pudding, and have a crappy job selling water coolers to companies who have no interest in having one in their office and just wish I'd leave them alone. It's not quite what I was expecting when I left uni, to be honest."

"What were you expecting?" My voice is sharper than I intended and Ed looks up, surprised.

"Well, I suppose I thought, you know, with a degree, even a crappy one in Geology, that it would be easy to find a job I liked doing. I guess the trouble was I didn't really know what I liked doing. Still don't."

"It's not exactly been that long, though. There's still plenty of time. Maybe if you didn't feel so sorry for yourself you'd find something."

"Whoa, where did that come from?"

"Sorry, I didn't mean to sound so harsh. It's just —" I stop and pick up a beer mat, aware I mustn't take out the frustration of the last fourteen years on the Ed who hardly knows me. I'll drive him away before we've even got started and then where would it leave us? "I just mean, there's plenty you're good at and that you could make work if you put your mind to it."

"Such as?" He puts his chin in his hand, waiting for an answer.

"Well, what about music? You loved the guitar. Could you not teach?"

He shrugs. "Maybe, but I'm probably not good enough."

"Well, what about cooking, then? You always loved making dinner for us all at uni. Isn't there something you could do with food? Or gardening, something practical. You've always been good with your hands." I flush at the double meaning. "I don't know. I'm not trying to tell you what you should do with your life, but, you know, there's plenty of things you're good at that you might find you loved if you just gave them a go."

Speech finished, I sit back and watch his face. He looks amused rather than cross and I'm relieved, aware I've probably gone too far.

"What's so funny?"

"Oh, nothing, Zo. It just sounds as though you've given this a lot of thought — more than I have. Maybe you should be a careers adviser rather than working in marketing. I reckon you'd be a hit."

"Oh, ha ha."

"But you are right. I do need to sort myself out, 'find' myself. Maybe you can help me do that."

His tone is flirty and I smile, glad to move on. "Maybe I can."

He leans closer and I'm aware of his hand on the table, right next to mine. I can almost feel the heat from it and am desperate to touch it, hold it. It's so all-consuming that for a minute I can't think about anything else. He glances down and I pull my hand away and twiddle my glass.

"So, enough about me," he says. "Tell me more about your promotion."

Back on safe ground, I chat happily about work, about moving to London, and about everything that's happened in the eighteen months since we've seen each other.

"And what about boyfriends? Been seeing anyone?"

I glance up. His face is serious, studying me.

"Um, not really. Well actually, I was meant to be meeting someone tonight . . ."

"But you blew him off for me?"

"No!" I glance at my watch. It's 9 p.m. "Well, er, yes, I guess I have. Oh dear. Poor Andy." I grin mischievously. "I hope he didn't wait too long."

"Why wouldn't he? I would."

His words hang thickly in the air, neither of us sure what to do with them. Anyway, there's something else I need to ask, whether I want to know the answer or not.

"What about you? Have you been seeing anyone?" The words sound stilted even to my ears.

He looks down at his drink, runs his finger absently round the rim of the glass, creating a low, insistent hum. He looks guilty as sin and I know what he's going to say before he speaks.

"I — sort of."

"Sort of." I try and keep the anger from my tone but it's hard. "What does that mean?"

"Just — I've sort of been seeing someone, but it's — complicated."

"Complicated?" God, I sound like a parrot. Get a grip, Zoe.

Ed rubs his hand over his face and breathes deeply.

"OK, Zoe, this is it, right. I have been seeing someone: it's been a few months, maybe five or six. We — she — is talking about moving in together —" He stops, drums his fingers on the tabletop. I wait. "The thing is, I haven't exactly discouraged her. But now . . . Well, now this, Zo." He waves his hand between us. "Now we're here and, well. As I said, it's complicated."

I let his words hang between us for a moment. "It doesn't sound that complicated to me. You're with

77

someone, it's pretty serious — serious enough for her to think you want to move in with her."

Ed shakes his head quickly. "No, you've got it wrong, Zoe. It's not that simple. Jenny — well . . ." He tails off, stares at his hands clasped tightly on the tabletop and lets out a rush of air. "It's not an accident, you know."

I frown. "What's not?"

"That we're here, now. Me and you."

"What do you mean?"

Ed carries on staring at his hands, refusing to meet my eye. "I rang you on purpose. You know, earlier."

I let his words sink in for a minute. "How? Why?"

Ed shrugs, uncomfortable. "I just — me and Jenny, it — well, it just felt wrong when there was someone else I couldn't stop thinking about. And then — well, then I did some detective work, found out where you work. And then — well, then this."

I stare at him a moment, willing him to look at me. And finally he does, and we sit like that for a moment, not speaking.

"Are you serious?"

He nods. "Yep."

"Oh . . ."

Ed laughs, a small, self-deprecating laugh. "So, you could say it's a bit of a mess. I suppose — well, I suppose I just need to sort it out."

I nod in agreement. Silence crackles between us and I don't know how to fill it. My mind's racing with possibilities. This is how this evening ended last time, apart from a kiss before saying goodbye later. I'd wanted to do the right thing, and so I had. But what if I didn't?

78

What if I wasn't that girl for a change, and, knowing that we get together in the end anyway, I say stuff it, and just be with him? It could be my last chance.

Before I can speak, Ed pushes his chair back and stands up.

"I need more booze. Same again?" He nods his head at my empty glass.

"Please."

I watch him at the bar again. I imagine going over there, snaking my arms round his waist and pressing my lips against the soft skin of his neck. Other people would. Jane probably would. But I know it would be wrong and I reflect that I'm not sure I want to be taking relationship advice from Jane either, given her future record. Then I feel guilty for the treacherous thought.

Ed returns with full glasses and seems to have composed himself a bit.

"Right, let's move on. What were we talking about before we reached that conversation cul-de-sac?"

Pleased to have the tension lifted, I smile and lean forward. We spend the next couple of hours chatting about friends, family, reminiscing. It actually feels pretty good just being with Ed again, free of burdens. I miss this Ed. It's been too long since our conversations weren't loaded with meaning, tiptoeing round each other to avoid a row.

The bell rings and the barman shouts, "Last orders!" I jump, looking round at the emptying pub. I'm quite drunk, and the room's spinning a little.

Ed looks at his watch. "Oops," he says, with a lopsided smile. "I think it's a bit late for dinner."

"Yes, a bit."

"I think I'd better get you home."

"Yes, I suppose so." I don't want the night to end, not like this, but I'm not sure what to do about it so I follow Ed's lead and stand and pull on my coat, wobbling a bit as I pick up my bag from the floor.

"Whoops." I grin and Ed grabs my hand and pulls me through the door. It's turned bitterly cold outside and our breath forms clouds around us as we stand slightly shocked outside the pub.

"I'm taking you home. To sleep," he adds, with a grin.

"Don't be silly, you live on the other side of the city."

"Doesn't matter. I'm not letting you go home on your own. I'll be all right."

We walk hand in hand to the Tube station and sit side by side on the train. I watch our reflections in the window opposite as we rattle through the tunnel. We look like any ordinary couple and I shiver. If only.

Ed doesn't let go of my hand the whole way. Then the train pulls slowly into Tufnell Park station and we both stand and get off. My heart's hammering with the possibility of what could come next. Last time we just said goodbye and I said I'd wait for him to sort things out. This time, with gin softening my thoughts, even I'm not sure what I'm going to do yet.

I turn to face him.

"You don't have to walk me home. It's late. You'll miss your train."

He glances at the clock on the board. It's 11.36. He nods, but doesn't move.

"I really enjoyed tonight," he says instead. Then he leans towards me and his lips gently brush mine. He pulls back and looks at me, as if to ask if it's OK, and I give him a tiny nod. He leans in again, and my legs start to shake as he kisses me, his lips cool against mine.

The station platform is empty but it could have been packed to the rafters and I wouldn't have noticed. For this minute, it's just me and Ed and no one else in the world.

Finally, he pulls away. "So?" The word is loaded with questions.

And suddenly, I know what I'm going to do. I shake my head, almost imperceptibly, but it's clear what I mean.

"I'm sorry, Ed, I just can't. Not now. It's not right."

Ed nods and takes a tiny step backwards.

"I know. You're right. Of course."

I shove my hand in my bag and find a chewed-up old biro, then I take hold of Ed's hand and carefully write my phone number across it, before letting it drop back to his side.

"Ring me when you can?"

He nods, and then before I can change my mind I turn and walk away, glancing back only once to see him watching me until I disappear from sight. It's the hardest thing I've ever done, knowing I may never see him again, but it's the right thing to do.

It's not until I'm back at home in my own bed that I allow myself to cry, as I remember Ed walking away from me, when all I wanted to do was hold on to him for the rest of my life. And never let him go.

And with my face comforted by my soft pillow, the tears subside and I drift off to sleep, hopeful for another tomorrow.

CHAPTER
FOUR

5 June 1999

A cup of tea sits cooling on the kitchen counter and I listen to Jane moving around in her room. She'll be through soon, so I'm enjoying a few minutes alone first.

When I woke up this morning and realized it was happening again, my heart soared. Another day with Ed. When I'd begged for more time with him in the dark days after his death, I'd imagined what I'd say and do in a few minutes with him: I'd tell him how sorry I was, how much I loved him, and how I would always love him. I'd pictured hugging him, kissing him, and just touching him: all the things I wasn't able to do any more. And now I was getting to do just that.

Despite myself, a smile spreads across my face.

"What are you grinning like a loon about?" Jane's shuffled into the room, her hair dishevelled and her eyes bleary. She's stifling a yawn.

"Nothing. Blimey, you look rough."

She chuckles. "Thanks. I feel like the walking dead." She glances at me again, suspiciously. "Unlike you. Why are you so chipper this morning?"

"No reason." Which is true. At least, not one I can remember.

Jane raises her eyebrows. "You're not —" her eyes flick towards my bedroom door — "*with* someone, are you?"

"No, nothing like that. I'm just happy to see you, of course." I grin and she picks up a cushion and throws it at my head. I duck just in time and it lands on the floor behind me, barely missing a lamp.

She pads over to the kettle.

"Coffee. I need coffee." She reaches up and pulls a jar of instant from the cupboard and spoons it into her mug.

"Let me make you a real one," I say, jumping up from my stool.

She looks at me again as if she's about to say something, then changes her mind and steps aside. "OK," she shrugs. "Thanks." She heaves herself onto a stool and lowers her head to rest on her arms on the tabletop.

"So what did you get up to last night?" I say, clattering around with spoons, hoping she'll shed some light on things.

She frowns. "What, after you left, you mean?"

Shit. "Yes, well, obviously. So did you go anywhere else?"

She sighs. "Well, after dinner me and Tom went to Turnmills but it was crap so we only stayed for about an hour. Then, well, he went home alone. Again."

Oh God, not Tom. Apart from being a total arse, he treated Jane terribly in the year or so they were together. Always messed her about, dropped her like a stone when it suited him. Turned out he was seeing

84

someone else at the same time, but we didn't find that out until much later.

"He's cheating on you. Just tell him to piss off." The words come out before I can think about them and too late I realize my mistake.

"What?" Jane's head snaps up.

"Well, you know. It's obvious."

"Is it? And what makes you so sure?" Her voice is cool, angry. I try to backtrack.

"Nothing, never mind. But he does treat you like shit, Jane. He always leaves you in the lurch, never wants to commit to anything. There's got to be something going on, hasn't there?"

She looks at me, hurt. "Has there?"

"Well, I don't know. It just seems . . . Listen, ignore me, I'm talking rubbish. I just don't like seeing you hurt, and you could do so much better. You deserve so much better."

She looks at me a moment longer, clearly deciding whether to forgive me. To my relief, she sighs.

"Sorry, Zo. I do know you're right, I just — I don't get it. One minute he seems to really like me, the next it's like he doesn't fancy me and can't get away quick enough."

"You shouldn't put up with it." I pour the water into the cafetière and almost scald my eyebrows on the steam.

She sighs. "I know, I know. But he's just so . . ." She looks for the right word. "Cute."

I roll my eyes. "That's one way to describe him." I perch on the stool again while I wait for the coffee to brew. "Irritating is more the word I was looking for."

She smiles weakly. "Yeah, I know." There's silence for a few seconds, then she grins impishly and adds, "Anyway, you can talk."

I sigh. I know what's coming. "Ed." It's a statement, not a question.

"Yes, Ed. Come on, Zo, you know what I'm talking about. You have a great night together, and then he buggers off and leaves you pining for four months, and still no word. That's more than irritating. That's just rude."

"I know, I know. But to be fair, he does have a girlfriend."

"So what? He promised to sort it. Don't you think four months is a pretty long time to wait around?"

"Yes, of course it is. But we've been over and over this. I'm not chasing him again. He can come to me."

"And what if he doesn't?"

"Well, then I'll be heartbroken for the rest of my life and never forgive myself and end up a lonely old spinster, pining for the man I lost."

"See, that's what I thought. So what are you going to do about it? It's all very well you giving me advice, but what about you?"

I sigh. "Yes, I know. I do. And maybe you're right. Maybe I should ring him."

Jane claps her hands together and bounces up and down on the stool. "See! This is what I mean. You've got to do something, you can't just let life pass you by. You know the old saying — it's better to regret something you did than something you didn't do."

"Isn't that a song?"

She grins. "Maybe. But it's still true."

I grin back. It might be ironic, her advising me in her situation, but perhaps, without knowing it, she's hit the nail on the head. Perhaps this is what I can do to change things this time. Perhaps I'm meant to ring Ed, hurry things along, stop waiting around. It can't do any harm, at least.

"OK, I'll do it."

"What, really?" She still looks suspicious.

"Yes, really." I nod for emphasis.

She jumps down and runs across the room, coming back with the phone in her hand. "Go on then, do it now, before you chicken out."

I take the receiver, my hand shaking. I think about speaking to Ed again, and I tense. I don't want to mess anything up. I'm still not exactly sure what day it is; how can I be certain he's ready to be with me?

"I'll do it later."

"Oh, you wuss. Why not now?"

"I just — I'm not ready. It's too early." It sounds lame even to my ears. "I'll do it later, I promise."

Jane narrows her eyes, disbelieving.

"I will. Honestly. Just give me time to get used to the idea." And to work out what I'm going to say.

"OK. But I'm not letting you get away with this, Zoe Morgan. I'm not sure I could stand listening to you banging on about it any more anyway." She grins as I swipe for her, and nearly falls off the stool. "Anyway, enough wasting a precious Saturday talking about bloody men. Haven't we got a day out planned?"

Have we?

"Course. Let's just have another drink, then I'm all yours."

I jump up and open the cupboard above the kettle and pull out a mug saying "I love to shop" on it and another plain blue one, part of a set. The blue one has a small chip on the handle. It's funny how I haven't thought about these things for years — the chipped mugs, the retro clock on the kitchen wall that ticked too loudly, the rarely used herbs and spices lined up neatly in the spice rack next to the toaster. Yet here they are, as familiar and normal as they ever were, as though no time has passed at all.

I pour the coffee and pass Jane her shopping mug, then pour myself a small cup.

"Why are you drinking coffee?" Jane says, the crease between her eyebrows deepening.

"Er . . ." I mumble. "Not sure, I'm not really with it yet." I pour the coffee down the sink, cursing myself. I never used to drink coffee, was almost evangelical about how I couldn't stand the bitter taste of it. Later I developed a bit of an addiction, but here, now, in 1999, I still hated it, and Jane knows that, of course.

She looks at me a second longer, then turns to switch on the radio as I busy myself preparing a cup of tea. "Hey Boy Hey Girl" by the Chemical Brothers blares out across the kitchen and the coffee incident is instantly forgotten as we grin at the choice of song.

"Chooon!" Jane yells, and we both bounce up and down for the next five minutes, giggling like children.

88

It turns out we've got a Saturday shopping day planned, followed by a night out drinking, and an hour or so later we walk to the Tube station arm in arm. I've slung on some jeans, Docs and a black vest top; Jane's in her usual girlie get-up of a strappy summer dress with a belt cinched in around the middle. The sun's warm on my face, the heat bouncing from the walls and pavement onto our freshly washed skin. For the first time I notice the freckles have come out on my arms and realize it must have been warm and sunny for a while now. London feels different when the sun comes out; it's as though it strips off its usual reservations and becomes a fun-loving teenager, ready for anything. Even the rustling of the leaves in the breeze sound like a low chuckle, and the birds tweet their reply in song. I love it.

We spend a lovely day browsing the shops on Oxford Street and Carnaby Street (I can't help glancing at the Shakespeare's Head as we pass, remembering the night with Ed), eating noodles, trying on ridiculous outfits. Even if I don't see Ed, today has been worth every minute of the time I've spent in it. I'd forgotten how to have fun, how to relax and just enjoy myself — and so had Jane. This day has been special.

Finally, about five o'clock, we head home laden down with bags, our feet aching from pounding the pavements all day. My heart feels heavy with the anticipation of the promise I made Jane this morning, that I'd ring Ed. I'm terrified of what this change might mean — and yet I'm excited too.

The flat feels cool as we come in, and I head to my room to dump my bags and get changed. I'm just admiring a new pair of jeans I treated myself to when Jane shouts my name. She sounds panicked.

I drop the jeans and rush to the lounge to see her stricken face.

"What? What's happened?"

She's starting to scare me. But then her face breaks into a grin. "Ed," she whispers, flapping her arms crazily in the direction of the answerphone.

"Ed?" I look at the phone as though I'm expecting to see him sitting there, then back at Jane's face. "What about him?"

Still grinning crazily she leans over and presses the play button on the answerphone. There's a bit of a crackling noise as though the person on the other end has dropped their phone, then a deep, familiar voice comes into the room, clear as a bell.

"Hi, Zo, it's me. Ed. I'm sorry it's taken me so long but I was trying to sort things out, and then, well . . . Well, ring me back, yeah?"

He leaves his number, then the phone makes a long, low droning noise, and goes silent. I stand there for a minute, staring at it, as though I'm expecting something else to happen.

"He rang!" Jane practically squeaks, jumping up and down next to me. "Zoe? Hey, Earth to Zo, are you hearing me? Ed just rang you!"

I look at her and can't help a grin escaping.

"He did, didn't he? He really did!"

90

"Well, don't just stand there, ring him back," she says. She grabs an old magazine from the side and rummages in her handbag for a pen, then presses the play button for a third time. We stand there as Ed's voice fills the room again, then at the end Jane frantically scribbles the number down across the top of the magazine cover, checking to make sure she's got it right.

She hands it to me. "Go on!"

I take it from her with shaking hands. "Bugger off, then, I can't ring him with you standing there earwigging." I swipe her arm with the mag and she grins, then scampers off towards her room and shuts the door with a dramatic slam.

My heart's hammering wildly as I pick up the phone and dial the number. Jane's writing is such a scrawl I can only just make it out, but finally I hear the ringing sound at the other end.

I'm fully prepared for the answerphone to kick in, so I'm taken by surprise when someone picks up, and I gasp.

"Hello?"

"Er, hi, um, it's me," I say stupidly. "Sorry, I mean Zoe. It's Zoe."

"Hey, you," he says, his voice warm. "I'm so glad you rang back."

I can practically hear his smile down the phone, and I feel myself start to relax.

"So . . ." I start, unsure how to ask him what I really want to know — whether he's available — even though I know the answer.

"Yes," he says simply. "It's over with Jenny."

My breath comes out in a rush and I laugh nervously. "Oh . . ." I trail off, unsure what else to say.

Ed steps in. "So." There's a pause and I listen to him breathing softly down the phone. Then he takes a deep breath and says, "Look —"

"I guess we should meet up," I finish for him.

"I guess we should. The question is, your place or mine?"

"Ha, you charmer." Then: "You're still in London?"

"Yes, still in London. So do you want to meet later, go for dinner?"

I think about it. All I really want to do is spend the night wrapped in Ed's arms and never let him go. But we have to have a first date and this is it; and dinner, well, dinner is normal. I could do with a little bit of normal. "Yes. I'd love to."

We arrange to meet in Covent Garden and go to a little Italian restaurant he knows. I know it well too, it's where we spent many dates over the years, but I pretend it's all new to me.

I put the phone down and before I've even turned round, Jane's out of her door.

"Well, where are you going?"

"You were listening!"

She shrugs. "Course, every word. Who wouldn't? So, where are you going?"

"Dinner. Covent Garden, at eight."

"So, blowing me out for a boy, are you?"

"Do you mind?"

"Why the bloody hell would I mind?" Jane glances at the clock. "But it does mean we've only got just over two hours to get you looking gorgeous and out of the house. Come on, let's go!"

She dashes into her room and I walk to the bathroom and start the shower going. As the room starts to fill with steam I watch my reflection fading in the mirror, my features smudging and blurring as the steam gathers. This is the first time today I've had a chance to stop and think, and I believe I might actually be happy.

Two hours later I'm ready and Jane's trying to bundle me out of the door.

"Come on, you'll be late and whatever you think, that's not cool," she says, handing me my bag. "Right, you've got your money, keys, make-up, toothbrush . . ." She grins wickedly as I shoot her a look. "What? It's best to be prepared, isn't it?"

I roll my eyes and grin back at her. "I guess it is. And Jane?"

"What?"

"Thanks."

"You're welcome." She looks at me for a second longer and I think she's going to give me a hug. But then she leans forward, moves a stray piece of hair from my forehead and says, her face serious, "Anyway, I couldn't let you go out looking like that, could I?"

I stare at her a second and then we both burst into giggles. "You cheeky mare." I lean and plant a kiss on her cheek, then stand and nervously smooth imaginary creases from my top. "Right, this is it. Wish me luck."

"Good luck. Hopefully see you tomorrow." She winks and practically pushes me out of the door.

And here I am, on my way to meet Ed again. As the Tube rattles towards central London my heart thumps wildly, thinking about enjoying a date with Ed again, a date when we still actually like each other.

Before, back in 2013, Ed and I had hardly been friends any more, let alone lovers. We were at breaking point. Life had become less about "us" and more about trying to get pregnant, and in the process, it was as though we'd forgotten who we were. Could it be that I've been given the chance to see where we went wrong and do something about that now — to tell him I still loved him and that it was him I wanted, and that I wanted to stop trying for a baby and be his wife again?

I feel dizzy at the thought.

The train pulls into Tottenham Court Road and I push my way to the doors before they close, joining the throng heading towards the exit. I'm walking the rest of the way, and as we stream onto the packed pavement the sun is still glowing in the hazy sky and I feel my spirits soar.

I'm meeting Ed!

I arrive at the restaurant a few minutes early and settle myself at a window table, happy to people-watch until Ed arrives. A couple stroll hand in hand down the road, stepping off the pavement to let a man in rolled-up chinos and boat shoes pass who's talking

94

urgently on his mobile. I let myself imagine, fleetingly, that chino man is going through the same as me, reliving a strange, parallel day from some other time, and wonder whether, if that were true, he'd try to make some changes to the first time around. Of course he would. Who wouldn't?

There's a gentle movement at my shoulder and I whip my head round. Ed's there, and the sight of him almost takes my breath away.

His hair is lighter than I've seen it in a long time, sun-kissed, and longer, past his collar and touching his shoulders. It flops sexily over one eye. He's also obviously made an effort and looks a little uncomfortable in a short-sleeved shirt and slim jeans. My heart contracts as I jump up and launch myself at him, engulfing him in a bear hug.

"Ooh hello, nice greeting."

We sit down and suddenly I feel shy. He looks so young, so much like the Ed I've held in my mind, that I can hardly speak.

I'm saved by the waiter's arrival.

"Can I get you any drinks?"

"Oh, I er . . . white wine, please. Large."

"Red, please," he says. "Large too."

The waiter bustles away and Ed turns to me, his eyebrows raised.

"Dutch courage, eh?"

"Definitely."

There's a silence and I pick at the corner of a paper napkin.

"I'm sorry it took me so long, Zoe," he says, after a few beats. "Jen — things were just harder than I expected."

I nod, tearing a strip off the napkin, then another. "But it's definitely over, now?"

He nods. "Definitely. And don't worry, I haven't been awful. She's OK. It's all fine."

He knows me well. But I'm still keen to move the conversation away from Jenny.

"Thank you."

"You're welcome." He peers down at the table. "Nervous?"

I look down and see the napkin ripped to shreds, and grin. "Sorry, bad habit." I pull my hands away and pick up the menu, but I'm hardly able to take in the words. Having Ed so close yet not being able to touch him is torture, and I can't seem to think about anything else. He's studying the menu, a line creasing his forehead in concentration. Every now and then his tongue comes out, dampens his lips, disappears again; his arms are lean, his skin warm and tanned from being out on his bike, the tiny hairs lightened and soft, the tendons standing out, tensed. One hand rests gently on the table, tapping out a muffled beat on the tablecloth, and my eyes are drawn to his long fingers, moving to a silent rhythm in his head. I long to reach out my hand and stroke them.

"Ready?"

I jump, and look up to find Ed watching me, the waiter waiting patiently by the table.

"Um, yeah." My face feels hot, and I'm glad Ed can't read my mind. I order the first thing that comes into my head: seafood pasta, the same as I always had when we came here. The waiter leaves and I turn to Ed and find him looking at me curiously.

"Are you OK, Zoe? You seem very — distracted."

If only he knew.

"I'm fine, really. Just happy to be here, with you."

"Me too." He reaches over and grabs my hand and his touch feels like I've been electrified. "So."

"So." I shrug.

"What now?"

That's the big question, isn't it? What now. Before, we'd spent the evening chatting about our lives, friends, work. But it doesn't seem enough now, it seems too everyday. It seems — the thing that's been playing at the back of my mind since I woke up this morning — that this is the perfect chance to have another go at trying to change something. It hasn't worked so far, but so what? Who's to say it won't? Who's to say the butterfly effect doesn't still stand?

My mind races through the possibilities. There are so many. Perhaps if I could bring up the subject of babies, make it clear from the beginning that I don't think I want them (even if it's not really true — I don't want them now, I've got too much I want to do first, but I might do one day), just maybe I could change something later. Maybe if Ed believed all along that I'm not sure about having a baby, it would be easier to cope with further down the line.

It's a serious subject to bring up on a "first" date, but I reckon I know him well enough. It has to be worth a shot.

"Let's talk. I mean really talk. You know, about the future, what we want, what we don't want." He looks surprised, so I plough on. "I mean, we've never really talked about what we want from life before, have we? And I'd like to know."

A cloud crosses his face briefly, then clears. "Right, blimey. OK." He looks worried.

"Shall I start?"

"Go on, then."

I take a deep breath. "OK, a boring one, this, but I've always wanted to travel the world, see different places. But I've always been a bit scared, worried that if I took a break from school, or uni, or work, I'd never get back into it, and so I haven't really been anywhere, apart from France on family holidays. So now here I am at the ripe old age of twenty-two, and I've hardly seen anything of the big wide world. I want to see more." I look up. "Your turn."

"Oh, OK, right. Well, I've done some travelling, obviously, so mine is a bit different. You know it's always been just me and Mum, right, growing up? Or as near as matters." I nod. "And it's fine, I mean, it's great. Mum's great. But the flat was always quiet, and I spent a lot of time playing on my own or with second cousins twice removed or whoever they were. I've always wondered what it would be like to have a huge family, a massive house in the country filled with kids, a huge garden to play in. I know it's a fantasy as nothing

98

is ever as idyllic as I picture it, but the kids bit — well, I'd love that."

My face must have paled because when he looks at me he shrugs. "Well, you did ask."

I smile weakly. "I did."

"So, what about you? Do you want kids, marriage, the works?"

The million-dollar question. My whole future might turn on a pin with the answer to this, but I don't have much time to think about it.

"Well . . ." I pause, gather my thoughts. This has to sound right, authentic. "I guess, I'm not sure. I'd like to get married, but kids, I don't really know. I mean, everyone always assumes they will, right, that they'll have kids one day even if not right now? But when I actually think about the reality of having children and what that would mean to my life, I'm honestly not sure. I love my life as it is, I love my job and, as you know, I'm ambitious. I want to work hard, work my way up, do well. I know I'm only twenty-two and people always think you might change your mind but the truth is — I can't see it. I just don't think it's what I want."

Speech over, I feel drained and sit back in my chair. Ed's looking at me with a curious expression on his face.

"Wow."

I smile weakly. "Well, you asked too."

"I did. It's just, you sound so sure."

"I am, for now. Who knows what will come in the future —" I wince at the irony of my words — "but for now, that's me."

It feels as though the silence that follows is going to stretch on forever, so I'm relieved when the waiter appears and presents us with our food. The fuss — the clatter of cutlery, the discussion about how good the food looks, the adding of parmesan, pepper, the pouring of more wine — all serves as a welcome distraction from the intensity of the conversation. I tuck into my plate of pasta, trying hard not to meet Ed's eye, sure he'll know there's something amiss.

I feel cruel, being so blunt, shattering the dream of a perfect family life he'd just so clearly laid out before me. With anyone else it wouldn't have mattered — nobody assumes on a first date that they are going to stay together. But me and Ed have history — quite apart from all the stuff I know about that is still to come — and this is more than a first date. This is us working each other out, planning to be together.

I have to hope my little speech didn't blow it completely.

"I hope you don't think I was being harsh."

Ed's eyes are unreadable.

"Not harsh, no." He seems to consider his words for a moment. "I just hope it's not a bad sign that we want such different things in life. I hope it's not a bad omen."

My heart hammers wildly.

"God no, I don't think so. I mean, people always work things out in the end, don't they? We're only young. There's plenty of time to worry about all that later."

He studies me a moment longer, then clearly decides to change the subject.

"You're right. Let's not start the date this way. Let's talk about something else. What about music? Are you still into that godawful metal stuff you used to listen to at university?"

"Godawful? You sound like my dad."

"That's because your dad has taste."

"That's because my dad wouldn't know good music if it smacked him in the face. Anyway, I thought you liked my music?"

"Some of it. But that loud, shouty stuff? Not for me. Give me a bit of Rolling Stones any day."

I nod. "I have to give you that. Which reminds me. What happened to your band? I take it the gigs didn't get you a record deal?" I try to hide my smirk but he sees it.

"No, they don't know what they're missing." He grins. "To be honest, Zo, I love playing guitar but we were bloody terrible. I don't think it's where my future lies."

"So where does it lie? Surely you're not planning to sell water coolers for the rest of your life?"

"No, not water coolers. It's a pretty soul-destroying job, cold-calling. Although it did me all right, because I found you again."

His face has turned serious, and I shiver with delight. "You did. Thank goodness for water coolers, eh?"

"I'll drink to that. To water coolers, and all who drink from them. And to us, and whatever this —" he waves his hand between us — "turns out to be." We clink glasses and take a drink, each lost in our own thoughts.

We finish eating and the restaurant starts to empty but we stay where we are, holding hands across the table, giggling. The owners of the restaurant must hate us but I can't bring myself to care. This might be my last day with Ed, and I don't want it to end.

But of course it must, and finally we can't eke it out any longer. The remains of our desserts sit on our plates, melted ice cream and smears of chocolate cake, and our wine glasses sit empty, smudged round the edges where our hands have been holding them all night. The rest of the diners have left, and the waiters are milling around, clearly desperate to shut up and go home but too polite to ask us to leave.

I don't want to leave Ed's side but I don't want to take him back to my flat — I can't subject him to Jane's interrogation, not tonight. I want him to myself. So I do something totally out of character.

"So, shall we go back to yours, then?"

Fuelled by wine and the certain knowledge that he's mine and he loves me — or at least if he doesn't now then he soon will — I feel bold.

"Come on, then." He pays the bill and pulls me by the hand all the way to the Tube, a sense of urgency in his actions.

Less than an hour later we're back at his flat, and Ed's pouring us a glass of wine each. It feels as though I'm floating outside my own body, watching things unfold like a film. Ed is here, and he's mine, and something inside me explodes with happiness.

I perch on the edge of the sofa, clutching my glass, and wait for him to sit down. But then he's standing in front of me holding out his hand and saying, "Come on, let's stop pissing about and go to bed."

I take his hand. "Such a romantic proposition," I say, smiling at him as I follow him across the room.

He shrugs. "Well, you know me."

He pulls me towards him and we fall onto Ed's bed, a tangle of limbs, and it feels amazing to be back in his arms. His lips almost burn my skin, I've missed him so much. I can hardly believe he's here and this is happening. I don't ever want it to end.

And then I'm lost, not caring whether this changes anything or not.

Afterwards we lie on the bed together, still, watching the shadow of a tree sway gently in the orange glow from the streetlight outside, and I'm the happiest I've felt in months, maybe even years. Never in my wildest dreams had I imagined I'd ever get the chance to be with Ed again and I still can't really believe it's happened. But for now I'm here, tucked safely into the crook of Ed's shoulder, and as I watch his chest rise up and down, up and down, I relax. And then, finally, I close my eyes.

When I open them again it takes a moment to work out where I am. I'm not sure what I'm expecting, but I'm surprised to find I'm still in Ed's bed, where we ended up last night. I'm still nestled in the crook of his arm, and his other arm is slung across the bed, opening his chest up to the room. Gingerly I pull myself into a sitting position and look around. It's dim, the sun seeping gently round the edges of the blinds, but there's enough light to see and I can tell instantly it's not only the room we were in last night, but it's the next morning, not weeks or months later: there are my clothes in a pile on the floor, Ed's next to them; across the room I can see our wine glasses in the brighter light by the window, half drunk, smudged and abandoned in the heat of the moment. My face flames at the memory and I smile.

I need a drink so I pull Ed's shirt on and wrap it round me and pad along to the kitchen to pour myself a glass of water. As the cold liquid hits the back of my throat I try to work out what's going on here. It's different from normal — or whatever has become normal — and I'm not sure what to make of it. Why have I woken up the next day rather than days or months later?

Who knows? But it means another day with Ed, so I can't complain. I walk back into the bedroom and climb into bed. As I do, Ed stirs and opens his eyes, squinting at me in the semi-darkness.

"Morning, you." His breath is stale but I kiss him anyway and he responds hungrily. When he pulls away he's fully awake and he smiles at me.

"So, last night was fun."

I rest my chin on my hand and look down at him.
"It was."

He sits up and adjusts his pillows so he's facing me. "So what do you want to do today?"

I meet his gaze. "How do you know I'm not busy?"

104

He shrugs, a smirk playing on his lips. "I don't."

I elbow him in the side and he falls backwards onto the bed.

"Oi!" he wails. I ignore him.

"As it happens I am free and it would be nice to do something, yes."

He grins again and glances at the clock. It's 9.30. "How about a picnic?"

"Ooh, yes." I clap my hands together. "I love a picnic."

"Great. Shall we go to Clapham Common?"

I frown. "I can't go out like this. Do you mind if I go home and change first? Then maybe we could go to Ally Pally?"

"Yeah, course." His eyes roam up and down my body and I feel myself blushing. "Anyway, I don't know why you need to change, I think you look pretty hot in just my shirt."

"Why, thank you young man." I flutter my eyelashes ridiculously and Ed throws his arms around me and pulls me tightly to him until I can hardly breathe.

"But you're not going anywhere yet. We've got loads of time for this first." And then his lips move down my neck and across my nipples and I gasp, lost in the moment all over again.

It's gone midday by the time I let myself back into my flat, Ed in tow. We're holding hands, giggling like teenagers, and I'm relieved to find Jane out. He waits in the living room while I jump in the shower and get dressed and I hope for his sake Jane doesn't come home and find him there all alone, prime for interrogation.

Half an hour later we're ready to go. I've shoved bread, cheese, crisps and wine into a bag and Ed hoicks it onto his back, then we set off through the sun-baked streets which wind up towards Alexandra Park. We hold hands all the way and his touch feels as though it's burning my skin, but I won't let go. I can't let go.

The park is busy on this hot, bright Sunday lunchtime. The sky is a hazy blue, the heat making everyone feel lazy. Roasting bodies glisten in the rare summer sun, hungrily soaking up the rays, while the odd person half-heartedly throws a frisbee or a ball through the thick, sticky air. From a couple of hundred metres away comes the sound of laughter and screams as a group of friends squirt each other with water pistols. We stop and spread out our towels on the grass in one of the few free areas of shade we can find, and Ed unpacks the food as I take in the familiar view. The rows of Crouch End houses in the foreground, reaching out to central London, dotted with spots of green parkland and trees, all the way to the soaring skyscrapers of Canary Wharf and, on a day like today, a hazy, shimmering south London. It's so stunning it takes my breath away.

"God, I'm starving," Ed says, grabbing a piece of bread and shoving it into his mouth. Crumbs spray all over the towel as he struggles to chew the enormous mouthful.

"Oh, that's a lovely way to impress a girl." I roll my eyes and attempt to flick crumbs from the towel where they've sprayed like bullets.

"Sorry," he grins mischievously, his cheeks puffed out like a hamster.

I grab some bread and cheese too and start making myself a sandwich, the heat making every movement feel like an effort. The air is full of a soft buzzing sound, a mix of distant lawnmowers, chatter and the odd wasp flying lazily past. I peer through the darkness of my sunglasses and take the opportunity to have a proper look at Ed while he can't see my eyes. He's still chewing furiously, the muscles of his jaw working hard to get through another huge chunk of bread. His hair, slightly sweaty, is stuck to his forehead, three dark strands trailing in his eyes so he has to keep pushing them away. His skin is lightly tanned, a mixture of sun cream and sweat making it glisten in the sunlight. He turns his head away to watch some kids playing a game of frisbee nearby and I allow my gaze to move downwards, taking in his strong, lean arms beneath the short sleeves of his T-shirt, the soft hairs lightened from hours in the sun. I blush as my eyes travel down further, trying not to think about what's under those clothes, instead checking out his legs peeking from the bottom of his shorts, the muscles taut. His head whips round and I tear my eyes away, hoping he'll mistake the redness flooding my face for overheating rather than embarrassment at being caught ogling him.

Ed leans back on his elbows and watches me.

"What?" I feel awkward under his gaze, scared he'll see right through me and know everything that's going on in my head.

"Nothing. Just enjoying the view." He grins, then lies flat on his back, his hands behind his head. I follow suit, watching the leaves above my head rustle gently in the almost nonexistent breeze, my mind full of questions — questions I don't think I'll ever be able to answer. Ed's body is so close to mine and I long to reach out and touch him. I shuffle round so my head is leaning gently on his thigh, and his hand reaches down to play with my hair. A shiver runs through me and I know, before it even happens, that sleep is going to take me away, leave me stranded in this moment. But I don't even mind because I'm so happy that even if this is my last moment with Ed, then it's OK. And then tiredness overtakes me, my eyelids droop and I'm powerless to stop them . . .

CHAPTER
FIVE

20 January 2000

I open my eyes and almost jump out of my skin. I can't see anything apart from a face extremely close to mine: tiny stubs of dark hair sprout from the pores of his chin like cacti in a desert landscape, and a slightly stale odour comes from his open mouth when he breathes out. I move away very slightly and study the tiny hairs that move in his nose as his nostrils flare, and the shine of his skin which is slick with sweat in the heat of the room. As I move further back still he starts to become a whole face, dark lashes splayed across his cheeks as he sleeps, a lock of hair stuck to his forehead, his lips squashed and full as his cheek sinks into the pillow.

My heart bursts with happiness at the sight of Ed, and the sudden rush of memory from the last time I was with him, in the sun in Alexandra Park. He's here, which means my little speech about not wanting children didn't scare him away.

It's been a long time since I've studied Ed's face in this much detail — have I ever done it? — and I'm making the most of it now, trying to commit every single detail to memory so that I never lose the image again.

After a few moments he stirs and shifts and, worried he's going to wake up before I've had the chance to orientate myself, I take the chance to look around the room.

From the bed I stare up at the ceiling. There are gaps in the plaster, and a single lightbulb hangs from the light fitting in the middle of the room. There's a door to my right, with a bolt across it and some fire safety instructions. I'm in a hotel of some sort.

I sit up and cast my gaze round the rest of the room: an open door in front of me through which I can see a toilet with the seat up, a picture of Jesus on the cross on the pale yellow wall, a wardrobe with the doors shut, a rickety wooden chair with a rucksack and a couple of jumpers hanging over the top of it, and that's it. I know where we are! A cheap hotel room in a town called Arequipa in Peru, where we stayed the night before heading to Lima. If someone had asked me what this room had looked like I couldn't have described it, but now I can see it I know exactly where we are. I shiver with excitement. Ed and I took some time out from work a few months after we first got together to go travelling, ticking something off my wish list, to see the world. I loved Peru, and I'm thrilled I'm getting to see it again.

But why this day? What was so significant about it? I can't work it out yet, but I'm sure I'll soon find out.

There's a notebook on the bedside table next to me and I pick it up and flick through it, leaning on my elbow as I read snippets of the diary I kept as we

110

travelled around the world. I haven't read this for ages and it makes me smile.

Oh God!!!!!!! Today has been MORTIFYING. We went to see the Taj Mahal and halfway back to the hotel this evening I got a bellyache. By the time we got there I knew something bad was happening and I had to race to the loo. Without going into TOO much detail, I was in there for some time and it wasn't pretty. But the worst thing was, Ed was just outside the thin, flimsy door and could hear EVERYTHING. I mean, I know we used to share a house, but the poor bloke's never even seen me on the toilet, let alone seen me with my insides FALLING INTO THE TOILET! And the smell. Dear God, the smell. In fact, oh God, I think it might be happening again. I have to go, I'm des—

The entry ended and even now, reading it back, I blush. I remember that day. It was probably safe to say it was the day that our relationship changed for good, the day he saw and heard and smelt me and my Delhi belly. I'd been utterly mortified, but Ed tried everything he could to make me feel better about it.

If only I'd known then that that was just one of many times all dignity would be thrown out of the window, with illnesses and fertility treatment stripping us of any reserve that might have lingered.

I put the diary back just as a muffled voice comes from beside me: "What time is it?" I turn to look at Ed and am confronted with a pillow instead of a face. I don't know how he can stand to put that thing over his head; it's rank, musty.

I reach for my watch.

111

"10.30."

Ed's body jerks awake and suddenly he's sitting up, looking at me, panic-stricken. "Shit, we're late!"

"Late for what?"

He frowns at me. "The bloody bus," he says, pushing the blanket off him and jumping out of bed. The sight of his naked body sends a shiver through me which I try to ignore. He strides across the room and starts rummaging in the pockets of his rucksack. I try not to stare at him. Then he pulls some crumpled-looking tickets from a plastic folder and squints at them.

"Shit," he says again, and thrusts the tickets at me. "The bus leaves at 11.30. We have to go."

I leap out of bed, not sure exactly where we're going but aware of the urgency. We throw some clothes on and clean our teeth, then shove everything else in our rucksacks and head to the hotel reception. The woman behind the counter doesn't seem to understand what a hurry we're in, taking ages to count our money and return our passports. But eventually she does and we run into the street and down a dusty pavement. I follow Ed blindly, across wide roads filled with ancient cars, past brightly coloured shopfronts, pretty churches and soaring palm trees, hoping he knows where we're going, and finally we turn a corner into the bus station. People are rushing around in the fume-filled air shouting loudly in Spanish, arms waving, buses beeping, suitcases being thrown about. How on earth are we going to find our bus?

But minutes later we're there, climbing on, our rucksacks being thrown into the hold while we settle ourselves into our seats. I pull out my Walkman and stick in the mix tape Ed had made me, then lean back and watch the chaos outside from the air-conditioned bus, breathing a sigh of relief. It's been a while since I went anywhere apart from London and it's been a bit of a shock to the system.

"Thank God for that," Ed says, fiddling with the overhead fan. "Couldn't afford another bus fare."

I say nothing, waiting for him to carry on.

"Only one more day left in Peru; can you believe it?"

"No," I say.

He glances at me. "You OK?"

I nod. "Yes, fine. Just tired." I yawn to prove my point.

We sit for a few minutes in comfortable silence. Then finally the bus starts to move, pulling out of the bus station and swinging towards the road. I sit back and watch the half-built houses whizz past the window. I listen to the hum of the engine, the muffled voices and the occasional shout in Spanish, and the rustle of the crisps Ed's eating beside me, and I feel myself drifting off.

It had been Ed's idea, this trip.

"Let's tick something off your wish list," he'd said over drinks just a few short weeks ago. There'd been a few of us — Jane, a couple of friends from work, and a cycling buddy of Ed's, Josh — squashed round a table in a pub in Camden after work. Our happy-hour drinks were lined up precariously on the sticky table in front of us, Blur's "Charmless Man" pounding from the speaker right next to our heads, our voices getting

113

louder and louder to compete with Damon Albarn's dulcet tones and the shouts of people around us.

"What?"

"Let's see some of the world. Let's go travelling."

"I can't just go travelling — I've got a job to go to, rent to pay."

"Oh, come on, Zoe, they're the excuses you've always made, which is why you've never done it."

I leaned towards Jane slightly as a dreadlocked man balancing three pints barged past our table, nearly knocking us all flying.

"Yes, but they're not excuses, they're reasons. It's different." I felt cross at the implication that I didn't really want to go, or was scared, despite there being more than a grain of truth in it.

Ed rolled his eyes. "Pedant. You know what I mean. I can get time off easily; there'll always be gardening work around. And you can get time off work, and we don't have to go for months and months. Three months tops, that's totally do-able, right?"

Jane, next to me, nodded. "He's right Zo, you can totally do this. Even if it does mean you have to abandon me, leave me all alone in that flat sobbing into a cold tin of beans every night . . ." She feigned crying, and I punched her on the shoulder.

"But what about work? I can't just up and leave. I've worked hard for this job. I'm in the middle of a campaign." The excuses came thick and fast, but Ed batted them all away.

"Listen, Zo, you can only ask, and they can only say yes or no. But think about how amazing it would be,

114

seeing some of the world together. We could go to South America, Brazil, Peru, Bolivia, climb mountains, take elephant rides, swim in the ocean. It would be amazing . . .”

My stomach contracted at the mention of all these places. Previously, I'd thought about travelling in the same abstract way you think about winning the lottery — something I hoped might happen one day, but just assumed never would. Now, faced with the reality of a list of places and a list of reasons for actually going, I felt terrified by the prospect. I took a large gulp from my glass of cheap white wine and banged it down on the table. Wine sloshed over the top, soaking into the beer mat and leaving marks on my jeans.

Sensing my reluctance, Ed turned to Josh for moral support. “Josh, tell Zoe how awesome South America is.”

Josh's face lit up. “Oh man, it's truly amazing. Had the best time of my life when I went. What do you need to know?”

For the next half hour the pair of them regaled me with stories about places they'd been, people they'd met. I'd been left feeling I had no choice, and so when work had agreed to give me the time off, unpaid, there was nothing else for it but to say I'd go.

And now here we were, and Ed and Josh were right. I was having the time of my life. I was grateful for the push.

Next to me Ed shifts and I lift my head, my neck stiff. I must have fallen asleep on his shoulder. Ed's dozing so I look out of the slightly grimy window and watch the scenery change, rubbing my sore neck. The run-down houses have turned into dusty fields and scrubby trees, miles of nothingness either side of us. Slowly, the road starts to wind up into the mountains and the trees turn greener, everywhere more lush. On the left-hand side of the bus the sheer cliff face rises up into the clouds, while on the right it drops off terrifyingly steeply into nothingness. There's only a flimsy-looking crash barrier between our bus and the enormous drop.

I try not to think about it.

We climb higher and higher into the mountains, and as we do the light mist thickens and becomes a dense, smothering fog until I can hardly even see the cliff edge at all. We still seem to be travelling fairly fast and I can't understand how the bus driver can see well enough to go at such a speed.

And then I gasp as a memory floods my mind.

This is the day we almost died. Or at least we truly thought we were going to. Blood rushes to my head and I grab hold of Ed's hand. He opens his eyes and smiles at me.

"OK?"

"Yes. But Ed?"

"Mmm-hmm?"

"Look out the window."

He glances out and I feel his body tense.

"How can the driver see where he's going?" I try to keep my voice steady but even I can hear the tremor.

"Well, he must know the road pretty well." Even Ed's voice sounds unsure, and that makes me even more

116

scared. He doesn't panic often. He tightens his grip on my hand and I squeeze his back until my knuckles turn white.

"Ow, you don't need to squeeze the life out of me just yet."

"Sorry." I loosen my grip and he moves closer so there's not even the tiniest space between us.

For the next few minutes we sit in silence, watching the bus's progress up the hill. It's slowed right down and every now and then the lights of an enormous lorry loom out of the fog ahead of us, and it feels as though the wind it creates is about to blow our little bus off the side of the cliff. Each time I hold my breath, certain that this time this is it — but every time we get past unscathed, our little bus going slower and slower as the driver is able to make out less and less of the road in front of him through the thickening fog.

"We could die up here. You read about bus crashes all the time. It could easily happen." My voice shakes uncontrollably.

"I know," Ed says.

He doesn't try to reassure me, or change the subject, or make a joke out of it, and that makes me feel worse. Instead he puts his arms around me and pulls me even closer. My ear is pressed against his chest and I can hear his heart beating quickly beneath the thin layer of his T-shirt. He's so alive, and he's here and I've got a chance to do something right now that I didn't take last time. I don't even stop to think about it.

I move my head so I'm peering up at him and he looks down, our eyes just inches apart. The blue of his irises has darkened to a deep, inky blue-black and his face is etched with worry, a crease lining his forehead.

"Ed?"

"Mmm?"

"I love you." It's hardly more than a whisper but I know he's heard me as his expression changes, softens. The words that I've longed to say to him since the day he died — that last time we took this journey I held back from saying despite being head over heels because I wanted him to say them first — they're out there and hanging in the air between us, taking away the terror and the fear and leaving nothing but us, me and Ed.

He lowers his face until our noses are almost touching and I can feel his breath on my cheek. It smells vaguely of mint and the warm, musky smell that I've missed so much it's like an ache.

"I love you too, Zoe. Always."

My heart almost bursts with happiness at hearing those words, words we haven't said to each other for too long. He kisses me, his full lips warm and slightly salty, and I kiss him back, holding him as though this is our last moment together.

Which it might be.

I don't want to cry, yet I can feel tears trying to escape and I blink them back furiously. But I can't stop them and they slide slowly down my cheeks and onto Ed's T-shirt.

"Oh Zoe, don't cry." We both glance out of the window, and he looks back, tightening his grip round my shoulders. "We'll be OK. We will."

I wipe my face with my sleeve and turn to look out of the window again, the terror of the journey back in my mind. I watch, numbly, as the bus continues its treacherous route, trying not to think about dying, about plunging down the cliff to our deaths. I can't think about Ed dying right now.

It feels like hours, but finally we start to drop down the other side of the mountain, and the fog slowly begins to lift, as though a blanket has been pulled away. Around us I hear the relieved murmurs of the other passengers, who I'd hardly been aware of before, as they realize we've made it, that we're going to be OK.

The bus rumbles along the open road, gradually picking up speed as it flattens out now that the danger has passed. I feel Ed's body next to me, warm and solid, as my head rises and falls with his breath, and happiness threatens to overwhelm me. I pull in as much air as I can, and let it out in a rush. Ed pulls away, looks down at me.

"You OK, sweetheart?"

I nod, the tears threatening again. "Yes, just glad that's over."

He nods, serious. "It was a bit dicey there, wasn't it?"

I smile at the understatement. "Just a bit." I pause, suddenly shy. "You know, I really thought we were going to die up there."

"Me too."

"So, you know, I'm glad I said — what I said." My face flames.

"Me too."

"Well, good." I glance at my knees, brush an imaginary crumb away and he takes my hand and pulls it to his mouth, planting a gentle kiss on the back of it.

"Don't be shy, Zoe. I'm glad you said it, and I'm glad I did too. I do love you, more than you can imagine, and I think I probably always have, from the very first moment I saw you, looking like a rabbit caught in the headlights — a very cute rabbit — in our student kitchen that day. It just took me a while to realize what an utter dick I was being, not being with you."

My breath seems to have caught in my throat and I swallow to clear it. He's always loved me. He never told me that, not in all the years we were together, and it takes a moment for the significance to sink in: this is new, which means something has changed. How much I don't know, but for now I don't care. This is enough. There's nothing else I can do today but make the most of our being together, of being with Ed again, and I vow that if this is our last day, at least we can make it a happy one.

Hours later, after a terrible, sleepless night, the bus pulls into a bus station and the driver kills the engine. Around us cheers go up and people clap with relief, and Ed joins in, his huge smile leaving lines etched round his eyes and mouth, his eyes sparkling.

We stand and he takes my hand, leads me from the bus and we collect our bags and make our way through the busy streets to our hotel. Neither of us says much on the way there, happy in each other's company.

120

But when we get to our room with its plain walls and hard-looking bed, exhaustion overwhelms us and despite plans to see some of the city, we both collapse on the bed.

"Well, that was interesting."

"That's one way to describe it."

"You know what, Zo, I don't think I've ever been on a journey that terrifying. I mean, I've been on scary flights where the plane shakes around so much it feels as though it's going to fall out of the sky, but even then, even the thought of falling thousands of feet from the air, I've never been as scared as I was today. And it was because of you."

I can feel him watching me and I turn to face him, lock eyes.

"Me?"

He nods. "Yeah. Before, it was just about me, and, well, obviously I don't want to die early —" my heart contracts at his words — "but if it happens, well, it happens. But the thought of losing you — that's the worst pain imaginable. It's terrifying." He stops, his cheeks reddening. "I know that makes me sound like a right dork, but it's true." He shrugs, embarrassed.

"Oh Ed, you don't sound like a dork. I feel the same. The thought of losing you makes me feel as though my heart has been ripped out. I'm not sure I can go on. Could go on." I quickly cover my mistake but he doesn't seem to notice.

We lie in silence for a few moments, then a smile spreads across his face. "Well, that was intense."

"Very." The moment's lost but I'm relieved. I need some light relief after the journey we've had.

He sits up, claps his hands together. "Let's go out."

"Out? Where?"

"I don't know. Food, walking. Alcohol. I think we need some."

I pull myself into a sitting position too, steady myself on the bed. "Edward Williams, for once, I think you might be right."

"For once? I'm always right."

We get up, throw on some clean clothes and head out into the busy city. We stroll past the cathedral and churches, do some window shopping and sit in plazas sipping too-strong coffee and wine. And for the rest of the afternoon and into the evening, I try not to think about anything but the here and now. Ed's here, we're young, we're having fun. We love each other.

There's nothing else I want more.

Later, back in our room, we stumble into bed and curl up under the duvet, drunk and happy. As I'm drifting off to sleep in Ed's arms I can't help feeling relieved that I don't actually have to live through tomorrow's hangover. But my heart feels full, content, and my last thought as I slip into oblivion is that I hope I get one more day with Ed. Just one more day.

CHAPTER
SIX

12 May 2001

I knew even before I opened my eyes this morning that I was back in the past, back for another day, and my heart beat so wildly I had to take several deep breaths to calm it down. I didn't care what day this was, it was just enough that it *was* another day.

It wasn't quite light outside so I'd scrambled out of bed, which was still the bed in the flat I'd shared with Jane, and come through to the living room with a blanket wrapped round my shoulders to keep out the slight chill. Now I'm sitting huddled on the sofa, surrounded by packing boxes and sipping milky tea, watching the inky sky slowly lighten behind the buildings across the street.

I know what today's going to bring — the boxes have given it away — and I'm excited about moving in with Ed, but already I'm wondering what I might try to change about it, whether there's anything I can do differently that might alter the course of history. That might stop Ed dying. I know there has to be something.

My tea finished, I leave the mug on the side table and stand, stretching my arms above my head. The blanket falls to the floor and I leave it there, the air warming now, the early-morning chill gone. I walk barefooted across the room to the tiny kitchen and stand in front of the fridge. It's covered with photos, stuck haphazardly to the door with magnets, as well as receipts, vouchers and anything else we don't know what to do with. It's so full you can hardly make out the white of the fridge door beneath.

The sight of the photos is familiar, but I'd never really examined them properly. Now, though, I stand and take a good look, trying to remember my life so far. My eye is drawn to a picture about halfway down, of me and Jane with two handsome boys. A long-ago holiday to Greece where we partied hard and scarcely saw the sunshine. Our eyes shine and our skin glows. We look very drunk. There are endless pictures of us round restaurant tables, holding up glasses of wine, smiling for the camera; there are graduation photos, birthday parties, pictures of me and Ed, me and Jane, Jane and boys long forgotten. It's a catalogue of our lives and loves and it makes me smile.

There's a voucher for a two-for-one meal at our local tapas restaurant, a Post-it reminding one of us to buy more milk, several receipts. There's a postcard from Barcelona and I pull it from its clip and turn it over.

Having a great time, have been shopping and had some lovely food. It's been sunny but quite cold, but better than home. You'd love it here, you should bring Zoe. See you soon darling.
Love Mum and Roger.

I smile at the memory. Susan rarely had a man in her life, but she'd been happy with Roger for a while. It had been this trip that had finished them off when she'd realized they wanted different things. His being mainly to sleep with other people, while she, selfishly, wanted him to be faithful. Poor Susan, she just seemed to attract that sort of man — including Ed's dad — and I didn't know why. The thought of it brings back another painful memory and I wince. It's of me and Ed when we first got back from our travels, buoyed up by the intimacy we'd shared, with the fact we felt secure with each other. Talk had turned to marriage: specifically, Ed's parents'.

"Well, after the disaster that was Mum and Dad's marriage I never want to repeat that mistake," he'd said. It had been a casual remark, I knew, but it cut like a knife.

"What, never?"

He shook his head. "What's the point? It didn't keep Mum and Dad together, and it clearly meant nothing to him. If people are cheats and liars then a wedding ceremony and a piece of paper isn't going to change that." His voice was harsh, vehement and I was taken aback by the strength of his feelings. I'd always known his parents' marriage had been unhappy before his dad had died, but I'd never known he felt this strongly about it.

I didn't know what to say. I wasn't desperate to get married but I always thought I would one day, and recently I'd been imagining it could be Ed I'd walk down the aisle with. Now, though, it seemed he had different ideas, and it didn't sound as though there would ever be anything I could do to change his mind. It didn't stop me wanting to try.

I shake the thought from my mind and turn my attention back to the photos. So many memories here, so many friends and family and happy times. There's a photo of my old work colleague and friend Lucy and her newborn baby, one of the first of any of us to get pregnant. For most of us it was something way off, intangible. Yet Lucy and her boyfriend Jake had planned it, wanted it, and were happy. My heart tightened a little as I traced my finger gently across the little girl's beautiful face.

"You're up early." Jane's voice cuts through my thoughts. I turn to find her looking bleary-eyed, hair sticking up like she'd been in a fight with a lawnmower.

"Could say the same about you."

"Yeah, couldn't sleep. Too sad about losing my best friend." She pulls a face, sticks out her bottom lip.

"Sorry."

"S'OK. Are you excited?"

"Can't wait." I'm moving out of the flat and in with Ed, and being reminded of it now brings back the excitement of that day.

It had been a big step, deciding to move in together, and surprisingly it was Ed who'd brought it up.

"I spend so much time at your flat we might as well live together," he'd said one day as we stretched out on the sofa watching TV.

"Mmm-hmm." I hadn't really been listening.

"So why don't we?"

I frowned, trying to tune in to the conversation, aware it was taking a different turn. "Why don't we what?"

Ed hesitated and I turned to face him properly, waiting for him to speak.

"We could — you know. Get somewhere together." He picked at a piece of imaginary thread on his jeans, refusing to meet my eye. He wasn't usually this shy and I knew what a huge effort it had been for him to suggest this. I decided to make it easy for him.

"Edward Williams, are you asking me to move in with you?"

He shrugged. "Well, yes, I just thought that, maybe, it would be easier if we actually, you know, lived together."

I let the words settle between us, find a home.

"Easier?"

"Yeah, well." He shrugged again. "Save having to schlep between each other's houses. We could keep everything in one place. And — well, it would be nice."

I couldn't help myself. A huge grin broke out across my face.

"Yes, it would be nice. It would be more than nice, it would be amazing. Ed, I'd love to."

And so we'd spent the next few weeks flat-hunting all around north London — from the scruffy streets of Tottenham to the leafy roads of Hampstead, where we could just about afford a shoebox — before deciding on Crouch End, just by Alexandra Palace. And then we'd broken the news to Jane.

"Abandoning me, are you?" she said, pretending to be cross. But I knew she wasn't, and the day we found our new place, she bought us a bottle of Prosecco to celebrate.

And now the day is here, and I'm reliving it all over again. I'd been so happy that day, and now a sense of nervousness is mixed with the happiness.

Jane's padding around the kitchen in our little Tufnell Park flat, spooning coffee into a filter paper. I watch her for a moment and smile. I've missed this, Jane's company, the ease of just being together. She turns and catches me watching her. "All right?"

"Yes, fine. Just going to miss you. Miss this."

She sighs dramatically. "Yeah, me too. Really really." She turns back and I'm about to tell her I'm sorry when she cuts me off.

"Crumpet?" She waves one in the air.

"Yeah, go on, then. Ta."

She pushes the toaster down and turns to me.

"Bet you Ed doesn't look after you this well. Sure you don't want to stay?" She pulls a ridiculous pout, pretending to sulk.

"Well, it's tempting . . . yeah, go on, I'll just ring Ed, tell him I've changed my mind."

She grins. "Ha, imagine if you did. He'd kill me!"

The crumpet pops up and she butters it and hands it to me. "Ta," I say, taking an enormous bite. "Mm, the girl makes a mean crumpet. You'll make someone a great wife one day."

"Oh piss off," she says, throwing a soggy teabag at me. I duck and it lands on the sofa behind me. "Ha, there goes your deposit," she laughs, and I stick my tongue out.

"So, what time's the van coming?"

"About twelve." I glance round the living room to see if there's anything else I need to pack. It looks as though I've been pretty efficient.

I wrack my brains to remember who moved in after I moved out. It would seem weird if I didn't mention it at all. I remember a strange girl called Ruth, who moved in for a few weeks and left again shortly afterwards when Jane found her nicking money from her purse, and I feel another pang of guilt. I shake it off.

"When's Ruth moving in?"

"Tomorrow. Hope she's not a total loser."

I say nothing, and Jane is immediately suspicious.

"What? Do you know something about her?"

"Don't be ridiculous, how could I?" I sound unconvincing even to my own ears and Jane gives me a strange look. "Just — well, just be careful. You never know if she's going to turn out to be a single white female psycho."

"Oh thanks, that helps."

"Anyway," I say, changing the subject as I polish off the last mouthful of my crumpet, "I need to get ready. Thanks for breakfast." I hop off the stool, taking my tea with me, and head to the bathroom.

Once again I find myself in front of the mirror looking at my reflection. My hair is light, and cut quite short, with a neat fringe. It's not very me, and it makes me look really young. I must be — what? Twenty-six? I look about thirteen.

I shower and get dressed in the clothes I'd left out for myself on the chair, then start heaving boxes into the front room. Jane's nowhere to be seen, but I can hear the shower pumping away.

Finally, midday arrives, along with Ed and the van we've hired for the day. As he bounds up the stairs to the flat he looks pleased with himself.

"What's wrong with you?"

"Oh, nothing." His eyes sparkle with mischief.

"Edward, what have you been up to?" His face breaks into a grin as he takes my hand and pulls me down the steps behind him. He leads me to the van and flings open the back doors. There, in the middle of the otherwise empty space, is a battered looking leather sofa.

"I found it in a junk shop. I know this place is furnished but I just thought you'd like it."

"Oh Ed, it's brilliant," I say, flinging my arms round him. It's just like the one I'd pointed out a few weeks before when we'd been out shopping for duvet covers and cushions.

"Do we really need all these cushions?" Ed had said.

"Yes," I replied.

"But what's the point of them?"

"They look nice," I snapped. "I'm not living in a bachelor pad."

Ed had shrugged and left me to it. But as we'd left the shop he'd caught me looking longingly at a gorgeous brown leather sofa. This one isn't exactly the same but it's pretty close, and it means he took some

130

notice, and that means more than what the sofa looks like.

I kiss his cheek.

"Right, are you going to come and help me lift these boxes, then?"

"Yes, boss." He follows me dutifully up the steps and we spend the next half hour heaving boxes from the flat to the van. I seem to have a lot of stuff for such a small room. But finally we're done, and ready to go.

"We're only going to be a bus ride away," I say to Jane, hugging her tearfully.

"Don't cry, silly. I'll be round every day for my dinner."

Ed goes quiet, a look of horror on his face.

"OK, every other day," Jane grins. "Ed, don't look so scared. I'm only kidding."

"Oh sorry," he says, flushing. "Sorry."

We say our goodbyes then climb into the van and we're off. Crouch End is only about two miles away from mine and Jane's flat — sorry, Jane's flat — in Tufnell Park, but it's still the end of an era and I feel sad as we sit in traffic on the hill down towards our new home.

There are moments when I just wish time would stand still, and that nothing, not even the tiniest detail, would change. And although it might not seem like much to anyone else, this, the first few hours in our brand-new flat, is one of those times.

My eyes are following a vapour trail across the sky and I wonder absently where the trail leads to. It's the only mark in an otherwise pale-blue expanse and I watch it until it starts to dissipate and my eyes begin to water. I squeeze them shut and shift my head slightly to the right, trying to ease the tension in my neck which has been stuck in the same position for far too long. Beneath the weight of my head Ed's stomach muscles tense, waiting while I move, and then soften as I relax against him, comfortable again. I can feel the soft pillow of his belly gently moving up and down in time with his breathing, and my head moves slowly up and down, up and down too.

This tiny square of garden that came with the flat had been the deciding factor for Ed. He longed for outside space, for greenery, clean air and peace and quiet. And while this didn't deliver all of those — it was still London and the sound of neighbours was impossible to ignore — Ed seemed happy for now. He had wanted to come straight out as soon as we got here, and so now we're lying on the uneven paving slabs, staring at the sky, and my whole body feels heavy, weighted into the ground; I realize that for the first time in a long time I'm experiencing what it's like to feel totally and utterly content. I refuse to let any bad thoughts enter my mind, and instead focus on how close I feel to Ed right at this moment. It feels like a miracle. My legs are stretched out in front of me, my arms folded primly on my chest, elbows touching the ground either side to keep me from tipping over. Ed's body is at right angles to mine; we form a T-shape across the decking. A half-drunk bottle of Prosecco sits next to us, the bubbles rising slowly, lazily, in the sun. Around us trees and plants rustle gently, sounding like a whisper, and the occasional shout pierces the otherwise relative peace.

My face feels warm and I can feel the heat radiating from Ed's body to mine, making me feel too hot, but I don't want to move. I want to stay like this forever, stuck in time. I don't want anything to change.

Then Ed's stomach muscles tense beneath my head again but this time he doesn't relax, he carries on moving upwards until I'm forced to lift my head, my neck straining with the effort. I prop myself up on my elbow and blink madly, shading my eyes with my forearm to look at him.

"What're you doing?" I mumble, as he sits right up and reaches forward, his arm moving towards me. Just as I think he's going to touch me, his hand goes right past and comes back seconds later holding a bottle of water which he unscrews and puts to his lips.

"Sorry, thirsty." He jerks his head back quickly, his hair flicking back with the action, and drinks greedily from the bottle, the water bubbling back inside between each gulp. A line of water escapes from his mouth and runs down the side of his cheek, dripping onto his shoulder, soaking into his T-shirt and leaving a dark-grey stain. Finally, the bottle half empty, he rights his head, takes the bottle from his lips and wipes the back of his hand across his mouth. His lips glisten in the sun and I can't resist. I lean forward and kiss him.

I kiss him deeply, his mouth moist and warm in response. Then I pull away.

"Sorry, couldn't help myself." I grin at him cheekily and a smile spreads across his face, gentle lines fanning outwards from the corners of his eyes.

"Well, who can blame you; I'm pretty irresistible." He shrugs and spreads his arms wide.

"True." I smile back at him and his grin falters. I know he's expecting me to tease him, the way I normally would. But I'm not going to, not this time. I don't want anything to spoil the moment, and so I keep quiet. Instead, I lie back down, stretching my arms behind my head to form a makeshift pillow and continue to gaze at the sky. Ed's still sitting up and his shadow falls across my chest. I can feel him watching me.

"This is great, isn't it?" he says after a moment.

"Hmm?"

"You know, this." From the corner of my eye I see him sweep his arm, taking in us, the tiny square of garden, the flat. I lift my head and look round, my eyes squinting against the light. Then I look at him; the hair that always flops over his eye no matter what he does, the lightly tanned skin from working outside all day, the dark stubble starting to sprout on his chin, and I know he's right. This is right.

I reach my hand out and press it against his cheek, feeling the roughness of two days' growth beneath my palm. He puts his hand on top of mine and holds it there.

"This is perfect, Ed."

134

He nods. "It is. Let's never let things change."

Of course I'm more aware than anyone that nothing lasts forever. Which is why we find ourselves just an hour later back in the house, unpacking boxes, the spell broken.

"I thought you said we were going to do this tomorrow," Ed grumbles, pulling out more plates and unwrapping the newspaper from them. "Jeez, how many plates do you need?"

"I like to eat. Anyway, how many houseplants do you need?"

"Three! There are only three!"

"Really?" I raise my eyebrows and look round the room. I can count at least seven.

"Some of these are for outside, Charlie Dimmock."

"Oh. Well, they all look the same to me."

Ed rolls his eyes. "God's sake, such a heathen. Tell you what, I'll take these outside, leave you to unwrap the contents of Habitat."

He turns and lifts one of the bigger pots from the floor behind him with a grunt and heaves it out of the back door. I watch him until he disappears into the bright sunshine, then I turn back to unwrapping plates, stacking them in a pile next to the mugs. Ed's shuffling backwards and forwards behind me, carrying plants out to the garden. He was thrilled when we found a flat with a garden. For him it was more important than the flat itself.

"Just think, we can escape outside whenever we want, get some fresh air."

"Ed, it's a tiny handkerchief of a garden, overlooked by fifteen other flats, in the middle of Crouch End. It's hardly Kew Gardens."

He'd shrugged. "Yeah, but one day we can have somewhere bigger, in the middle of nowhere. This is just the start."

I hadn't said anything at the time but now I couldn't push it from my mind. Ed loved the countryside, and although he was happy in London right now, for him it wasn't a long-term thing. The problem was, for me it was. I couldn't imagine living anywhere else, had no desire whatsoever to live in the countryside. But instead of talking to him about it I'd buried my head in the sand and hoped it wouldn't matter.

But of course it would, one day.

But what if I could bring it up now, give him some warning that, actually, I was unlikely ever to want the big house in the country filled with kids that he dreamed of? Would it stop the rows, later?

"Ed?"

He stops in the middle of carrying a plant outside, his breath coming quick and fast. "Yep?"

"I love living in London."

"Me too."

"But you don't want to live here always, do you?"

He adjusts his grip on the flowerpot, rests it on the counter.

"Zo, this is heavy, do we need to talk about this now?"

"Yes. It's important."

136

"Hang on a sec, then." He bends down and rests the plant on the floor, wipes his hands down his jeans. "Right, all yours. What's up?"

"I just — I worry this isn't going to be enough for you, one day."

"What, me and you, or this flat?"

"Us, in the city. I worry you think this is just for now, that one day I'll want to move to a massive house in the middle of nowhere. But Ed, I don't think I'll ever want that."

Ed leans on the counter, takes a deep breath and lets it out in a rush. He's looking at something in the distance, thinking.

"You pick your moments, don't you?"

I shrug. "Sorry. It just felt important, you know, to mention it."

"Well, tell you what, let's just enjoy today, enjoy being here, and worry about that if it happens. Yes, it would be great to live somewhere else, somewhere with air to breathe and space, but it's not everything." His eyes turn to mine, latch on. "It's you I want, Zoe, and to be honest we could live in a mud hut in the middle of the desert and I wouldn't care."

I can't help it. A grin crosses my face. "Ed, I don't think they have mud in the desert. I think it's just sand."

Quick as lightning he picks up a piece of scrunched-up newspaper and throws it at my head. "You're not funny, Morgan."

"I am, Ed, I'm hilarious. You'll learn."

He stops, suddenly serious. "I guess we'll learn a lot of things about each other over the next few years, hey?" His voice is gentle now and tears prick my eyes. He's right, we do have a lot to learn about each other, about what the future holds. At least, he does. I know too much.

"Yes, I guess we will."

Later, when the darkness has descended and we've unpacked everything we own, Ed and I flop, exhausted, onto the new leather sofa.

"I'm bloody knackered."

I snuggle into his shoulder and he wraps his arms around me protectively.

"Me too."

He picks up the remote and flicks the TV on and we sit in silence, staring at the images on the screen. And soon I can't hold on any longer, I have to let go of this day and move on, and just hope I get another one. My eyelids droop and my breathing steadies and slowly, finally, I drift off and let the darkness take me . . .

CHAPTER
SEVEN

26 January 2002

"Zoe, it's me. Mum."

I rub my eyes groggily. The sound of the phone ringing had woken me up and I'd just got to it before it stopped.

"Mum. Hi."

"Are you OK? Did I wake you up?"

"Mmm-hmm. S'OK, though."

I glance at the clock through bleary eyes. 7.15 a.m. What's Mum doing ringing me at this time of the morning? And where am I?

Before I can work it out, Mum's talking again and I struggle to tune in.

"I just rang to say good luck today. Me and Dad will be thinking about you all day; promise me you'll let me know how it goes as soon as you get out?"

Unsure what she's talking about, I look around the room, scrabbling for clues, grasping for snippets of memory before they flit away again like butterflies, just out of reach.

"Zoe, are you still there?"

"Yes, sorry, I'm still here."

"You're not crying, are you? Oh sweetheart, please don't cry. You'll be OK. You will." Mum's voice catches on the last words and my heart flips. What the hell is going on?

"I'll ring you, I promise."

"OK. Good. Right, go and get yourself ready and we'll speak later. Good luck. Love you."

"Thanks, Mum. Love you too."

Mum hangs up and I'm left holding the phone, confused. My feet are cold on the wooden floorboards and I realize I'm shivering. Grabbing my dressing gown from the back of the door, I pad through to the kitchen, hoping to find a clue. Ed's nowhere to be seen but it's our flat, at least our old flat, the one we moved into "yesterday". A few plates are balanced on the draining board, clean, and a cafetière of half-drunk coffee sits cooling on the worktop. Ed's favourite mug is next to it, a ring of brown round the inside rim. There's nothing else out of place that I can see. I move my eyes over to the kitchen table. For a change it's clear of papers and bills and envelopes — but there is a note, and I recognize Ed's scrawled handwriting immediately. My heart stops at the sight of it.

Have gone to work. Didn't want to wake you. See you at the hospital at 2. Love you. Ed.

Hospital.

My legs feel weak and I pull out a chair to sit down. I've spent many, many hours and days in hospital over the last few years being poked, prodded and examined. What's it about this time? What am I going in for — good news or bad news?

I know one way to find out.

140

I stand and walk, legs shaking, into the flat's tiny bathroom. There's no natural light in here but it doesn't matter. I flick the light on, stand in front of the mirror, and lift my pyjama top up.

And then I know. There, on the side of my right breast, is a small scar. It would be hardly visible to most people but I can see it. And that, along with the pain I can now feel in my breast, tells me exactly what today's going to bring.

It's January 2002: the previous Christmas I'd found a lump in my breast. I'd been sitting in a boiling hot bath, the steam rising round me, filling the bathroom so I could hardly make out the cabinet on the wall, could barely see my toes at the other end. I was lazily rubbing body wash over myself, when suddenly I stopped. I rubbed my right breast again. Could I ...? Was there ...? Did I have a lump there?

I stood up, water and bubbles whooshing down my body with the sudden movement, and almost jumped out of the bath. I grabbed a towel, wrapped it round myself, and went drip, drip, dripping into the front room. Ed was slumped on the sofa, exhausted after a long day gardening, a blank look on his face as he stared at the TV, a glass of wine in his hand. He glanced up as I walked in, his forehead creasing slightly at the sight of me.

Before he had a chance to speak I blurted, "I've found a lump." I threw myself on the sofa next to him and took the towel off. "Look," I said, pointing at my boob. "Feel this. Does this feel right to you?"

Ed knew this was no time for jokes, and he dutifully ran his hand gently round the curve of my breast. He stopped when he got to the lump, and I knew he'd felt it too. My body stiffened. "It's not right, is it?" I said, my voice almost a whisper.

He shrugged. "Zo, I honestly have no idea."

I knew he was just telling the truth but it wasn't what I wanted to hear, and I burst into tears.

"Ed, I've got breast cancer!" My voice wobbled precariously.

"Zo, don't you think you're being a bit dramatic? It might be nothing. It probably is nothing. Don't get upset before you even know if there's anything to get upset about."

"It's easy for you to say," I said.

"How?"

I stopped. "What?"

"How is it easy for me to say?" he said, his voice hardening. "Seeing you crying and getting all upset and panicking and the possibility you could be ill? That's not easy at all. In fact it's bloody hard. But there's just no point in getting yourself in a state because you've found a lump until you know what it is."

I stared at him, shocked by the emotion in his voice.

"You're right," I said, wiping my face with the towel I'd wrapped back around my now-shivering body. "I'm really sorry. I'm just scared. It's just — you know, you always read about these things, and it's always bad news, and, well, I . . ."

"You what?" Ed said gently.

"I couldn't bear the thought of leaving you." My voice was quivering.

Ed leaned over and put his arms around my shoulders.

"Oh, you silly sod," he said, and I could hear the smile in his voice. "You're not going anywhere. I won't let you." He pressed his lips gently on the top of my head and, even though I had no idea whether his words were true, I felt comforted. I felt safe. My Ed wouldn't let anything happen to me.

It was Christmas a couple of days after that, so there was nothing I could do. We were spending Christmas Day with my family in Doncaster. We hadn't seen them for months, and had really been looking forward to it.

"Let's not tell Mum and Dad until we know a bit more," I said.

"Are you sure?" Ed knew how much I hated lying to them.

I thought about it. What good would it do, telling them about it before we even knew whether it was something to worry about? "No, let's wait," I insisted. "Let's have a happy Christmas and deal with this in the new year."

And that's what we'd intended to do. But when I was there, surrounded by the people I loved, I'd realized I needed their support. I needed them. And so I'd told Mum over the sprouts, as I was preparing them for Christmas dinner.

"Mum, I've got — some news."

"Ooh, good or bad?"

I paused. "Um. Not good."

I heard her put down the knife she'd been chopping carrots with. "Zoe, what is it? What's happened?"

Suddenly she was behind me, her hands on my shoulders, and I turned and faced her, buried my face in her chest. Tears ran down my cheeks and soaked into her reindeer jumper and she held me for a moment, quietly.

I pulled away and wiped my face, sniffing. "Sorry. It's just, I haven't really talked about it much. Not yet. I — I'm going for some tests. In the new year. I've found a lump, in my boob, and I need to find out whether it's cancer."

I felt Mum's body tense but she said nothing, smoothing my hair back from my face and kissing my forehead gently. "I'm scared, Mum." My voice was barely a whisper.

"I know, darling. I know. But everything will be OK."

I didn't know whether her words were true but I was grateful for them, grateful she didn't quiz me too much, want too much detail.

I asked her to tell Dad and Becky, and later, over dinner, the mood was subdued.

As we passed the vegetables round the table in silence, I stood up. Everyone turned to me.

"Right, that's enough tiptoeing around. I know Mum's told you my — our news." I glanced at Ed, and he smiled weakly. "But I don't want it to spoil today. I don't want it to spoil anything. So can we just pretend it's not happening and enjoy Christmas dinner? Please."

144

There was a beat of silence and then Dad picked up a cracker. "All right, pull my cracker then."

I smiled at him and leaned over and pulled the end of the cracker with a bang, and just like that the tension was gone.

We'd hardly spoken about it any more, apart from a few good luck wishes as we'd left to drive home, and I was grateful to them for trying so hard.

Then the new year had come and I'd gone to see my GP and been referred for tests. I'd had an ultrasound scan and a biopsy, which had left me with the small scar, and Ed had been with me at the appointment, holding my hand. I was glad he was. Mum had wanted to come too, but I'd been insistent. "I'm fine, honestly. I'll let you know the minute I have some news, I promise."

And now here we are, just a week later. The day of my results.

Even though now, more than ten years later, I know what results I got on that day, I have a tight feeling in my chest at the thought of going through it all again. And who knows whether the results will be the same the second time around?

I could die before Ed. The realization hits me like a train and I stay sitting for a few more minutes, just taking in the details of the kitchen in our old flat. It still strikes me as strange how something can be so ingrained in your memory that, even when you haven't seen it or thought about it for more than ten years, or even twenty, it can still feel utterly familiar.

There's a chipped tile above the sink that we always meant to fix; there's one ring on the electric hob that doesn't work, and never will; I know if I open the cupboard on the wall there will be seven or eight mugs, none matching, a box of teabags and a jar of coffee. I know the good coffee, the cafetière coffee, is kept in the fridge. I know the fridge light flickers and that eventually it will give up the ghost completely, and that there are two ring marks on the wooden tabletop where Jane and I left our glasses after drinking too much one night. I know there's a gap in the floorboards that, if I place my chair at the wrong angle, its leg will get wedged down.

I know all these things intimately, despite not having been in the flat for years, despite having lived somewhere else for years since.

If the mind is a strange place, then mine is even stranger.

My chair scrapes on the floor as I lean on the tabletop and push myself up to stand. All the other times I've woken up my body has felt younger, sprightlier, than it does at the age of thirty-eight. I hadn't noticed myself getting older physically, but being reminded of how I used to feel has made me realize I'm stiffer, creakier, than before.

But this time, my body feels old. I don't know if it's the fear or whether it's because I truly am ill this time, but I do know for certain that today is going to be a lot tougher than the last day I spent with Ed.

The clock on the wall says it's only 9 a.m. Usually I'd be at work, but I have the day off.

It's cold in the flat and I get dressed carefully in several layers — vest top, long-sleeved top, jumper, jeans and thick socks. I switch the radio on as I make some breakfast and eat it mechanically at the kitchen table.

When I've finished I wash the dishes and place them carefully on the draining board. I wipe the surfaces down even though they don't need cleaning and cast my eyes round the room for something else to keep my hands busy. I've got the day off work but I still have four hours until I'm meeting Ed and I don't know how to fill them. But I do know I can't hang around the flat any longer, thinking. It's too cold for a walk, so I decide to take myself off to an art gallery. There's something soothing about walking round quiet galleries. It doesn't matter what art is on the walls — I know nothing about art anyway — but it's a good way to distract myself for a couple of hours, and lose myself in the throng of tourists.

An hour later I'm in the huge, cavernous space of the main hall of Tate Modern. I've been here many times in the years following this day and the sheer scale of the place never fails to put things into perspective for me.

I spend the next hour wandering through the rooms, staring at paintings and installations. Colours blend before my eyes, textures merge, and I wonder how the artists who spent their lives creating these pieces would feel if they knew they were all blurring into one; that their soft shapes and colours were helping to calm my nerves.

I make my way to the downstairs café and order a cappuccino and a piece of carrot cake — there's no one here to see me ordering the coffee I used to hate so much — and sit at a table by the window, watching the grey clouds slide slowly across the London skyline. It's only 12.30 and already it feels dark outside. The sky's so heavy it looks as though it could snow at any minute, and part of me hopes it will.

I sit a while longer, then walk outside and stand at the barrier on the South Bank overlooking the Thames. A few boats dot the mighty river. The water is so dark, reflecting back the colour of the sky, that it looks bottomless, and for a second I wonder what it would be like to jump from the riverbank into the freezing water and just be carried away. Would the real me, asleep back in 2013, just drift off, and never come back again?

I'm not prepared to risk it. Even though Ed is gone, and the pain is too much even to bear thinking about, I have other people to consider too, other people who need me.

I check my watch and walk briskly along to Waterloo Bridge, run up the steps and hurry across the river to Embankment Tube station. The gentle rumble of the train washes over me, and when I step onto the platform twenty minutes later at Archway, I feel calmer.

I walk slowly up the hill towards the Whittington Hospital where I'm going to hear my fate. I scan the entrance as I approach but can't see Ed anywhere. It's too cold to wait outside, so I pull my coat tighter round me and walk, head down, to the front door. As I step inside the wind stops and warm air hits me. I feel the tension seep from my body. And then I spot Ed. He's standing by the hospital shop, looking idly at the magazine selection. I gasp loudly, glad of the background noise that swallows the sound. He looks older than he did last time I saw him, and yet still so achingly young. His hair is shorter, but it still hangs sexily over his eyes. He's holding a coat and dressed all in black, as though he's going to a funeral. I watch him in awe for a couple of seconds then stride towards him purposefully. I need a hug. He spots me before I get there, and opens his arms wide as though he can read my mind.

"You OK?" he says softly, pulling away.

I nod mutely.

"Let's get this over with, then."

We walk, hand in hand, to the lift, and stand in silence as it glides up to the fifth floor. My body is tense, my stomach wound tighter than a ball of wool, and I'm gripping Ed's hand like I never want to let go. He squeezes it gently as the lift reaches the floor we need and we step out.

We sit down on the hard green plastic chairs. "You OK?" Ed whispers again. I nod tightly. There are three other women in the waiting room; one woman on her own, a flowered scarf wound artistically round her head, and two women sitting together, one older than the other. They hardly speak, except for the odd whispered word which is impossible to make out from where I'm sitting. They're holding hands, their knuckles white. Probably mother and daughter. I wonder which one is waiting for news. I smile weakly at them and they both smile back. Then we look away. Knowing other people are going through the same thing doesn't help, not really. It doesn't take away the utter terror.

I stare blankly at the details of the waiting room. The pale-green walls, the posters offering counselling, help, advice; the rows of green chairs nailed to the floor, as though anyone was going to sneak one under their coat and walk out with it; the piles of magazines on the low tables between the rows of chairs, dog-eared and out of date. I read a coverline over and over again: *Dumped for losing weight.* I wonder briefly how that woman must have felt, telling her story to the whole world. Would anyone believe my story if I told them what was going on?

And then my name's being called and Ed's pulling me gently to my feet and we're walking into the surgeon's office and sitting down again and the surgeon is looking at me with kind eyes and Ed is clutching my hand and my heart is hammering so hard against my ribcage it feels as though it's going to jump right out of my chest and land on the doctor's desk. I take a deep breath and it catches in my throat, sounding like a sob, and Ed tightens his grip on my hand. I don't dare look at him.

I stare blindly at a poster on the wall behind the doctor's head. This all seems like so long ago, and yet still so fresh in my mind now I'm here again, reliving the terror. The silence in the room before the doctor speaks is probably only a few seconds but it feels like a lifetime as I sit there, squirming in my chair, trying not to guess what she's going to say as the silence is filled

150

by a deafening roar in my head. I put my hands to my ears to try and stifle it.

And then the silence is broken. The doctor has a soft voice and whatever she says sounds kind, cushioning any blow she might have to deliver to her patients. It's a good quality to have, I think. All through this process she's delivered news I don't want to hear: *Zoe, you need a biopsy; Zoe, we need to hurry you through; Zoe, we have your results.* It's never been good news so now as I hear her familiar tone, I'm expecting the same again, so much so I'm hardly listening. So when she stops and I realize she's looking at me expectantly, waiting for me to speak, I don't know what to say as I can't remember hearing anything at all. And despite what happened last time, I can never assume this is the same.

Nervously, I glance at Ed. His eyes search mine, a small crease between his eyebrows, waiting for me to react.

"I — I'm sorry, what did you say?" I stammer.

The doctor's face breaks into a warm grin. "You're clear," she says, soft as feathers. "You don't have cancer."

"Oh!" It comes out as a strangle, a sob, the tension and relief flooding out of me with this one syllable, and I feel as though I'm going to fall off the chair. I turn to Ed and he wraps me in his arms as I cry and cry. The tears won't stop, and this time it's more than just the relief of the all-clear from cancer, which I half knew was coming anyway. This time, I'm letting myself sob for everything I've lost since, everything I haven't let myself cry about until now.

Finally, three, four, five minutes later, I pull myself together and listen to what the doctor has to tell me. She explains that the biopsy showed the lump was simply a benign cyst, and that it's nothing to worry about. I don't need an operation, it should just go away by itself. They're the same words I've heard before but the relief is still as immense. I don't have cancer. I'm going to be OK.

Nothing has changed. I'm not going to die before Ed. I'm not sure how happy this makes me feel.

I stand, my legs still wobbly, but feeling strong.

"Thank you." I stick my hand out and shake hers firmly.

"You're welcome."

We say our goodbyes and walk out of the office, through the waiting room, trying not to catch the eye of anyone there who might not get the same news as me, down in the lift, then out into the crisp, grey day.

The wind that had felt so cold before now feels fresh on my face, and the dark clouds feel comforting rather than threatening.

I look at Ed. Tears are shining in the corners of his eyes. He wipes them away with the back of his sleeve.

"Well, that was a surprise," he says.

"It was."

He says nothing for a second, his breath coming in puffs in the biting air. I shiver.

"Let's get out of here, I'm frozen." He takes my hand and we head to the nearest place we can find out of the cold, a coffee shop on the corner. The heating hits me as I walk in, and I unbutton my coat and sit down at a table to wait. Ed orders drinks and, among the warm buzz of the coffee shop, with the cappuccino machine whirring and banging in the background, I tap Mum's number into my mobile.

She snatches it up before I've even heard it ring. "Zoe?"

"Mum. It's OK. I'm fine. I haven't got cancer."

Her breath comes out in a rush. "Oh, thank God, Zoe. Thank God. I was so worried. Hang on." There's a rustling sound and I hear her speaking to Dad in the background. "John, she's fine. She's going to be OK."

I don't hear Dad's response, but then Mum comes back to the phone. "Don't tell anyone but Dad's crying."

"I'm bloody not." Dad's voice is gruff but I laugh. It feels good to listen to Mum and Dad bickering as though nothing is out of the ordinary.

"Tell him my lips are sealed."

There's a beat of silence. Ed places the paper cups down on the table and smiles as he sits opposite me. I smile back gratefully. Then there's a sniff down the line. "Mum, you're not crying as well, are you?"

"No love, not crying. I'm just so — oh, Zoe, I'm so relieved. I love you so much."

"I love you too, Mum."

I make a snap decision then, something I didn't do enough of before. "Why don't you come down and stay? It would be good to see you; we don't see you often enough."

"I'd love to, love. Be good to spend some time with you. Let me speak to Dad and we'll sort something out, OK?"

"OK. And Mum?"

"Yes, love."

"Can you tell Becky for me? I'm not sure I can keep having this same conversation over and over again." I take a sip of my drink and wince as the hot liquid burns my lip through the plastic spout.

"Course."

"OK, Mum, well, I'll ring you later, have a proper catch-up, OK?"

"OK, sweetheart. Your dad sends his love."

"Give him a sloppy kiss back."

Mum laughs. "He'll love that. Bye."

We hang up and Ed watches me across the table, sipping his coffee quietly. The voices and sounds in the coffee shop are soothing and I can feel the tension in my shoulders release as I sit there cupping my hot chocolate in my hands. A sense of contentment washes over me and I realize how stressed I'd been. I can only imagine Ed feels the same way.

"Do you fancy going out to celebrate?"

I sip my drink again, remembering last time, when we'd gone out and got drunk on champagne, eaten budget-busting food. It had been lovely, but having Ed here now, I just want to spend some time with him, alone. Who knows if I'll get another chance?

"Do you know what, I think I'd just like to go home and relax, maybe get a takeaway. Does that sound boring?"

"Yeah, terrible." Ed grins. "It sounds perfect, Zo."

"Good."

We finish our drinks and stand, make our way back outside. It's turned bitingly cold and a gust of wind almost takes my breath away. We walk quickly to the bus stop, hand in hand, and huddle ineffectually behind the plastic shelter, but the wind seems to go right through it. Ed wraps his arms round me tightly and I bury my face in his chest, slip my arms round his waist under his coat. He rests his chin lightly on my head and despite the cold I feel warm, loved. I want to stay like this forever.

Plastic takeaway boxes cover the rug and the light from the TV flickers across Ed's face, giving it a deathly glow. I shiver at the thought.

"Shall we go to bed?"

Ed looks at me sleepily. "Yeah. I'll just clear this up."

"Leave it. We'll do it in the morning."

He doesn't need telling twice and I stand and hold my hand out to pull him up. In the bedroom we take our clothes off and let them fall on the floor, then climb under the duvet. Ed holds his arm out for me to snuggle into and we lie there, drifting off. His body is warm, his skin slightly damp despite the chill in the air. I breathe in his scent, trying to commit it to memory, just in case. I can hear his heartbeat, thump, thump, thump, in my right ear, and he feels so vital, so alive, I can hardly believe he's gone now. How can he be, when he's right here next to me?

"Ed?"

"Mmm-hmm?" His voice vibrates through his chest and into me.

"You know I'll always love you, right?"

"Mmm. Me too." His voice is thick with sleep, but I'm not ready to leave him yet. There's something I need to do first, to try to get him to understand.

"Did —" I pause, unsure. "Did you really mean it when you said there was no way you wanted to get married, ever?"

His body tenses and he pulls away slightly, peers down at me.

"What?"

"You said you thought marriage was a waste of time, and that it wasn't for you. I just wondered if — maybe, you think you might change your mind one day?" I'm aware this has come out of nowhere but it feels important. He's looking at me and I don't want to catch his eye, scared of what I might see there. So instead I keep my head down, eyes trained on his chest, studying the tiny hairs and the smooth, soft skin.

"I did mean it, Zo. I just don't see the point."

My heart contracts, squeezes tightly. "But —" I stop, wriggle to a sitting position so I can look at him properly. This is something that needs to be said, and he needs to listen, whether it makes a difference or not. I cross my legs and lean my elbows on my knees.

"Listen, Ed. I know you said you think it's meaningless because it meant nothing to your dad. But you're not your dad and I'm not your mum. I'm not saying I want to get married now, and I definitely don't want to scare you off. But to be honest I find it pretty

156

hurtful that you're so adamant, so against the idea that you won't even talk to me about it, won't even consider it as a possibility."

He opens his mouth to speak but I cut him off.

"I know it's just a piece of paper and that it shouldn't make any difference, and I can't explain why it does, but it just does, Ed. And that's it. One day, I'm going to want to get married and I want you to be prepared for that. I don't want it to drive us apart, but you need to know." I stop, shrug. "And that's it."

Ed stares at me as my words press down on us, and I wait for him to process them. The air is heavy and I rub my head, feeling the effect of the wine.

"I don't know what to say, Zo. I guess I've never really thought it mattered that much to you."

"Well, it does." I sound petulant, but I don't care.

"Clearly."

He sits up, wraps the duvet round his shoulders and looks me right in the eye. "OK, listen. I promise to give it some thought and I promise I won't just dismiss it right out of hand. But you've got to give me some time, Zoe, OK?"

I nod. It's a step forward, at least. He reaches his hand out and grabs mine. "But if I do decide it's not for me, for us, does that mean you'll leave me? Because I couldn't stand that."

The truth is, I have no idea. I couldn't imagine not being with Ed forever, and if it meant not getting that piece of paper, did it really matter all that much? I wasn't sure.

"No, I don't think so." It's the best I can give him, for now. I can't explain why it felt so important, but his dismissal just felt like a rejection of me, of us. Maybe it was my insecurities that were the problem, rather than his. "No, probably not," I add.

"OK, good." A few seconds pass, then Ed pulls his hand away and says, "Right, let's get some sleep." He lifts the duvet for me and I climb under it again gratefully, suddenly cold. Ed flicks the light out and I lie staring at the grey ceiling. Beside me I hear Ed's breathing, uneven at first, then slowly deepening into a regular rhythm until it's clear he's asleep.

I turn to face him and lie there for a while, watching him. His arm is slung above him, his head turned slightly to the side, and he looks so peaceful. I wish I could pause this moment forever, and never have to leave him.

Finally, though, exhaustion takes over and I can put it off no longer. So, despite everything today has brought, I give in to the pull of sleep, and I let go . . .

CHAPTER
EIGHT

5 October 2002

My eyes snap open to the sight of Ed's face hovering inches above mine, grinning, and my heart surges with happiness. Another day with him: I can hardly believe it. It hardly matters where or when it is.

"*Bonjour, ma chérie, tu as bien dormi?*"

"Wha — what?" I struggle to prop myself up on my elbows. There's still a blur round the edges of my vision, and I rub my eyes to clear them.

"*Bonjour, c'est le matin, il faut* — er, get up-pay . . ."

Ed's French deserts him and I can't help smiling. He wasn't known for his language skills.

"*Bonjour, chéri, ça va? Pourquoi tu me parles en français?*"

"Er, what?" He scratches his head.

"Why are you talking to me in French?"

"Oh, er, well, I thought I'd better give it a go, as we're in Paris. Sorry for murdering the belle language." He shrugs nonchalantly, but I'm not really listening. We're in Paris! I peer round the room, taking it in. The curtains are drawn so I climb out of bed and walk over to the window and poke my head out. I gasp.

"Paris! We're really here!"

"Well, yes, we were last time I looked." Ed tugs the curtain from my hand and peeks through too. The view is nothing special, just more hotels and buildings across the street, but I know where we are and my heart contracts. Paris, the city of love and romance — this could be fabulous.

Except that, last time, it wasn't. Not at all. Last time, I'd spent the whole trip expecting Ed to ask me to marry him. Every time we went for dinner, at the top of the Eiffel Tower, on the Champs-Élysées, on the banks of the Seine — I saw a significant occasion, a moment to remember. It drove me mad and, by the end, it drove Ed mad too.

"What the hell is the matter with you?" he snapped finally, on our last day there as we ate crêpes from a van on the pavement. "You've been a grumpy old cow all day. Actually, scrub that: for the last three days."

"I have not." A piece of crêpe fell from my mouth and landed by my foot. "Fuck's sake." I kicked it away angrily.

"See, you're even angry at a piece of food."

Thunder roared in my ears.

"I'm not angry at a piece of fucking food, I'm angry at you!" I stamped my foot like a petulant child.

"Me? What the hell have I done, apart from book a lovely holiday to Paris to cheer you up after a cancer scare? God, what a bloody terrible, selfish boyfriend I am."

I didn't reply. I knew I was being an unreasonable bitch, but it didn't mean I could stop it. I felt I wanted

160

to punch something, someone, at the injustice of it all. The rage had to come out somewhere and it seemed that here, on this innocuous street in the middle of Paris, was where it was going to come out, like bile.

"You *are* selfish. The whole time we've been here I've been convinced you were going to propose, to ask me to spend the rest of my life with you, but oh no. Edward Williams couldn't possibly imagine that taking his girlfriend to Paris might make her think that he wanted to marry her, could he? You know how much I want to get married, you know how much it means to me, but you're *still* refusing to even think about it. You're a bloody selfish bastard, Ed, and I'm — fucking furious."

The tears were coming thick and fast by now but Ed just stood there, his crêpe in his hand, staring at me. I needed a hug, for him to tell me everything was going to be OK, but he wasn't budging. He stood there, stock-still in the cold autumn air; then he turned, shoved his uneaten crêpe in a nearby bin and stalked off. I watched in horror and fury as he walked away from me, willing him to come back, to hug me and tell me everything was going to be OK. But he didn't. He just went, leaving me standing there alone.

Now, of course, I understand his hurt, confusion and anger. But then — well, then I was devastated. I walked around for hours as the sun went down and the air got chillier and chillier. I couldn't face going back to the hotel and seeing the disgust on his face. I thought I'd ruined everything.

161

And for a while, I had. We hardly spoke for the rest of the day and by the time we got home we agreed, after a stilted conversation, that we probably needed to spend some time apart. I was heartbroken. He'd gone to stay with his mum for a few weeks while I rattled round the flat by myself, empty, bereft.

Eventually, of course, Ed and I had sorted things out. But I couldn't go through that again. I wasn't going to ruin it this time. This was my chance to make amends.

I turn from the window and slip my arms round Ed's waist. He buries his face in my hair. "You're in a better mood today."

I flinch, remembering last time. "Yeah, sorry. Amazing what a good night's sleep can do." I smile up at him apologetically.

"So, where do you fancy going today?"

I stare out of the window at the grey skies, the clouds sliding over the rooftops. We were in the most romantic city in the world and I didn't care where we went. I would have been happy to stay in the hotel, just me and Ed. I shrug. "Dunno. The Louvre?"

Ed's face twists, his expression unreadable. "Er, we saw that yesterday."

"Oh. Oh yes, sorry." Oops, hopefully he put it down to tiredness. "I don't really mind."

"Well, how about the Sacré-Cœur? You said you fancied going there." He peers out of the window, wrinkles his nose. "Although it looks like it might rain."

"We could always stay here, order breakfast in bed . . ."

162

"Ooh, now you're talking." Ed grabs the room service menu and we order a continental breakfast to be brought to our room.

Half an hour later the breakfast arrives and we spread it out on the carpet like a picnic and sit cross-legged. I spread some jam on a croissant and watch Ed doing the same. "Thanks for this, Ed."

"What, breakfast?"

"No, this. Paris."

He shrugs. "I just wanted to cheer you up, after the cancer scare and everything. I wanted you to know how much you mean to me. How much I love you."

I smile happily. "I love you too." I take a bite of croissant but miss slightly, and end up with a huge lump of jam on my chin. I lean over to give Ed a kiss.

"Get off me!" he screeches, laughing and pushing me away. "You're covered in jam!"

"I know." I carry on moving towards him.

Ed jumps up and runs across the room. He grabs a hairbrush from the dressing table and holds it in the air.

"I have a weapon and I'm not afraid to use it," he yells, backing up against the chair.

"Aha, you think you can defeat me, do you?" I purr, smearing jam all over my mouth and chin and padding slowly towards him, licking my lips.

"Get away from me, Jam Girl," he shouts. "You will be defeated!"

He swipes the hairbrush round in circles like a sword. I carry on, dodging him, backing him slowly away from me and into the bathroom; then I grab the back of his neck and plant a huge smacker on his lips, covering his face in sticky red jam.

"Oh, gross!" he yells, wrapping his arms round me. I think he's cuddling me and I sink into him, laughing. Then suddenly I feel water pouring down my face and realize he's not finished yet. He's holding a soaking wet facecloth above my head, the nearest thing he could find, and is just letting it drip, drip, drip all over me.

"You little git!" I yell, pulling away from him. "Right, this is war!"

I grab the shower gel from the bath and squeeze it down his arm and across the front of his T-shirt. He grabs the shampoo and squirts the contents all over me. A huge lump lands on the top of my head and slides down over my eye and onto my cheek. Undeterred, I wipe it away and reach over to his face and smudge it on his eyebrows and nose.

I walk back to the bedroom to find something else to throw at him but as I take my eyes from him for a second he follows me and scoops up a handful of butter and throws it at me. It's soft and it slides down my chest and lands on the carpet. I gasp, then grab the bowl of strawberries and yogurt, charge up to him and dump the whole lot on his head. He looks shocked and for a few seconds we stand in silence, watching the strawberries that haven't been squashed into his hair roll across the floor.

And that seems to break the spell and as we stand there, sticky, wet and covered in food, we start to laugh hysterically. We're laughing so hard we can hardly breathe, and finally we're both sitting in the middle of

164

the floor trying to catch our breath, covered in our breakfast.

"You stupid bugger," he says, laughing. I look at him, covered in yogurt, jam and strawberries, and start to laugh again.

"You look so ridiculous."

"Have you seen yourself?"

I look down. My previously clean T-shirt is covered in smears of yogurt and is wet through. My pyjama bottoms are just as bad and I can't begin to imagine how my hair looks. I can feel it plastered to my head.

I look round the room. "I think we'd better get cleaned up."

I step across the mess to the bathroom and strip off and climb into the shower. The warm water pummels my head and I close my eyes. Then I hear the bathroom door open and Ed joins me in the tiny shower cubicle and wraps his arms round me from behind. I can feel his firm body pressed up against me and I reach round and cup his bum cheeks in my hands. He kisses my neck and I turn round so that our bodies are crushed against each other. My heart hammers in my chest. I've missed him so much; I've craved his touch, I've missed the feel of his strong body against mine. Now he's here, it's like an ache and I know I need him, I need to feel him inside me, to let myself go and really feel it. And so, in the confined space of the steamy shower cubicle, Ed and I make love. It's not like in the movies: the cubicle is too small and we both keep banging our elbows on the glass, and then the water turns cold and we have to turn it off, and Ed has to change position several times because his legs are aching. But it doesn't matter, because it still feels amazing.

Afterwards, as we're drying off, I feel shy. Even though it wasn't the first time we'd been this intimate in the days I'm reliving, I'd thought I'd lost the chance to ever be with Ed again, to feel him on me, inside me, and now I don't know how to behave. I get dressed quickly, and when he hugs me I smile with happiness.

"Well, that was fun." Ed grins wickedly.

"It was."

"I think I like the less grumpy you."

"Oi!"

"You know what I mean." He peers out of the rain-spattered window. "It doesn't look like it's getting any better. Do you want to go out?"

I shove an undamaged piece of croissant into my mouth and nod.

"I guess we should."

And so we spend the rest of the day as you should in Paris; we stroll hand in hand up the Champs-Élysées, we do some shopping and we walk up the hill to the Sacré-Cœur. At the top of the steps we stand; the rain has stopped and the clouds scud across the sky as Paris and all its endless possibilities spread out before us. I squeeze Ed's hand and he squeezes mine back and smiles at me.

This time, I refuse to think about marriage. This time, I want to be happy.

We wander back to the hotel, stopping for coffee and cake at the gorgeous Café de la Paix. It feels like such a treat. We stroll along the banks of the Seine, along walkways and through pretty gardens. At Pont Neuf we take a boat trip, Notre-Dame rising up before us, and the Eiffel Tower always in the background, reminding us where we are, in one of the most romantic cities in the world. I feel like the luckiest woman alive, being here with my Ed by my side.

That night we enjoy a romantic candlelit dinner overlooking the river, and this time I don't spend the whole meal a bundle of nerves, waiting for a ring to drop out of my glass or for Ed to drop down on one knee. This time, I just have fun.

Later, as we snuggle up to go to sleep, I think back over the day and feel happy. This is so different from last time. I can only hope it's enough to make a change. I can only hope I've done enough.

CHAPTER
NINE

19 October 2002

The room is totally unfamiliar and I feel breathless with panic as my eyes dart wildly around. The curtains are tightly drawn, making it hard to see details clearly, but in the murky grey light I can make out walls covered in generic paintings of landscapes, windmills, a lake; there's dark wooden furniture, thick, flowery curtains, a standard lamp in the corner. I have no idea where I am.

What does it mean, that I don't recognize this room? Has something changed in the past, or am I back in the present in a whole new day? And if I am, what does that mean — that I've changed something? That Ed might not be dead? I feel light-headed just at the idea.

But my thoughts refuse to settle, flailing around like a kite in the wind, and I frown as I struggle to pin them down into something coherent, tangible.

I lie still a few more moments, trying to steady my heart, taking in deep gulps of air. This is crazy. Where — and when — the hell am I?

Rolling over, I stand and walk to the window and pull open the curtains. The angry iron sky is dark, heavy, pressing; the clouds are low and still, reaching down to touch the sea, the line between the two dirty, smudged as though they can't decide where one ends and the other begins. My eyes are drawn to the sea, the rolls of white surf like folds, the dull, bottomless water that stretches out forever. I flick my eyes to the left, and the right. In front of the house there's a road, slick with rain, the light from the lamp post that's still glowing reflected along the black tarmac. A car rolls slowly past, spray from its tyres splashing up, creating ripples long after it's moved along. There's a small fence with a gate, a path through a garden that in summer must be full of light and colour but today looks grey and lifeless. Leaning forward, I look to the left and see a pier, no lights flashing, nobody on it; to the right the road rises sharply, stretching between the sea and the row of houses. I can't see the beach from here but I know it must be there, empty except for the odd dog walker, huddled against the chill.

I turn and find a jumper hanging on the back of a chair. I wrap myself tightly in it and open the door cautiously, peering out. Straining my ears for sounds of movement, I listen carefully but there's nothing. It's totally silent.

I walk past two other doors — the bathroom and another bedroom, empty — and down the stairs to the kitchen, where I busy myself finding cups and teabags, boiling the kettle. Then I take my cup of tea and sit at the table, overlooking the sea and the view I've just seen from the bedroom window. There's a hushed, early-morning feel to the cottage, as though everyone else in the world is still sleeping and it's just me awake,

169

watching the steam rise from my cup and dissipate in the cool air.

A bag sits on the other chair, containing my laptop and some notes from work. I'm clearly planning to be here for a while if I've brought my work with me. My handbag is hanging from the back of the chair and I lean over and pick it up, looking for my phone. When I locate the old Nokia — definitely my old phone — I glance at the display. 7.14a.m. Early still. There are no missed calls, no text messages. The date says 19 October 2002.

I'm in the past, the day before Ed's twenty-eighth birthday. But it's not a past I've been in before.

The room tilts at the realization and I grab the table for support. What on earth is going on? And how am I going to find out?

I sit for a few more minutes, my mind calming, and try to bring some order to the thoughts racing round my brain. It's only two weeks since we were in Paris and we were happy. Last time had been so bad we'd agreed to have some time apart when we'd got home, and I'd stayed in the flat while Ed had gone to stay with his mum for a bit, and later with Rob.

We'd arrived home and Ed had hardly spoken to me since our row the day before, on the streets of Paris. The journey home had been tense; we'd been polite but cool. I'd hated every minute of it and hoped everything would be fine when we got home. But Ed had other ideas.

"I don't think I can do this." We were in the kitchen; I was shoving clothes into the washing machine, Ed was

170

chopping mushrooms. He'd turned, knife still in his hand, to face me, his face set, drawn. I'd never seen him look so miserable and my stomach flipped over.

"Do what?" I hated the high pitch of my voice but it didn't seem to want to work properly. My heart hammered against my chest and I prayed he wouldn't say the words I knew he was going to say.

"This. Me and you. I think —" He paused, licked his lips, looked at the ceiling, the window, the door, anywhere but at me. "I think we need some time apart, to decide whether this is what we really want."

His words were like bullets in my chest and I felt winded. I stayed crouched by the washing machine, not knowing what to do, what to say.

"I — I don't want some time apart. Surely — surely we can talk about it, sort this out?"

Ed nodded, briefly. "Maybe. But I think we need to be apart for a bit, get our thoughts in order. You made it clear, when we were in Paris, that nothing but marriage will make you happy, and I — I haven't worked out yet whether I can do it. Even for you. I need some time to think."

He'd seemed so cool, detached. I felt the world tilt on its axis, as though everything I'd thought was real, solid, was about to slip away, out of reach. I couldn't let this happen.

"But — I can live without it, Ed. I can. I just want to be with you. Please. Please don't do this." I stood and stepped over the piles of clothes towards him. As I reached him he stiffened and I hesitated.

"I'm sorry, Zo. I love you, but I've got to get my head sorted. I'll — I'll go and stay with Rob for a bit, maybe go to Mum's."

I stared at him, feeling as though my heart was going to snap in two. There was nothing I could say. He'd made up his mind.

And so I'd let him go. Those weeks without him had been terrible, as though there was a hole in my life that couldn't be plugged. It had filled me with terror, the thought of not having Ed in my life. It would be like living a half-life. When he eventually came back, it was such a relief that we just sort of reached a silent agreement not to talk about it, to move on.

But now, remembering it, I realize I'd felt the same terror since he'd died, too — and this time there was no way back. Life had stretched out before me like a blank, featureless desert; but then I'd been given these "second chance" days, these days to be with Ed again, to maybe change something, and it had been like seeing an oasis and realizing it was real.

My mind snaps back to the present. Nothing that has happened so far could explain why I am in this house. Could it be that what I did in Paris has actually changed things? And if so, what? I frown. I'm clearly here alone; there's no sign of anyone else staying here. So what on earth can this be about?

Grabbing my cup, I stand and march back up the stairs. I run the shower until it's scalding and jump in, trying to dispel the chill that's descended over me, into my bones. The room fills with steam and afterwards I stand, dripping wet, in front of the mirror, waiting for it to clear. Impatient, I rub a smudgy circle in it and lean in and peer at myself. I look exhausted; dark circles ring my eyes, the skin tight and drawn across my face. I frown, and the small crease that appears is deeper than it's been before.

I get dressed and dry my hair, apply some make-up. It feels pointless, getting ready for the day when I have no idea what it's going to bring. But I feel the need to be prepared.

Downstairs I pull on boots and my coat and head out of the door. I need to do something, get out of the house, find out where I am. I march along the seafront towards the pier, my hands shoved in my pockets. It's started to rain now: fine, drizzly rain that fills my eyes, my face, so it feels as though I'm breathing underwater. I reach the deserted pier and walk to the edge, leaning over the barrier to watch the water swirl a few feet beneath me. I walk on until I reach a shop. A sign outside reveals where I am: Lowestoft. I frown. I've never been here before; why would I be here now?

I duck inside and buy a paper, then head back to the house along the seafront, past the rows of half-empty guesthouses. There are a few people around now, walking dogs, and some nod at me as I walk past, my hood pulled tight round my face. I nod back. I let myself into the house and close the door behind me, immediately aware of the silence that presses down around me. I'm totally alone.

I pass the next hour or so reading the paper, then use it to get the fire started. I poke around, trying to stop the flame from going out, and place some more wood on it from the pile in the corner. A warmth begins to seep into the room and I sit down and switch on the TV, desperate for some company.

I must have fallen asleep, because I wake to the sound of banging. Someone's knocking on the door, insistently. Jumping up, I head to the window and peer around. And when I see who's there I gasp.

It's Susan. Ed's mum is here.

I hurry to open the door and a whoosh of cold air comes in with her. As soon as she's inside she opens up her arms and throws them round me, holding me tightly against her damp coat. I breathe in the familiar smell of her perfume. Then she pulls away and grips the tops of my arms, holding my gaze. Her eyes are the same deep blue as Ed's and I struggle not to look away.

"Zoe, what on earth is going on?"

I squirm uncomfortably, not sure what to tell her. How can I explain what's happening when I have no idea myself? I hope she'll elaborate.

"Can we go and sit down?"

I nod as she shrugs out of her coat and I hang it on the peg by the door and lead her to the kitchen.

"Can I get you a drink?"

"I'd love a coffee, please."

I busy myself making coffee as I wait for her to speak, but she stays quiet. Finally, drinks made, I sit down at the table opposite her.

"So . . . ?" I trail off, unsure what to say.

"Oh Zoe, I'm so sorry. Firstly I'm sorry about stalking you — nobody knew where you were but I made Jane tell me. I needed to speak to you. Mostly,

174

though, I'm sorry about Ed, and I — need to be able to help fix this because — well, I feel responsible."

"Responsible? For what?"

"For this — mess." She drums her neat nails on the table. A frown lines her face. "Listen, Ed's told me what's been going on. That you want to get married and that he — well, he just doesn't want to."

Ah. So I was right. I nod, trying to keep my face blank, unreadable.

She leans forward as though to tell me a secret. "The thing is, Zoe, it's not about you. Ed adores you, anyone can see that. He'd do anything for you. It's his bloody father that's caused all this."

"His father?"

She nods briskly. "Yes. It seems that my son is worried he might turn into his feckless father if he agrees to get married, mad as that sounds."

"But he's not his father — and from what he's told me he's nothing like him, is he?"

Susan holds my gaze, then looks down at her hands, shakes her head. "No, he absolutely isn't anything like him, thank God. Listen. Henry was a total bastard, always had been, and always was until the day he died. I knew he was a cheat when I married him, but I loved him. Pathetic, I know, but I thought I could change him; I thought getting him down the aisle would turn him into the perfect husband. But of course it didn't. If anything, he got worse. Always sneaking off, "working late" — shagging his secretary, more like. It was all such a sordid bloody cliché, and I let it happen. But Ed is absolutely nothing like him, and I've told him that."

She looks up and I hold her gaze. "I've told him. If he doesn't marry you, and he loses you, he'll be a bloody idiot."

For a moment we sit, letting her words settle round us like confetti. I'm shocked. I'd always known how Ed felt about his dad — the dad he rarely saw, who was always out, who left his mum fighting back tears every time he did bother to come home. But I'd never heard Susan speak about him like this.

"What did he say, when you told him that?"

She shrugged. "He said he knew. He loves you so much, you know, Zoe. I think you two need to talk."

"I think so too." I pause, my voice barely more than a whisper. "But there's still one thing I don't understand."

"What's that?"

"Ed's desperate for a baby." I flush, feeling embarrassed talking about this in front of his mum. But it's too late for that now; she already seems to know everything. "I've told him I don't think I want children, that I love my job and I don't think it's for me, but he seems to have this vision of a house full of kids running around. How can he be so scared of commitment, if he wants all that?"

"Oh, it's not the family thing he's scared of. To Ed, having a huge family is the sign of a perfect life — well, it would prove that he's not like his father, wouldn't it, because we only had him, as you know. It's not commitment he's afraid of, Zoe, it's just the idea of marriage. He's got it into his head that it might turn you two into a carbon copy of me and his father."

176

I nod, starting to understand. "Do you — do you know where he is, now? Is he at your house?"

Susan's face flushes and she looks embarrassed. "Well, actually, he's here."

"Here?" I look around stupidly, expecting him to jump out like a jack-in-the-box.

"He's gone for a walk; he's waiting for me to ring him. I'm sorry, Zoe, I just thought if I could make you two talk you might be able to sort things out rather than you staying here alone in this — cottage in the middle of nowhere and him moping about my flat with a face like a wet weekend." She smiles, hopefully. "So, will you talk to him?"

"Yes. Yes, I'll talk to him. As long as he'll listen."

"Oh, he'll listen, don't you worry about that. Otherwise he'll have me to answer to." She grins. "So, can I ring him? Or do you want to?"

"I will. And, Susan?"

"Yes?"

"Thank you so much. For everything. For telling me everything."

"You're welcome. I thought it was about time someone started talking around here, what with you two being so stubborn."

I dig my mobile from my bag and dial Ed's number with shaking hands. There's so much at stake here — our future, our lives together — that I have to get this right.

It stops before it gets to the end of the first ring.

"Zoe?"

"Ed."

A pause. A silence heavy with expectation.

"So. Can I come and see you?"

"Yes please."

I tell him the address and Susan makes herself scarce. As I wait for him I feel like a silly little girl, waiting for the boy she fancies to ring her. My stomach hurts and my shoulders are tight. I sit, I stand, I pace, I wipe imaginary dust from the mantelpiece with my finger.

And finally there's a knock at the door and when I open it I see my Ed standing there, his face serious, his wet hair plastered across his face. I walk forward and throw my arms around him and I feel the tension fall from me as we stand there, holding each other as though we never want to let go.

Eventually we have to, though, and I lead him by the hand into the kitchen. I don't bother with pleasantries like drinks and chat about the weather. Instead we sit and I say: "So. Your mum says we need to talk. I think she's right, don't you?"

"She is. And we do."

"OK. So you start."

"Right." He wipes his hand down his face, pushes his hair out of his eyes, leans his arms on the table, drops of water falling onto the surface like tiny rivers. "I've talked to Mum. We've talked a lot, about Dad, about how he behaved. It probably sounds stupid but somewhere inside me was this feeling that, if I allowed myself to get married, to settle down with someone I loved, that I'd turn into him, become a cheat, a liar. Someone I never wanted to be. And so I thought it was

178

easier to shut myself off, tell myself — and you — that I didn't want to get married, that I didn't need it. That I was happy as we were."

"And we are happy."

He nods. "We were. But look at us now, Zo. We're falling apart, and all because I'm being a stubborn git."

"You had your reasons. I do understand them Ed, I do. I understand, now, that it wasn't about me. But it always felt like it. I felt like you didn't want to marry me because you weren't sure I was the one, and you were waiting, making sure there was no one better waiting in the wings. It felt like a rejection."

"I can't believe you'd ever think that."

I shrug. "What else could I think?"

"I don't know, but definitely not that I was waiting for someone better." He pauses, looks down at his hands cupped on the table in front of him. His voice comes out quiet and I have to strain to hear his next words. "There is no one better, Zoe. It's always been you. Always."

My heart explodes with happiness. "Oh Ed, I feel the same. I just love you so much." Tears are falling down my face as he stands and comes to envelop me in his arms, but I don't care. We stand there for what could have been a minute but could have been days, and all the tension of the last few weeks, months, seeps away.

Finally, spent, we pull away and sit back down again.

"So, does this mean you want to get married, then?"

He takes a deep breath.

"Yes, I think so. This is a big thing for me. Anyway, you can't ask me that, not like this. I want to do it properly, not just agree it in a conversation. You know, the grand gesture, the big proposal. A proper, traditional proposal. This —" he gestures between us — "this isn't a proposal. This is a conversation."

"You big softy."

"Well, you know, if you're going to do something, you may as well do it right. It's what you always tell me." He grins and I can't help smiling back.

"You're right, I do."

The muffled ring of a phone breaks the moment and Ed rummages in his pocket to find it before it stops. He glances at the screen before answering.

"Hi, Mum . . . Yes, all OK . . . Yes, it's safe to come back . . . I will, I'll do it now. See you soon."

He hangs up. "Sorry, Mum's getting cold, wondered whether it was safe to come back yet. And she wants me to put the kettle on."

"I think we can manage that."

A few minutes later Susan is back. The tension has lifted and laughter fills the room as we make dinner together then sit and eat it from our laps in front of the fire in the living room. I'm so grateful to her I want to hug her. But finally, she stands. "So, I suppose I'd better be going." She yawns dramatically and looks at Ed pointedly. "I'm assuming you're staying here tonight?"

He nods sheepishly, looks at me. "If it's OK?"

"Of course it's OK." I soften. "More than OK."

"Right, well I'll be off, then." Susan gathers up her coat and bag and we see her to her car. The rain has eased and we stand and wave her off, holding hands,

180

until she disappears round the corner. And then we go back inside.

The day has ended where it began: in the bed in a room I don't recognize. Only this time, as I lie on my side, Ed's body is wrapped around mine, his chest pressed into my back, his legs following the contours of mine, his arm draped across my waist. I can feel his warm breath on my neck and it makes me shiver. I'm trying to commit the feel of his body to memory, to hold this in my mind forever, so that if I don't get to see him again, at least I'll always have this. I can't imagine ever forgetting it, but I know I will, eventually.

We're lying still but my mind is busy, trying to lend some order to what's happened today. Something has changed, shifted; today was a totally new day. Last time we'd been through this I'd stayed in the flat, alone; I'd gone to the office and worked late, worked like a maniac, trying to avoid going home to an empty flat. A flat without Ed in it. This time, I'd come to this house, in this town I don't know, and Susan had come to see me, helped us sort things out. I don't know what this means, but I can only hope it means that, if I've changed something small like this, then maybe I might have changed something bigger; maybe I've already tweaked things enough for Ed not to die. After all, it would only be a matter of a few seconds' difference in timing, that terrible day. Who's to say it couldn't work?

"You OK, Zo?"

"Yeah, I'm fine. Thinking."

"About what?"

"Just how happy I am."

"Me too. Really happy." His arm tightens round me.

We lie like that a while longer and I listen as Ed's breathing slows.

"I love you, Ed. Promise me you'll never leave me. Promise me you won't die."

But there's no answer; he hasn't heard me, and the steady sound of his breathing is my only reply. And so I drift off too, hoping that this won't be the last memory with him I'm able to create, hoping I'll have at least one more day . . .

CHAPTER
TEN

13 December 2002

Pink's "Let's Get the Party Started" is thumping from the stereo, the bassline pulsing through my body. I'm standing in the corner of a room sipping a glass of wine, watching the party in full swing. I can't see Ed but the room's full of people, and Jane's standing by the Christmas tree talking to a vaguely familiar man with a strange goatee beard who I feel certain she ends up snogging the face off. She seems animated, young.

I smile. We're at a party at Rob's flat in Tooting; I remember it well. He'd held a party a couple of weeks before Christmas 2002 and we'd all got wildly drunk, not even making it home until the next morning. It was one of the last big blowouts I can remember before we got all sensible and grown-up. I glance at .my watch. 10p.m. Still early.

"You look thoughtful." There's a voice at my elbow and I jump and whip round. Simon's there, a beer in his hand, a crooked smile on his lips.

"Hello, stranger, how are you?"

He smiles sheepishly, shrugs. "You know, not bad. Pretty busy, but —" He looks round the room.

"It's good to see you. It's been too long. How's the lawyer training going?"

"I know, sorry, I've been crap. It's fine, it's good but — work is just so bloody busy I hardly even have time to fart any more, let alone go out."

I grin. "I know the feeling. I always seem to be at work these days too."

"Marketing, isn't it, you're in these days? Über-successful, Ed tells me, head of the department or something?"

"I don't know about that, but I do love it."

"Great, great. I always knew you'd do well, Zoe. I wish I'd done something easier though, like Ed. You know, goofing around, doing a bit of gardening here and there."

"He's not goofing around, not any more." I sound sharp without meaning to, but I feel defensive. "He's just trying it out for a while, deciding whether it's what he wants to do, you know, as a career. Not everyone's as focused as you, Si."

"No, point taken. Sorry, I didn't mean it. I just sometimes wish I had more of a life, got out to see my friends more." He pauses, takes a sip of beer. "So anyway, how are you — you and Ed?"

"Good." I nod and take a sip from my own drink. "We're really good, thanks. Happy."

And we were. Since the huge row about getting married — the first time round — Ed had come back from staying with his mum and we'd reached a kind of plateau; we seemed to be doing OK. Tensions had dropped and I'd begun to accept that it might never happen, that he might never propose. I was even starting to think I might be OK with that.

And then, the day after this party, we'd gone out for dinner. He'd been moody and grumpy and I'd put it down to our horrendous hangovers. But then he'd got down on one knee and asked me to marry him and I'd nearly fallen off the chair with shock.

I'd said yes, of course. I don't remember many days I'd ever been happier, before or since.

But what I've been trying to work out since I woke up this morning is why, if other days I've relived have been so significant to me and Ed, I've come back to this day and not tomorrow, the proposal day. Nothing's really happened today, apart from this party — we've both been at work, we had dinner and then we got ready and came here. I'm hoping all will soon become clear. I can't shake a nagging doubt, a feeling somewhere deep inside that something's going to go horribly wrong.

I'm pulled back to the party by the sound of Simon's voice. He's been saying something and I haven't heard a word.

"Sorry, I was miles away." There's a woman standing next to Simon. She's a good few years older than him, her hair shiny and make-up immaculate. Her eyes are sparkling with happiness and I recognize her immediately as Joanna, who very quickly becomes Simon's wife.

She holds her hand out. "Lovely to meet you."

"You too." I shake her hand and smile. I'm about to say something else when I spot Ed across the room, fiddling about with the CD player. It's not the first time I've seen him today but my heart skips a little beat anyway.

"Sorry, excuse me a minute." I scurry over to Ed, not caring how rude I seem, wrap my arms round his waist and press my cheek against his warm back. He spins round to face me. "Hello, you."

"Hello yourself. What're you up to?"

"Oh, just seeing if there's anything better than this bloody racket." He rolls his eyes. He's holding a few CDs in his hands.

"And is there?"

"Nah, load of old crap. You know what Rob's taste's like." He grins. "Shall we go and get another drink?"

"Good plan."

We wander into the kitchen, hand in hand. Most of the surfaces are covered with bottles and a growing pile of empties sits by the back door. There are a couple of people I don't recognize and they smile at us as we come in. I smile back.

Ed opens the fridge and pulls out a bottle of wine, pours me one, then finds himself a glass and pours in some red. We both take a sip and wince. "Jesus, it tastes like mouthwash." He glances at the bottle then takes another gulp, his mouth pinched. "Oh well, beggars can't be choosers."

"True. And you know the best way to stop noticing the taste?"

"Drink it quicker?"

186

"Exactly." I grin and we tip our heads back in unison and drain our glasses. I slam mine back down on the counter, breathless. "That was gross. More, please."

Ed obliges and we stand quietly for a moment, the bass from the music thumping through our bodies as we lean against the kitchen counter. My head is spinning from drinking the wine too fast. Ed's face is serious, thoughtful, as he watches me intently, and for a moment I wish I could read his thoughts.

"Penny for them?"

"What? Oh sorry, I was just thinking."

"About?"

"Just — you know, this. Us. How great we are." He turns to me with a wicked grin. "Especially me."

"Ha bloody ha." I punch his arm gently.

"Seriously, though. It's true. Since we had our chat, I've been thinking —"

"Zoeeeee!" Jane bursts through the door, stumbling a little, holding hands with goatee-beard man, a wild, drunken smile on her face.

"Hey, you." The moment's broken and I glance at Ed and raise my eyebrows in question. He shrugs.

She stands straight and looks at me, then at Ed. "You having your own little party in here, then?" She indicates the now-empty kitchen with a sweep of her arm.

"Yeah, you could say that." Ed's voice is flat.

"Sorry to interrupt, but this —" a wave of her hand — "is Adam. Adam, this is Zoe and Ed. My best friends."

Adam raises his beer bottle in greeting. "All right."

Ed nods a greeting back. "Nice to meet you."

"Adam's an old friend — used to work with me . . ." Jane links her arm through his territorially. "Anyway, we've just come to get a drink, I'm bloody parched." She leans over and plucks a couple of beers from the counter and passes one to Adam, then they both turn and stumble from the room as quickly as they'd entered.

The kitchen's suddenly quiet again and Ed's looking at the floor, worrying his shoe over an imaginary stain on the tiles. He seems anxious and I'm desperate to know why.

"So, before we were rudely interrupted you were about to say something?"

His eyes flick up to meet mine, flick down again.

"Yeah, it — it doesn't matter. Not now."

"Oh, OK. It's just — you said you'd been thinking, so I thought it might have been something important."

"Yeah, it was. It is. It's just — I'm not sure it's something I want to talk about here, now, after all."

"Why not?" I look around the kitchen and smile. "What's wrong with this lovely kitchen?" There are dirty plates and cups littering most surfaces, and overflowing ashtrays. Ed smiles back.

"Good point. It *is* pretty salubrious."

"So?"

"You're not going to let this go, are you?"

"Nope."

He inhales deeply, lets the air out through his mouth in a hiss, his cheeks puffing out. "OK. So, I have been thinking. A lot. About us." He pauses, looks at his feet,

188

shuffles uncomfortably. "I've been thinking about our future, about the house in the country, the kids, the marriage — everything we've talked about." He pauses and my heart hammers wildly in my chest. What's coming next? What if this time around he's decided he can't do it, he can't be with me? Where would that leave me now, in the present? I feel the room spinning as he takes a deep breath and I feel as though I'm going to pass out. The strip lights over my head become a whirl of rainbow colours, and my vision blurs. And then I realize Ed's holding something in front of him, and waiting for me to speak, and I try to focus on him, on his face.

"Zoe, are you OK?"

"I — I'm fine. Wh-what did you just say?"

Ed nods his head, indicates the thing he's holding out in front of him. It's a box and in it is — I squint more closely at it. It's a ring! A tiny, glittering diamond ring, and Ed's looking at me expectantly, waiting for an answer.

"I just asked you to marry me, Zoe." His face is serious.

And so I give the only answer I can give, the only answer I'm ever going to give. "Yes." My voice is barely more than a squeak.

"Was that a yes?"

I nod. "It was." I brush the tears from my face but it's soaking wet now and there's no stopping them.

Ed opens his arms and I fall into them, soaking his T-shirt. He buries his face in my hair. "Thank God for that."

I look up at him, his face so close to mine I can hardly make out his features. "You didn't really think I'd say no, did you?"

"No, I didn't, not really. But to be honest, Zoe, this wasn't really planned, not tonight. I had it all arranged for tomorrow, you know, when we go out for dinner. I've been carrying the ring round for days because I didn't want you to find it in the flat. But tonight you just looked so happy and beautiful and — well, you know. I just thought, why not? Why not now? And at least it's not a cliché." He grins sheepishly.

"It's definitely not that, Ed. And I'm sorry, I didn't mean to scare you. It was just pretty — unexpected." I stand on tiptoes and reach up and plant a kiss on his lips. They're warm and soft, and taste slightly of red wine. It's lovely.

I pull away and look at him. "So what made you change your mind?"

He pauses a moment, licks his lips. "I think it was the thought of losing you, Zoe. I kept thinking, how would I feel if I refused to marry you and you left me and married someone else, and it just — I just couldn't imagine it. I couldn't let it happen. Plus, Mum told me I was being a total idiot for refusing to marry you." He grins. "Not that I listen to my mother, of course."

"Course not. But she does talk a lot of sense."

"She does. And she's right, you know. Just because my bloody useless father couldn't commit to anything for more than five minutes, it doesn't mean I'm the same. I'm not the same. I hate him for what he did, but it's not me."

"No, it's not." I squeeze him. "We're going to be great, you'll see." I wish I could tell him what's to come — the good times and the terrible times. This is such a major thing that's happening to me, and yet I can't share it with the one person I share everything with. It feels wrong, almost as though I'm cheating.

But what would he say if I did tell him? Is it worth a go?

"Ed?"

"Mmm-hmm."

"What would you do if you got the chance to meet me all over again?"

He pulls away and looks down at me, a line creasing his forehead, and I know I've made a mistake. "What?"

"Well — you know. What if we could do this all over again, up to this point. Would you do anything differently?"

"I — I dunno. Why, would you? Are you trying to tell me something, Zo?" His face is pinched in confusion and I wish I'd never started this.

"No, no, nothing. It's nothing. Forget I ever said anything."

I've looked away but I can feel his eyes boring into me, searching for a clue to my thoughts. But I'm giving nothing else away. It's too risky.

Finally, he shrugs and turns to pour another glass of wine. "I think this calls for a celebration, don't you?"

"Definitely." I hold my glass up and we clink them together. "To us!"

"To us."

We both take a sip and stand, slightly awkwardly. "So, are you going to actually let me put the ring on, then?"

"What? Oh, sorry, Zo, I totally forgot." His hands are shaking as he slides the ring carefully onto my finger.

"Thank you. I love it."

It fits perfectly, as I knew it would; it's the ring I've been wearing every day for the last eleven years. I stare at it for a moment, lost in memories. And then I kiss Ed deeply, and we go and tell everyone our good news.

It's been an interesting day, one that hasn't worked out quite as I'd expected when I woke up this morning. The new proposal was great, and I'm thrilled. But as I drop off to sleep in the early hours, my head swimming with too much cheap wine, I can't help wondering what it all means that new things keep happening.

I can't help hoping that, in some way, it means that everything has changed.

CHAPTER
ELEVEN

14 December 2003

A banging on the door wakes me up and I sit bolt upright, my heart pounding. Seconds later Becky crashes through the door.

"Going to the chapel and we're gonna get ma-a-arrieeeed," she squawks as she plonks a cup of tea down next to me and throws herself on the end of my bed. "Morning, Mrs Williams." She grins happily.

"Not yet," I mumble, propping myself up on my elbow. "And morning yourself."

I rub my eyes and look round the room. It doesn't take long to work out where I am: this is the second time I've woken up in my childhood bedroom and it looks almost exactly the same as it did before, apart from the packing boxes. It only takes a few more seconds to work out what day it is too, as my wedding dress is hanging on the wardrobe opposite my bed. My stomach flips over at the sight of it. This was one of the happiest days of my life. I never dreamed I'd get to do it all over again.

My forehead creases briefly as a thought crosses my mind. This day was almost perfect — no, it *was* perfect. I can't imagine there's anything I'm going to want to try and change. I'll just have to wait and see.

I cross my legs and take a sip of the tea Becky's brought me. She sits next to me and we're lost in thought for a moment, two sisters, cross-legged on the bed. I smile as I remember asking Jane to be my bridesmaid.

"As long as you don't make me look like a toilet roll holder. In fact, better than that, I want to look hot."

"Of course," I'd said, grinning. "Aren't you meant to find the love of your life at your best friend's wedding or something? Or at least get a great shag out of it. You can't do that if you're looking like a lampshade."

"Exactly. All right then, I'll do it."

Ed and I had agreed we didn't want a massive wedding. Well, I wouldn't have minded, but Ed was firm. "I'm not dressing up like a penguin and poncing about on the dance floor. I just want the day to be fun."

And I knew what he meant. The day was about me and him, not about whether our napkins matched our tablecloths or whether everyone got a voile-wrapped sugared almond on their plate at dinner. So for the last few months we'd been quietly getting on with sorting the details out. We were having a low-key civil wedding at the Mount Pleasant Hotel near Bawtry, and had booked a buffet and a band. Decorations only needed to be minimal because the whole place was already decked out with Christmas trees and lights, and we had about fifty people coming. It was going to be perfect.

It had been perfect. And now I was getting to enjoy it all over again.

"So, are you excited?" Becky's looking at me over the top of her mug, steam curling in front of her face.

"Terrified." I take another sip of tea, gulp it down. "But yes, excited too."

"Me too."

I blow my tea gently. "Becky? Thank you for being my bridesmaid. I'm so glad you're here. I've missed you since I moved out."

Her face clouds over for a moment. "It's OK. Anyway, like you could have stopped me — I'd have killed you."

I grin. "True. But I'm still glad."

"Good."

We sit in silence for a few more minutes until Mum's voice floats up the stairs.

"Come on, you lot, come and get some breakfast."

"Yes, Mum," we chorus.

"We'd better go, Mum's made enough food to feed a small army." Becky swings her legs round and walks out of the door. But before I head down I go into the spare room and wake Jane up.

"Mum's made breakfast," I whisper, shaking her gently.

"Hggghhghh," she mumbles, and rolls over to face me. "Are there pancakes?"

"This is Mum we're talking about, of course there'll be pancakes."

"OK then, I'm there." She rolls out of bed, shoves her fags in the pocket of her dressing gown and follows behind me down to the kitchen. As we step through the door Mum shouts, "Surprise!" and hands me a glass of champagne. Dad's standing by the dining table munching on a piece of toast.

"John, put that down, we haven't started yet."

"I have. Anyway, you've got enough to feed the whole street; one piece of toast won't matter." Crumbs spray from his mouth as he pops the last piece in, and Mum looks furious. I have to stifle a laugh.

I look at the table, where Mum's stacked piles of pancakes; the toast rack is rammed full of toast, there are pots of jam, marmalade and honey, butter, croissants, boiled eggs, boxes and boxes of cereal and a jug of milk. There are also tea and coffee pots and there's more coffee brewing in the machine.

"Wow, thanks, Mum. But — I'm not really that hungry . . ."

Mum's face turns red and Dad almost chokes on his tea. "You have to eat someth —" she starts; then she sees the look on my face. "Oh ha ha, very funny." She claps her hands. "Now come on, sit down, tuck in."

We do as we're told. As we chew on toast and croissants, drink gallons of tea and far more champagne than we should at eight o'clock in the morning, we chat and laugh and I have to fight back the tears. I've missed this so much. Things had been so tense with Ed towards the end that I hadn't wanted to talk about our problems with anyone, not wanting to admit we were failing. But in doing so I'd shut out the people that mattered, the people I love. My family. And this is what I've been missing.

After breakfast I shower, and Becky does my hair and make-up, as well as Mum's, Jane's and her own. I slip into my dress and Jane zips it up at the back and I turn to look at myself for the first time this morning. Seeing

196

myself as a bride almost takes my breath away. The photo that will later stand on our mantelpiece doesn't capture the happiness that radiates from me like sunbeams, or the glow that's settled round my face. My dress clings to me in all the right places and my shoulders look lean and tanned.

"You look beautiful, love," Mum says, as she peers at my face in the mirror.

"So do you." And she does. She looks so young, and the electric blue of her dress lights up her face. She blushes and turns away.

"Right, let's get going," she says, and then we're off. We pile into the car. As we rumble along I stare out of the window, trying to steady my heart. After the excitement of the morning this is the first chance I've really had to think, to take in what's happening. In a few minutes' time I'm going to see Ed again, in front of dozens of people, and I'm not sure how I'm going to do it. Every time I see him it makes me feel weak with pain and desire. I feel dizzy.

But before I know it we're pulling up outside the hotel. Outside the front door my Aunty Jo hurriedly scrunches her cigarette out under her shoe then bends to throw it in a bush before scurrying inside. Rob is standing nearby looking smart and uncomfortable in his black suit, tugging at his collar and adjusting his tie as he scans the approaching cars. When he spots me his face breaks into a grin and he raises his hand in a half-wave and makes his way towards the car. He arrives at the door as I climb out and offers his hand to help me stand up straight. He's looking at me with an expression in his eyes that's hard to read.

"Everything OK?"

"Yes, everything's great," he says. "I'm just so relieved you're here. Ed's been like a bear with a sore head all morning. I've never seen him so stressed and nervous."

I smile and hug Rob tightly. "Thanks for looking after him."

"You're welcome, Zoe."

Dad is at my elbow now. "Right, shall we get you married, then?" he says gently. Rob takes Mum by the arm and leads her inside ahead of us. Then it's just me, Dad, Becky and Jane, standing outside in the bitingly cold December air. I want to remember this moment forever and so I take in all the details — the pale-grey sky; the leaves edged with white that cling to the evergreens; the look on Dad's face, half proud, half sad. Then a shiver runs through me and I take a deep breath and say, "Right, let's do it."

We walk slowly across the gravel and towards the door, Jane and Becky following behind. There's a roaring in my head that's making it hard to think, and I focus on placing one foot in front of the other.

And then we're there, at the door, and everyone is standing and waiting for us to walk down the aisle, watching me expectantly. I can't catch anyone's eye and I keep my eyes trained on the floor as we walk slowly towards the front of the room. Finally, I look up, and there's Ed, and the sight of him is so overwhelming I feel my legs give way beneath me and I stumble. Dad's arm tenses, holds me up, and someone gasps. The room is spinning but I keep going, one foot, then another, and another, until we're there and Dad's letting go of my hand and Ed's face is in front of mine. I look him in the eye, hold his gaze, drink in the details of his face: the piercing blue eyes, the hair cut shorter than usual, neater. His shoulders are hunched and he looks pale.

"You OK?" he mouths and I give a tiny nod.

The registrar starts to speak and Ed reaches out his hands, takes mine gently. His touch is like an electric shock and I flinch as I let the familiar words wash over me, trying hard not to cry.

And then we're married — again — and as we walk down the aisle hand in hand everyone cheers, and yet I feel as though my heart is going to break: we were so happy today, but I'm not sure we've ever been this happy again. And now, now he's gone, and this could be the last time I ever see Ed.

It's even colder outside now and as we stand and have a few photos taken I'm shivering uncontrollably, unsure whether it's from the cold or the terror that's descended.

"Come on, let's get you back inside, you're freezing." Ed pulls me by the hand and holds me in his arms to warm my frozen body. I blink wildly, trying not to let the tears fall. This is meant to be the happiest day of my life, but it's hard to behave like the blushing bride when I'm really a grieving widow.

Ed kisses the top of my head and pulls away. "You'd better go and meet your public."

I nod. "Yes, OK." I look up at him. "Ed?"

"Yes, Zo?"

"Promise me you'll never forget how happy we are right now? Promise me you'll never forget how much we love each other?"

"Of course not. But what's this all about?"

"Nothing. It's just — I don't want this to be it. I want this to be just the beginning, not the end."

Ed watches me for a moment, obviously trying to work out what to say. But the moment's lost when Dad walks through the door.

"Come on, you two lovebirds, come and join us, we're starving."

I take a deep breath and plaster a smile on my face. All I want is to stay here with Ed and never let this moment, this day, end. But I know it's impossible, and that everything has to come to an end sometime. And so I make a decision: if I'm going to go through this day again then I may as well make the most of it and enjoy it.

I grab Ed's hand. "Come on, let's go and eat, drink and be merry."

And so we join everyone; people offer their congratulations, people I haven't seen for many, many years, and I feel a pang of guilt. They were my friends, we liked them enough to invite them to our wedding, so what happened? Did I really become so self-obsessed that I didn't value them enough to stay in touch? I vow to change that, if I ever get the chance.

We sit down to eat and my eyes wander round the room. Jane's sitting with Simon and Joanna and a couple of Ed's friends from home, both male although

200

both of their names escape me now; there's my Aunty Jo and her partner Richard and her grown-up son, my cousin Josh. I smile as I remember the end of the evening, when Josh and Jane dance drunkenly together before snogging each other's faces off. Aunty Jo was mortified.

Just like the first time, the day passes in a whirl of excitement: our first dance to Pearl Jam's "Smile" — one of my favourite songs and one that has always made me think of Ed; chatting, drinking and dancing, and before I know it, Ed is holding me in his arms and we're swaying together on the dance floor. We're drunk on champagne and it's nearly the end of the day. I lean my cheek on his chest and he holds me a little bit tighter and the lights blur around us. I lift my head and look up at him.

"I love you, Edward Williams."

"I love you too, Zoe Williams."

I feel so close to him at this moment that I have an almost overwhelming urge to tell him everything. To tell him about us, our future, his death, the rows, the highs and the lows. And, of course, about me, reliving our significant moments together all over again. It's such an amazing, important thing, it feels wrong to keep it from him. But it's impossible. I can't even begin to imagine what he'd say if I tried to explain it. How would I have reacted if he'd said the same to me?

As we sway there gently, I can't help wondering again whether this is all leading up to something, why this has happened to me. Is it because things are going to end up differently? Although the days haven't been exactly the same, detail for detail, as they were the first time round, the result has been the same so far. But that doesn't mean things can't change. That doesn't rule out the possibility that, if I keep trying to do things differently, Ed might be OK and we might get the chance to grow old together, just as we've promised to do today.

The song comes to an end and I pull away from Ed and wipe a tear from my eye before we walk, hand in hand, to sit down. I glance at the clock. It's 11p.m., almost time for everyone to go home. I'm not ready for the day to be over, not yet.

One by one, friends and family come to say goodnight and congratulations. And then the music stops, the lights come on, and we're heading up to our room. I want the day to mean something, I want to try to do something different, but I don't know what. I'm running out of time.

"I know this sounds weird, but can we just sit and chat," I say as Ed and I stumble into the room and switch the lights on. We look at the bed; it's covered in petals and there's a box of condoms with a note stuck to it. Ed picks it up. "Be careful, you've only just got married."

I roll my eyes. Rob.

"You mean you don't want to ravish your new husband on your wedding night?" Ed pretends to pout, and I pick up the box of condoms and throw them at him.

"I just feel a bit — overwhelmed. Do you mind?"

"Course not, if that's what you want to do. Your wish is my command."

"Help me out of this, then," I say, and Ed unzips my dress and it falls to the floor. I'm standing in the lingerie I bought especially for today and as I climb into bed and under the covers to wait for Ed I feel shy. A few moments later he climbs in next to me and wraps his arms around me.

"You happy?"

"Utterly," I say. And I mean it. I am.

"Just not in the mood, eh?" He grins at me.

"Nah, just don't fancy you."

He slaps my bum playfully and I giggle and suddenly I am in the mood after all. I don't know whether it's the niggly feeling that I may not see him again, but right now I want this man more than I ever have in my life. I sit up and throw my leg across him, kissing him passionately on the lips. He responds eagerly and for the next hour we lose ourselves totally in each other. It's so good it makes me long for those days again.

When we're finished we lie in each other's arms and talk about the day.

"Did you see Mum on the dance floor?" Ed laughs. "She was mental."

I burst out laughing. "What about when your Uncle Ted fell over. He was so drunk he lost his footing, dropped his drink then slipped on the wet floor. It was a total clusterfuck."

"It was usual Uncle Ted behaviour."

A few seconds pass and we lie in silence.

"Rob said you were a nightmare this morning," I say.

"Did he, now?"

"He says you were really grumpy."

"Huh, charming." He pauses for a minute. "I suppose I was, though. I was just terrified you weren't going to turn up and I honestly didn't know what I'd do if you'd changed your mind. I don't think I could have gone on."

I look at him.

"Really? You thought I'd change my mind?"

"Well, you never know."

"Edward, I love you more than anything else in the whole world. You're my calm head in chaos, my fun in sad times. You're everything to me."

He props himself on his elbow and looks down at me. "You don't know how glad I am to hear you say that." He looks so serious that it doesn't feel like the right time to make a joke, so I stay quiet. Then he leans down towards me and kisses me deeply once more and then we fall into each other again, more deeply and passionately than we ever have before. And afterwards I finally feel ready to fall asleep and leave this day behind and see what comes next. It finally feels right.

CHAPTER
TWELVE

19 May 2005

Breakfast plates are piled in the sink, and streaks of jam smear the wooden surface of the table. I run my finger lazily through the crumbs, listening to Ed singing along loudly to the radio in the shower.

My shiny new phone has already told me it's 19 May 2005, which means I'm thirty years old. Unfortunately it hasn't told me exactly what's going to happen today. That's still buried somewhere in the junkyard of my memory.

I need to go for a run, clear my head. Running has been my tension release since the wedding, my way of unwinding after a long day at work. I stand and walk back to the bedroom, pulling out the running trainers that I knew I'd find there.

By the time I'm ready to go the shower's stopped and I can hear Ed moving around in the bathroom. I need to see him before I leave in case I don't get another chance later, so I open the bathroom door and peek my head round. Ed's wrapped a towel round his waist and his chest is bare, and the sight of him makes my heart almost stop. I want to reach out and touch him, run my fingers lightly over the dark hairs that scatter his chest, trace them down across his belly button, follow the darker hairs down —

"Earth to Zoe."

"What?" I jump, look up guiltily.

"You were staring at me, not speaking. You look like you've seen a ghost."

"Oh, I —" I stop, my face hot. I feel like a voyeur, as though Ed's body, eight years ago, isn't something I should be allowed to look at. I feel like an impostor in my own life and it's not a feeling I'm enjoying.

"I just came to say I'm off for a run. Will you be here when I get back?"

He grabs a towel and rubs it over his hair, his chest muscles flexing as he does. I try to concentrate on his words. "No, I'm taking Mum to the Chelsea Flower Show, remember?"

"Oh yes, course. Sorry." I hadn't wanted to go, but now wish I could. I wish I could spend the whole day with Ed. "Do you have to go?"

Ed frowns, his damp hair sticking out in all directions. "What do you mean? Of course I have to go. Mum's looking forward to it. So am I."

"But she wouldn't really mind if you cancelled, would she? Stayed here with me for the day — we could, you know, go to bed . . ." I tail off. The look on Ed's face makes it clear my tactic isn't working.

"Zoe, what's wrong with you? You're acting very odd."

"What's odd about wanting to see my husband?"

"You know what I mean. You've known about this for ages and you didn't want to come. Why are you being all weird now?"

I shrug. "Dunno."

He looks at me for a moment, then turns to pick up his toothbrush. "Listen, I've got to get ready. Have a good run, OK, and I'll see you later." He leans over and gives me a peck on the cheek and turns away, back to the mirror. I've been dismissed. I have no choice but to leave now, and hope I see him later.

I tuck my laces in, clip my iPod holder to my arm, stick the white headphones in my ears and head for the door. The pavements are damp from this morning's rain, but it's dry now and the sun's struggling to show its face from behind the iron-grey clouds. I set off along the road, the sound of the Prodigy's "Firestarter" filling my ears as my feet pound the pavement and I listen to my breathing getting faster and faster and then settling into a steady rhythm. It's been a long time since I've felt this free, without the sense of doom that's settled heavily on my shoulders over the last few years. I've missed it.

Slowly my mind settles into a rhythm too, until the running and the sounds of London become just background noise. I trawl my memory back through the years to this day, and try to remember what happened, why I'm here. There must be a reason.

And suddenly it hits me like a bus.

This is the day that changed everything between us forever. This is the day Ed said he wanted to start trying for a baby. And I'd said no.

I'd known Ed had been thinking about things for a while — he'd even tried bringing it up a couple of times but I'd swept it away, pretended it wasn't happening. But I'd seen the hurt in his eyes every time someone asked, "So, when are we going to hear the pitter-patter of tiny feet, then?" *Mind your own business!* I felt like yelling. But I'd kept quiet, and ignored what was bubbling along below the surface of our marriage. Babies weren't on the agenda yet; life was too busy. I was working hard and loving doing so well, making money, going out drinking. I loved living in London with Ed and I didn't want anything to change.

But today — the first today — when I'd got back from a day out with Jane and he'd been out with his mum, he'd been sitting on the sofa, quietly. The TV wasn't on, and he had an open magazine on his lap, which he wasn't looking at. Instead, he was staring straight ahead at the blocks of wood stacked up in the fireplace. He didn't move when I came in, didn't appear to hear me, so I moved around in front of him and knelt down. There was a knot of tension rising from my belly, snaking its way up to my throat.

"Ed?" I took hold of his hand. "Ed, what's wrong?"

His eyes slowly came into focus and he looked at me and smiled weakly.

"Hi, love," he said.

I peered at him. "What is it? Are you ill?"

He looked at me blankly, then finally he spoke. "We need to talk."

His words, those words, sent spikes through my heart — because I knew exactly what he was going to say. I nodded, looked at the floor and sat next to him on the sofa, stiffly.

"This is about having a baby, isn't it?" My voice was flat.

I could see him turn to look at me from the corner of my eye but I didn't look back. I couldn't meet his eyes.

"Yes. It is."

I waited for him to say more.

"It was just — today, being out with Mum. There were families together everywhere with their kids, and they looked so happy and I felt so — lonely. I don't know how to explain it. I felt like I did as a little kid, seeing everyone with their brothers and sisters having fun, while I was all alone, and I realized I just didn't want to feel like that any more. I know I've been saying it for a while but it really came home to me today, Zoe. I really want a baby. Your baby. Ours."

My whole body felt like a coiled spring as I sat there under his gaze, ready to snap. The silent seconds became minutes, hours, weeks, until it felt as though the tension couldn't stretch any more.

"Ed, I can't." The words came out in a rush, like an explosion, as if it would somehow make hearing them easier. I turned to face him, tried to soften the blow. "I know what you're saying but I'm just not ready. I'm — I need some time."

His face crumpled and he rubbed his hand across it, trying to hide the hurt. But it was too late.

"I'm so sorry, Ed. I know you want a baby, and — But I just can't. Not yet. Not now. I'm sorry . . ."

"It's OK. I knew you were going to say that. I just hoped, I guess, that you might have changed your mind. You know, after we've been married a while, after everything . . ." His voice was small, lost. I longed to reach out and comfort him but instead I sat still, hoping the moment would pass.

But of course it didn't.

"I really am sorry, Ed, but nothing's changed, not for me. I know you want a baby, I know you think it's what will make us a family, but I don't feel that way. As far as I'm concerned we *are* a family, me and you. I'm sorry, sweetheart." What I didn't tell him was that I was scared. Scared that having a baby would spoil everything I'd worked so hard for; it wasn't part of the plan, not for at least a few more years. It sounded too selfish even to my own ears.

He nodded, then stood, looking down at me.

"I get it, Zo, I do. I don't mean to pressure you and I'm sorry. I promise I'll stop it if you promise me something too."

"Anything."

"You'll at least start to think about it? Not just dismiss it out of hand. Promise?"

I nodded. "I promise."

"Thank you." He leaned down and kissed the top of my head, stroked my cheek with his hand, his skin slightly roughened.

And over the next few months he'd kept to his promise, and I'd tried to keep to mine. But the subject became our elephant in the room, the strain pressing down on us daily until we could hardly bear it any more.

As I run along now, past the run-down estates, palatial mansions, stations, shops, woods, fields and railway lines that make up the fabric of the city, I know I can't let the same happen again this time. I resisted and resisted trying for a baby last time until it almost destroyed us, which, in hindsight, was pointless as in the end we wanted the same thing anyway.

So this time I'm going to do something to try and stop all the heartache; something that might, just might, change things enough to keep Ed with me.

I know what I need to do.

By the time Ed gets back, darkness has pulled itself like a veil over the day, the lights across the street igniting one by one as people settle in for the evening. I'm almost beside myself with impatience, desperate for him to get home.

I still went out with Jane today; I needed to do something to pass the time until Ed got home. I decided against telling her what was on my mind, though; it was far too complicated, and I was worried I'd say something I shouldn't, give myself away. Instead, I just made sure I got home before Ed, and got myself prepared.

I'm in the kitchen stirring a pan of home-made tomato sauce when I hear Ed's key scrape in the lock, and my heart rate picks up pace. A few seconds later he walks in: he looks tired, drawn; it's clear something is weighing on his mind.

A frown crosses his face when he sees me.

"I thought you weren't home until later?"

"Yeah, I came home early. Thought it would be nice to have dinner together." I hold the spoon up. "It's not as good as yours, but want to taste?"

He shakes his head. "No, thanks." I know not to be cross at his surliness, because I know what's on his mind.

"OK. Well, this will be ready soon, so would you like a glass of wine while you wait?" I'm aware my voice is slightly too high and unsteady, but Ed doesn't seem to notice. He sits down heavily on the chair and grabs the bottle of red wine that's already open, slugs some into the glass and tips his head back, gulps it down.

"Zoe, listen —"

"It's OK, Ed, I know what you're going to say."

He frowns. "I don't think you do."

I turn the heat down and sit opposite him, my elbows resting on the table. He's hunched, his shoulders tight, his face grey and drawn. "I really do. This is about the baby thing, isn't it?"

His face flashes briefly with surprise, and he gives a tight nod. I carry on. "I know it's been on your mind, and I guessed it's what you've been talking to your mum about today, am I right?"

"Yes, but —" He stops, rubs his hand over his face. "How the hell do you know that?"

I shrug. "Just a feeling. You've mentioned it a few times now and I suppose — well, it's been eighteen months since we got married so it's about time we talked about it . . ."

212

He nods again. "Yes, it is. But you've thrown me a bit, to be honest, Zo. I was all prepared to come back and talk to you about it, expecting you to say no way, throw it back in my face. I wasn't expecting you to be the one to bring it up. So what's brought this on?"

I take a deep breath. "I've just been thinking. About me, and you. And yes, I do think we're a family, just the two of us, and to be honest, it doesn't feel like a great time, what with work being busy and everything. But — well, when *is* a good time? And who's to say we'll even be able to get pregnant straight away anyway —" My voice cracks at this and I cough to cover it up. "I suppose — I suppose what I'm trying to say is that maybe we should think about giving it a go. Trying for a baby, I mean."

Ed's eyes are wide, his mouth slightly open. "You mean — you want to have a baby? Now?"

"I mean I think we should start trying." I reach across the table and take his hands. "What do you think?"

"Shit. Sorry, Zo, but I'm in shock. I — this is the last thing I expected from you. But I'm — I'm so happy." Tears are shining in his eyes and I stand and walk around the table to him, perch awkwardly on his knee. I cup my hands round his face and kiss his lips gently.

"I'm happy too. I love you so much, I just want us to be happy, always."

"Me too. Thank you, Zoe."

He wraps his arms around me and we stay like that for a few moments.

"Um, Zo, can you smell burning?"

"What? Oh, shit, the sauce."

Smoke is billowing from the saucepan; there's an ominous sizzling sound, and a strong smell of burning. The sauce is black, totally ruined.

"Oh, um, whoops." I hold the pan up for Ed to see. "Fancy a takeaway?"

Ed laughs. "Tell you what, I'll go and get Chinese, you clean this mess up. Deal?"

"Deal."

Then he kisses me and is gone, almost skipping out of the house. And as I scrub the saucepan under hot water I can't help thinking that maybe, just maybe, this has been the best thing I've ever done. Maybe I've just changed everything.

Later, as we watch TV, our bellies full of food, I glance across at Ed at the other end of the sofa. He smiles at something and the corners of his eyes crinkle gently. His skin shines in the glow from the screen, and without him even realizing he's doing it, his fingers drum gently against the edge of the sofa, sending soft vibrations through from his body to mine. The evening is warm and he's wearing long shorts, the muscles of his calves flexing sharply as he taps his foot in rhythm to his fingers. He's never still, even when he looks as though he is.

He notices me looking at him and turns his face towards me.

"OK, Zo?"

"Mmm," I mumble. "Yes, just looking at you."

214

He leans over and plants a soft kiss on the end of my nose. "I love you, you know," he says. And before I can answer he pulls away and turns back to look at the TV.

"I know. I love you too."

I tear my eyes away from him and realize my face is wet with tears. The day is almost finished and although I want to find out if I've changed anything today, I don't want to leave him. I don't want the day to end, to find out that that's it, that I'm back to never seeing Ed again.

But I have no choice. My work for today is done; I need to move on.

I stand. "I'm going to bed."

"Already? It's only —" he squints at the clock on the wall — "ten o'clock."

"Yeah, I'm just tired. It's been a long day."

"OK, gorgeous. Sleep well."

I walk over and give him a kiss and he catches my shoulder. "Thank you, Zoe. For everything. I love you."

"I love you too. More than you'll ever know."

And then I walk into our bedroom, pull on my pyjamas, climb into bed and pull the duvet over my head, and slip into oblivion . . .

CHAPTER
THIRTEEN

16 December 2007

Sometimes things happen that really surprise you. Eight months ago, at my mum and dad's house as Becky and I were drinking tea and raiding the biscuit tin, something happened that I never would have expected in a million years. My baby sister told me she was pregnant.

"You're *what*?" I screeched when she told me the news, nearly choking on my ginger nut.

She looked at me with her wide-open eyes and shrugged. "Pregnant," she said. "You know, got a bun in the oven, up the duff, knocked up, with child —"

"I know what it *means*! I just . . ." I genuinely didn't know what else to say. The news had knocked me totally for six. Becky was only twenty-eight and had only been with her boyfriend, Greg, for about five months. How could she be bringing a baby into the world already?

The silence between us stretched a bit longer. Finally, I had to fill it.

"How . . . I mean, does Mum . . . ?"

"No, Mum doesn't know yet, so don't say anything. You're the first person I've told. Apart from Greg, obviously. I just needed to talk to you about it."

I let her words sink in for a minute. "So this wasn't planned, then?"

"Not exactly." She looked sheepish. "It was a bit of a drunken night out and, well, you know . . ."

"Oh Becky."

"I know. But it's OK. Me and Greg have talked about it and we definitely want to keep it. I mean, it's not as though we're sixteen and too young, is it? We both have good jobs and, well, we really love each other. We just thought we might see the world a bit before this, but now it's happened, well. It just seems like it was meant to be."

I couldn't argue with her. She'd made her mind up and actually seemed happy about it. So instead I stood up and threw my arms around her and held her tightly until I thought she was going to burst.

And now, here I am, reliving the first time I met my niece. Compared to the last day I had to relive, I feel blessed.

She was born less than two days ago and Becky is now back home, at the flat she shares with Greg. They've decided to call her Gracie, and as I walk into the room and see Becky for the first time since she had the baby I feel as though I've had a blow to the stomach. Becky's sitting on the sofa propped up on pillows, leaning back. She looks tired but there's a glow about her that I've never seen before. Then I notice the little bundle on her chest, and my heart skips a beat. Gracie is fast asleep, dressed in a stripy Babygro, her face squashed into Becky's chest, her nappied bottom sticking high into the air.

Becky smiles and her eyes crinkle at the corners as she sees me.

"Hey," she says, her voice a half-whisper. The room is in semi-darkness and the TV flickers silently in the background. "She's just dropped off so I'm trying not to wake her."

I nod and creep carefully to sit down next to her, planting a kiss gently on her forehead — the only part of her I can reach without squashing Gracie — before I do.

"So," I start, shrugging my shoulders, unsure what to say.

"I know. I'm a mummy. Mad, isn't it?"

"Totally. So, how was it?"

Gracie wriggles in her sleep and Becky adjusts her position to accommodate her daughter.

"It was bloody horrendous." She looks at me and smiles, but I can tell she means it. "It was worse than I ever thought it could be. But it was worth it." She looks down at her daughter with a look of complete and utter love and I feel a spark of jealousy. What must it feel like to love someone so utterly and without question like that?

We sit quietly for a while, watching the people on TV selling things from their homes at auction, trying to lip-read what they're saying. Every time there's a bang or a small noise Becky tenses, then settles down again, breathing a sigh of relief.

"It's taken me all morning to get her to finally drop off," she explains. "I need the peace to last as long as possible."

218

I nod as if I understand but of course I don't really. And anyway before too long it becomes irrelevant when Gracie starts to stir.

"Bugger, she's going to be starving when she wakes up," Becky says, shifting awkwardly into a sitting position as Gracie opens her eyes and takes in the world around her. For a few seconds I wonder what the fuss is all about, as there is nothing but silence. Then suddenly she launches into an ear-piercing cry, her little face screwed up and getting redder and redder.

As quickly as it started, the noise stops and I'm left with a ringing in my ears as I wonder how Becky managed to stop the screams so quickly. And then I notice Gracie attached to my sister's breast, sucking happily, and I look away again quickly. It doesn't matter how natural it is; it feels wrong and awkward to watch. Instead I concentrate on Becky's face, on the picture on the wall behind her, on the TV screen still playing away to itself on the other side of the room.

"Ah, silence," Becky sighs. "The best sound ever."

As Gracie feeds, Becky tells me all the terrible details of the birth. The pain, the screaming, the dilation, the epidural, all of it, and I listen in awe. My baby sister has been through all this, something I've never experienced. And amazingly, I know she gets over it quickly enough to go through it all again in a couple of years' time. But for now I just listen, and let her get it all out, and try to ignore the ache in my heart at the fact that my little sister has had a baby when I've been unable to.

Finally, Gracie stops feeding and her eyes start to droop again as she falls into a happy slumber.

"Tough life, being a baby," I say.

"Terrible," Becky agrees. Then she looks at me. "Do you want to hold her?"

I pause. I'm longing to hold her but I'm terrified. What if I break her? What if she brings back all the pain of the last few years before Ed died? I'm not sure I can cope with that.

But on the other hand it might be comforting. And really, there's no way I can actually say no.

"Yes," I whisper, and Becky half stands and sort of tips Gracie into my arms. Her head lolls into the crook of my arm and she makes a small mumbling sound, and then she's asleep, contentedly snuggled into me.

I feel the warmth of her tiny body through my arms. I look down at her scrunched-up face, her eyes closed tightly against the light, her chest rising and falling gently with each breath, and I think about the first time I ever met Gracie. My niece is getting close to six now, and I haven't seen her for a few weeks. Seeing her as a tiny baby again I feel a surge of love, mixed with regret. These past few years and months I'd been so caught up in my own grief and worries I'd forgotten about the other things that mattered in my life. I still see my sister and her children, but not enough. I realize now that I just thought it was going to be too painful — when actually the truth was, it might have done me good.

After about half an hour I notice it's growing dark outside and it's time for me to head home.

"I'd better get going," I say, shuffling upright as Becky moves forward to take her daughter into her arms.

"OK," she whispers, as Gracie settles herself into her new environment in her mummy's arms. I don't really want to leave. I want to stay here and hold her forever, protect her from the world, never let anything happen to her. But I need to get out of there and be on my own for a while, take some time to work out how I'm feeling.

I bend down and pick up my bag from the floor where I dumped it when I came in, then lean down to gently kiss my sister's and my niece's heads.

"I love you," I whisper, and Becky smiles, then smooths her hand softly over Gracie's head and I can see they're both going to be fast asleep as soon as I leave. I creep out of the living room and open the front door. The cold air hits me like a train and I close the door behind me and wrestle my arms into my coat. I wish I had my scarf. The weak December sun was giving a little warmth when I arrived, but now it's turned wintry and a hint of frost hangs in the air. I shiver and clumsily do up the buttons on my coat, hook my bag over my shoulder and start to walk. I'm not sure where I'm walking to. I don't want to go home yet, and so I work out a general direction and just keep putting one foot in front of the other. It gives me time to think.

The first time I met Gracie was the day that things changed for me. As I'd held her tiny body in my arms, and watched her breathing gently, happily, it had made me realize that I wanted this too; that I wanted Ed's baby.

This time, of course, I've told Ed I want to start trying for a baby already, so things are different. Or at least they should be. But after this morning I'm not so sure.

I'd seen Ed before I'd left to come and meet Gracie today.

"Are you sure you don't want to come?"

"No, you go, have some time alone with her." He'd seemed distracted but I couldn't work out why.

"You sure?"

"Yes, I'm sure." His voice was sharp, snappy. He didn't seem to want to look at me.

"Ed, what's wrong?"

"Seriously, you're asking me that?"

I didn't know what to say. I had no idea what had been happening, but it obviously wasn't great.

"Zoe, just go and see Becky, OK? I'm not sure I can handle being with you today after all the shit you've put me through in the last few weeks."

"What shit?" I had to know.

Ed's face was furious. "What shit? You mean you don't remember promising we can start trying for a baby and then changing your mind again, and then refusing to talk about it for the last six months? You don't remember the constant arguments and the confusion and the — the stress? Well, then, maybe you'd better try and remember, because quite frankly I don't even want to be in the same room as you right now . . ."

He'd walked away from me then, shutting the front door firmly behind him and leaving me standing in the

222

hallway, feeling terrible. Obviously, I can't remember any of this, and I can't believe, after everything I thought I'd achieved, that we're back to square one. In fact, worse than square one, because at least last time I hadn't given him any false hope. What was wrong with me? I had to make this right.

My head's spinning and I stop and lean against a wall for a minute. Bile rises in my throat and I lurch forward, thinking I'm going to be sick.

"Are you all right, sweetheart?"

I look round to find an elderly man cupping my elbow in his hand, concern etched on his face. "You took a funny turn, are you all right?"

I stand up and feel the nausea subsiding. I wipe my hand over my mouth. "Yes, yes, I'm fine, thank you. Sorry, I just felt a bit . . . I'm OK now, thank you."

"OK, well, you look after yourself," he says.

"I will." I smile weakly to let him know I'm fine. He seems reassured and starts walking away, his cane tap-tapping on the pavement as he walks.

I look around and realize I have no idea where I am, or how long I've been walking. A blanket of darkness has been pulled over the sky, leaving half of it bathed in a whitish-blue light, the rest a dark grey above the buildings. I pull my phone from my pocket and glance at the display. 4.50p.m. I've only been walking about half an hour but have managed to get myself totally and utterly lost.

I look round for signs, some indication of which direction I need to head in. Middle of London, and nothing. I peer up at the shopfronts. Nothing is familiar. I know I don't visit Becky very often, but this is ridiculous. I try not to panic as I keep walking, praying for a familiar landmark, anything to give me a clue where I am. And then, finally, it's there, like an oasis in a desert — the familiar red circle and blue line of the Underground, and I scurry towards it as quickly as I can and descend the grimy stairs towards the Tube, and home.

It's late when I walk through the front door. The light from the hall spills over me and I can hear the tinny sound of the TV. As I close the door Ed appears in the doorway of the living room. "Hey, how was she?"

His hair is ruffled and his eyes are red as though he's been asleep. He looks unbelievably handsome.

"She's great. Gracie's beautiful."

He nods, steps towards me. "Listen, I'm really sorry about earlier. I didn't mean what I said. I was just angry."

"You did mean it, Ed."

"But —"

"No, it's OK. You had every right." I pause, take a breath. "Listen, I don't know why I've been acting the way I have. It sounds as though I've been a bit of a bitch —"

"You make it sound like you haven't really been there, Zo."

"Maybe I haven't, not really. I don't know what's been wrong with me, Ed, but whatever it was, seeing Gracie today has made everything much clearer."

"In what way?"

224

"As I held her, I kept thinking what it would be like if she was ours, and I realized I wanted to find out. I don't want to regret never having one. I think it really is time, this time."

Ed looks at me, his eyes narrowed.

"What? What's wrong?"

"Are you sure you mean it this time, Zoe? It's not just the excitement of meeting Gracie today? Because, to be honest, I don't think I could face going through all that again."

"I am sure, Ed, absolutely one hundred per cent, I promise. I won't let you down again."

He looks at me a moment longer, then holds out his arms for me to walk into. "In that case, you've just made me the happiest man in the world. Thank you, Zoe." My shoulder feels damp from his tears but I pretend not to notice. I know I should feel happy that we've finally decided to do this — and a part of me is excited about the thought that maybe this time things will be different. But I can't help worrying that, after today, I'm just going to mess things up again, and that despite all my efforts nothing will have changed. That I'll just end up hurting him all over again.

Later that night as I'm dropping off to sleep I wake up with a jolt. I've been dreaming about a baby. I'm holding it in my arms and it's screaming and screaming and then Ed's trying to pull it from my arms, shouting, "It's not yours, you have to give it back; it has to come with me," and then I'm crying and Ed's ripping the baby from my arms and running away with it and I'm left sobbing, my arms empty, with no baby and no Ed, and no hope. Fully awake now, I'm breathing heavily and my heart's struggling to slow down, and I'm shivering in the cold. I toss and turn for what feels like hours, desperate for sleep to come so I can wake up another day and find out if I've done the right thing. And finally, I fall into a fitful sleep, without dreams . . .

CHAPTER
FOURTEEN

14 December 2009

I'm not sure whether it's the sound of a cup smashing onto the floor, the swearing, or the overhead light flicking on and almost blinding me that wakes me up, but I'm awake with a start this morning, my heart racing. I sit up in bed and as my eyes adjust to the light I squint through my half-closed eyelids to see Ed, on his hands and knees next to the bed. My stomach does its usual flip at seeing him again and it's all I can do not to shout out his name at the top of my voice.

"What on earth are you doing down there?"

Ed's head snaps up to look at me. "Oh bugger, you're awake."

"Lovely to see you too."

He looks sheepish. "Sorry, love. I was trying to surprise you with breakfast in bed, but then the bloody cup slipped and — well, this happened." He held up his hands, one holding a cloth soggy with tea, the other holding my favourite mug, in pieces. "Your toast is on the floor, if you want it."

"I think I'll pass, but thanks." I shuffle over and pat the bed. "Come back to bed instead."

He climbs in next to me and gives me a peck on the cheek. "Happy anniversary, anyway. Can you believe it's been six years already?"

Six years. That means two years have passed since I last woke up in my old life. I have a lot to catch up on, but I've no idea where to start.

"Happy anniversary to you too." I return the kiss. Then Ed pulls away and stands up.

"Wait there a sec." He disappears, then returns moments later, brandishing a bunch of white lilies and a white box with a handle. He thrusts the lilies at me and sits down again. I take them from him and place them on the bed.

"The lady in the shop said these were traditional for a sixth wedding anniversary," he says. "I assumed she was right." He grins then picks up the white box from the floor. There's a scrabbling noise and I know instantly what's inside. I watch as he opens the top of the box and pulls out a wriggling, squirming, black and tabby kitten and places him gently on my tummy. I gasp with excitement and scoop him up in my arms. "George!"

Ed frowns. "You've decided his name already?"

"Oh, er, yes, it — just seemed right . . ." I trail off weakly, aware I sound odd. It had just slipped out when I saw him, the little kitten that became like a surrogate baby for so long, that we'd showered with love.

Ed looks at me for a moment then shrugs. "OK, George it is."

"Thank you, Ed, he's perfect," I whisper, squashing my nose into the kitten's soft fur.

228

"Hey, what's the matter, why are you crying?" Ed leans forward and wipes a tear from my cheek.

I hadn't realized I was. "Nothing's the matter." I sniff, trying to force a smile to my face. "It's just such a lovely surprise. Thank you."

"You're welcome."

He leans forward and plants a soft kiss on my lips, and I struggle to fight back the tears again. For a few minutes we lie there, watching as the kitten investigates his new home, sniffing his way round the room, pushing open doors with his tiny paws. My heart swells with love, and for a moment it almost feels as though everything is going to be OK.

But I can't help wondering, again, why I'm here. This had been a bittersweet day, the first time round. We celebrated our anniversary, gave all the signs of being happy. But there had been an undercurrent of tension, rippling away, waiting to cause waves, that we'd chosen to ignore. We both knew what it was — how could we not? — but we skirted around the issue, as we always did.

But now it's clear nothing has changed from last time: here we are, six years into married life, and there's still no baby. If it's been the same as last time we've been trying for two years, with no success.

And, if it's like last time, I've become totally obsessed with the idea too. Every month had become a trial to be endured, waiting to see if my period would arrive. And every time it did: heartache.

"I know it's hard, Zo, but you've got to stay positive," Ed had said after one particularly bad month.

My period had been a few days late, and its arrival had triggered a meltdown.

"Positive?" I spat as I sat on the toilet with the lid down, my head in my hands. "This is a nightmare, Ed. What the hell is *wrong* with me?"

He stepped towards me but I turned my back and he stopped. "I just mean — listen, Zo, remember what you read in that magazine the other day? Stress can make it less likely you'll fall pregnant. I know you're upset — I am too — but you need to try and do something to relax. I don't know. Yoga? Meditation?"

"You're joking, right? Medi-fuckin-tation?" I knew even as the words came spitting out that I was being totally unreasonable, but I just couldn't help it. It must have been a bit much for Ed to take in: one minute I was adamant I didn't want a baby; the next, I was obsessed. But I hated the fact that this was something I couldn't control, something I couldn't get right straight away. Every time I saw someone with a baby I felt a surge of resentment, a pain rising in my chest until I could hardly breathe. It made me so angry, at the world, at myself, at Ed, that I couldn't even stand to spend too much time with Becky and the baby.

And then Becky fell pregnant again.

I knew she was scared to tell me.

"Zoe, I need to talk to you," she said, her face as white as a sheet as we sat in my living room together drinking tea one morning. And I knew without even looking at her what she was going to say.

"You're pregnant, aren't you?" I tried not to make it sound accusing. I was happy for her, after all. It wasn't

230

her fault I couldn't conceive and she could, and I was determined not to make her feel guilty about it.

She nodded. "I'm sorry, Zoe," she said.

"Becky, don't ever say you're sorry," I said, standing up and throwing my arms around her. "I'm thrilled for you, I really, really am."

I felt the tension drain from her body as she realized it was all going to be OK. And I put on a good show, I really did. But after she left later that afternoon — after I'd strapped Gracie into her car seat and kissed her warm forehead, after I'd hugged Becky and told her I loved her, after I'd waved them goodbye as they drove away down the road — only then did I fall onto my bed and bury my face in my pillow and sob and rage until I had no more tears left to shed. Ed didn't know what to say. I knew he was hurting too, but somehow, even though he'd been the one to want a baby all along, it didn't seem to be such an utter obsession for him as it was for me.

I was furious about it, and even though I knew it wasn't fair to take that anger out on Ed, it was the easiest way.

That was two months ago now and as Becky's belly bloomed I was still no closer to becoming a mummy. Before, we'd left it longer and longer before admitting we needed help. Perhaps, if I could bring it up today, suggest we get some help now, it might change things, give us more of a chance.

I turn to Ed. He's cradling George in his arms, rubbing his nose gently with his own nose. He looks so happy, I know I have to give us this chance.

What do I have to lose?

The trouble with fertility treatment is it's so utterly devoid of what a marriage is about — love, emotion, feelings. It's clinical and unromantic and sometimes downright embarrassing. You have to lose all your inhibitions and just let your body become a machine.

It can also cause terrible mood swings and even worse arguments. And that's what I was terrified might happen again.

But despite all this, I know I have to give myself and Ed the chance we deserve for things to work this time.

Which is why, when we sit down in our kitchen-diner later that evening to eat the meal I'd bought in our local deli, my heart is thumping against my ribcage as I think of how to bring up the subject.

In the end I just blurt it out.

"I think we need some help."

Ed looks up from his dinner, his fork, spearing a mushroom, halfway to his mouth.

"What with?"

"Having a baby."

Ed pops the mushroom into his mouth and chews slowly, watching me across the table. Finally, he swallows, wipes his mouth on the back of his hand. "Seriously?"

I nod. "Ed, it's been two years. Nothing's happened and probably nothing's going to happen. I think we just need to go and see someone, talk about our options." I take a gulp of wine and watch him carefully. He's holding his wine glass by the stem, turning it slowly one way and then the other. Music plays gently in the background.

"I think you're right." He pauses, takes a breath. "So what do we do now?"

I shrug, hoping I'm not giving away my fear. Because I know what comes next; the hospital appointments, the tests, the prodding and poking; the injections, the moods swings, the stress, the arguments, the almost marriage-busting tension. But I can't say any of that.

"I guess we need to see the doctor, find out if there's a problem."

"Yes," Ed says. He goes quiet as he chews. "What happens . . ."

"If what?"

"If, well, what if we find out we just can't have a baby at all?"

"Well, then we deal with it. But Ed, there's no reason why that should happen. It might just be that we need a bit of help."

I feel like a fraud, like I'm playing the part of his wife. Because I'm lying to him: I know we need more than a bit of help. But I also know that we were never told to give up all hope. So it has to be worth a go.

"I hope so."

We eat our dinner in silence for a few minutes, both of us lost in our thoughts.

"You know if we can't have a baby I'd never leave you, don't you?" Ed's words come out in a rush, as though a plug has been removed and there's nowhere else for them to go.

"I know," I say. And I do know he means it. It doesn't mean it won't happen though, despite our promises. There's only so much a marriage can withstand.

"If it comes to it, we can always adopt."

"Ed, let's not talk about that. Let's just take it one step at a time. Let's make an appointment to go and talk to the doctor and see what he has to say. If we need tests then fine, but let's just see what happens."

"Yes, you're right," he says, staring at his dinner. Then something snaps inside him and his face lights up. He lifts his glass. "To the future. To *our* future." I lift my glass to his and clink. "To the future."

I can only hope we have one.

CHAPTER
FIFTEEN

10 December 2010

When I wake up I'm bolt upright in bed, sweating and shaking, my heart pounding as though it's trying to escape from my chest. The room is dark and as my breathing slows I turn to Ed, desperate for comfort. But he's not there. I reach my hand out and smooth it over the crumpled sheet, as though I need confirmation that he's not where he's supposed to be.

I frown. Where is he?

My heart races as my mind trawls through the possibilities. He rarely went away, so it can't be that. He could just be up already, but it's the middle of the night and that doesn't feel right.

Oh no. It couldn't be — could it? My eyes move around the room like a searchlight, trying to see details in the dark room to disprove the theory. No, this isn't a hospital room; I haven't woken up in 2013 to find Ed is dead. This is still the past. I just need to work out when.

The room is cold and I shiver as I roll onto my side and push the duvet away. I grab my dressing gown from the floor next to the bed and wrap it round myself. I pull open the bedroom door and pad through to the front room. The floor-boards creak under my feet and the orange glow from the streetlight outside the front door shines through the glass panel, lighting my path. I push open the living-room door quietly and peer inside. At first I can't see anything. The blinds are fully closed and not a peep of light is getting through. But as my eyes adjust to the gloom I see a shape on the sofa.

Ed's curled up on his side, a thin blanket over him, snoring softly. I flick on the light in the hallway so I can see him better without waking him, and sit down in the chair opposite. As I sit, Ed stirs a little, and pulls the blanket higher up his face so that all I can see are his eyes over the top. I watch him for a few minutes in the darkness, the blanket rising and falling gently with each breath, and I wonder why he's sleeping in here, and not next to me where he belongs. Have we had a row? It only happened a few times, but each time it was terrible. I have no desire to relive one of those days again. What would be the point?

I pull myself up from the chair and go through to the kitchen. The clock on the cooker says 4.05. I know I'm not going to sleep any more, so I fill the kettle and perch on a stool while I wait for it to boil. As the hum fills the air I look around and realize with a start that this is the flat we lived in when Ed died; that I live in now. It's a different flat from the one I woke up in last time, and I can't believe it's taken me this long to notice.

There's a calendar on the wall and I peer at it in the dim light. It's December 2010. My God, only three years until Ed dies. Time's passing so quickly, this could be the last day I ever have with him. My head spins at the thought.

My eyes scroll down the calendar: "Dinner with the girls"; "Ed work Christmas do"; "Mum and Dad" — my handwriting. Then they stop on 10 December. There's one word here, no exclamation marks, no notes, no nothing. Just: "Results". And then I know. That must be today. That must be why I'm here. It's the day for the results of our first fertility treatment.

That means it's a whole year since our lives became about nothing more than reproduction. As agreed, we'd been to see our GP. He'd asked us lots of personal questions, and we'd been referred for tests. But none of them had told us anything. There didn't seem to be any reason why I wasn't pregnant. And yet I still wasn't.

We were given one chance at fertility treatment. One, before we had to pay for it ourselves. And despite not wanting to pin my hopes on it, I'd been sure that it would work. After all, why shouldn't it?

The treatment was harder than I'd imagined.

"I think we should try something called Intrauterine Insemination, or IUI," the specialist had told us.

So we were placed on a waiting list and a few months later the call had come. It was our turn.

From the beginning the whole thing felt as though it was happening to someone else. From Ed giving his sperm sample to me being inseminated with it, to the hormone drugs, the cramps and the waiting. None of it had seemed real, not that first time.

And now here we are, back to the day when we found out whether it had all been worthwhile.

Despite myself, despite what I know, I can't help wondering whether it might all be different this time; whether this might be the reason I'm back here. I almost fall off the stool at the thought.

The kettle reaches a crescendo and, with a shaking hand, I stand and reach for a mug from the shelf and stick a teabag inside before pouring the boiling water over it. I'm on auto-pilot, swirling the teabag with a spoon, getting the milk from the fridge, pouring in a generous glug, replacing the milk. As I close the fridge door I nearly jump out of my skin. Ed's standing there, bleary-eyed, behind the fridge door.

"Jesus, Ed, you nearly gave me a heart attack!"

"Sorry." He rubs his eyes. "What are you doing up?"

"Couldn't sleep. I could ask you the same."

"I just . . . well, you know, the sofa isn't very comfortable . . ." There's an awkward silence which I can't fill because I don't even know exactly why he's on the sofa. I wait for him to speak again.

"I'm sorry," he says. "I didn't mean any of the things I said last night. I just . . ." He rubs his hand over his face as if to clear it. "Well, I just lost my temper." He holds his arms out as an invitation and I don't hesitate. I don't really care what he said last night, or what I said. The fact is it doesn't matter, not any more.

"It's OK."

He pulls away, peers down at me. "So does that mean I can come back in, then?"

I pause, pretend to think. "I suppose so."

Ed grins. "Good."

238

"The only thing is, I'm really not tired." I sit at the table and take a sip of my tea. "I might just stay here."

Ed pauses for a minute, looking hurt. "In that case, I'll stay with you." He switches the kettle back on, pours himself a cup of tea and sits down on the stool next to me.

"So, are you ready for today?"

I sip my tea. "Yes, I think so. Are you?"

Ed nods. "I know you've got your hopes up, Zo, but there was one thing I meant last night. If it doesn't happen this time, please don't be too disappointed. The doctor told us, there's no guarantee — it's only our first go."

"I know. But let's just see."

"Yes, let's wait and see." His voice is soft.

I stare down at my tea. I can feel Ed looking at me but I can't meet his eyes in case I start to cry. Instead I slide off my stool and tighten the belt on my dressing gown.

"I'm going for a bath."

"I might go and get a bit more sleep."

"OK." There's no way I'll sleep now. My mind is too full of *what if*s. Maybe a bath will clear it a bit.

An hour later, wrapped in a towel on the sofa, I sit staring at the black square of window onto the street. It's only 5.30 and still dark outside, unusually quiet, the only sounds the distant rumble of trains and the squelch of tyres from the odd car driving down the wet road. My diary sits on the table, and I turn to today's date. *Results, 3p.m., Whittington.* I've underlined the word *Results*, used exclamation marks too. The excitement, the hope, is heartbreaking.

I close the pages again. It's going to be a long day. I need to do something to fill it.

Quietly, without waking Ed, I get dressed in my favourite skinny jeans, and several warm tops, slide my feet into my boots then wrap my thick parka round me with a scarf, gloves and bobble hat, grab my bag and keys and softly open the door. The cold air takes my breath away and I breathe it in deeply, letting it fill my lungs, then breathe out in a quick puff and watch the steam rise and disappear into the air. I pull the door shut behind me and shove my hands into my pockets. There's a slight frost on the ground which makes my boots crunch against the concrete, and I listen to the rhythm of my footsteps as I march down the road quickly, trying to keep myself warm. I don't really have a destination in mind, but I just need to get out of the house and into the fresh air. I need to feel alive.

I walk down well-known streets, turning randomly until the houses are no longer familiar. My body's warm under my layers and I pull my gloves off to let the air cool my hands.

It's still dark but there's a soft glow behind the buildings, giving a hint of the day to come. As I pass a café with its windows steamed up I realize I'm starving, so I pull my hat off and undo my coat and duck inside. It's a typical greasy spoon; the mumble of voices, the sizzle of bacon, the smell of greasy eggs fill the room, and it's just what I need. No one notices me and I order fried egg on toast and a mug of tea and take a

240

seat at one of the tables. The café is hot and steamy and I watch people, the early risers, shift workers, night workers and people on their way home from a night out, all together in one place.

My eggs arrive and I wolf them down then sit and nurse my tea for a bit, waiting for it to cool. And then and only then do I allow my mind to wander.

I think about Becky, and her two beautiful children — Gracie, who now, in 2013, is six, and Alfie, who's four and who looks just like his daddy. I love those children to bits but it hurts every time I see them, reminding me of what I can't have. And so I keep my distance.

A conversation comes back to me, from around this time the first time round. Becky's number had come up on my phone and for a change I'd answered it. But it was three-year-old Gracie's voice I'd heard rather than my sister's.

"Purleeeeeease come and play, Aunty Zoe, I miss you! I've got all my dolls for you."

A lump formed in my throat so I could hardly speak. Becky had tricked me and I was cross, but I couldn't be cross with my niece.

"I'll come soon, Gracie, I promise." My voice had been barely more than a whisper.

"But you *always* say that. Can you come now, please, please, please?"

"I'm sorry, not right now, sweetheart. But soon, I promise. Can I talk to Mummy now?"

"OK. Bye, Aunty Zoe, I love you!"

"Bye." There'd been a few moments of silence, then Becky's voice.

"Sorry, but I thought you might listen to Gracie more than you listen to me. You haven't been to see us in ages. Is everything OK?"

I couldn't stay angry at Becky: she was right. I had been neglecting them.

"Yeah, everything's fine. I just —" I stopped, not wanting to say too much. Nobody wanted to hear me moaning on and on. It wasn't interesting to anyone else; it was my own little drama — mine and Ed's.

But Becky saw straight through me.

"Zoe, you do know everything will be all right, don't you? Doctors can do amazing things these days. You'll see. Nothing would be right with the universe if you weren't allowed to be a mum."

I swallowed the lump in my throat and tried to speak but it felt as though my vocal cords had been tied together.

"Are you crying? Please don't cry. I didn't want to make you cry. We just miss you. Please can we see you soon?"

"Yes. Yes, of course. I miss you all too. It's just — it's just hard, Becs, that's all." I didn't want to say any more.

"I know. Really, I do. Listen, Alfie's just done a massive poo, I need to go and sort him out before I pass out from the smell. But I'll see you soon, promise?"

"Yes, you will."

242

I'd hung up vowing to stick to my promise. But I hadn't managed it. I'd still stayed away far too much and by 2013 it was even worse. I did the same to Mum and Dad, and Jane too. They all tried to help me, to talk to me about things, but I shut them out, stopped answering their calls, stopped going to see them.

I feel ashamed. This time, if I get the chance, I won't make the same mistake again.

I look up and see that it's already light outside. I can't see the sky but there's a low grey-blue light hanging over the buildings, and the people walking past are bundled up tightly. It's time for me to head home. I leave a fiver on the table and pick up my coat and leave. I don't know where I am but if I keep walking I'll find a Tube station eventually. I pull my phone from my bag and send a message to Ed.

On my way home. See you soon. X

Then I turn my phone off and start to walk.

On the way home I made a decision. I wasn't going straight home: Ed would probably have left for work anyway, I realized, and I didn't want to be alone. Instead, I sent him another message to let him know where I was and I went to see Jane. I couldn't see what I could do to change the outcome of today — it was pretty much out of my hands. But I had an overwhelming urge to do this, to see my best friend, the friend I'd neglected so much recently.

Which is why I now find myself shivering and stamping my feet on Jane's doorstep, waiting for her to let me in.

Finally, Jane's fuzzy voice comes over the intercom, indecipherable, then there's a loud buzz and I push the door open and make my way up the stairs. Jane's door is ajar and I go through and find her stooping over her coffee machine, swearing, while it emits strange choking sounds. She hears me come in and looks round, her face flushed.

"Fucking thing is buggered," she says, yanking her hand backwards and pulling out a piece of the machine and smacking it on the counter, hard.

"I don't think that's going to help."

She grins. "Won't make it any worse." She wipes her hands on a towel and walks towards me, arms outstretched, to envelop me in a tight, warm hug. I hug her back and we stand like that for a few moments until Jane pulls away. Her hands still grip my upper arms.

"So, stranger, where have you been?"

I hang my head in shame. "I'm sorry I've been so shit. I don't really have an excuse."

"Don't be daft. I didn't mean it like that. I know you've been having a rough time. I know it sounds soppy, but I've missed you."

"I've missed you too." I blink back the tears that threaten to escape down my cheeks.

"Right," Jane says, turning back towards the broken coffee machine. "Coffee's off the menu. How about tea?"

"Tea sounds perfect," I say, and as she roots through the cupboard looking for teabags I take milk from the fridge and cups from the mug tree. It's almost as familiar to me as my own house.

244

Tea made, we go through to her living room and I tuck my feet underneath me on the sofa. I catch sight of the clock above her TV and am shocked to see it's still only 8.30 a.m. I've been up for hours.

"So how come you're not at work today?" I ask.

"I called and told them I was going to be late."

"What, because of me?"

She shrugs. "Course. You sounded like you needed me, and you haven't sounded like that for a long time."

"God, now I feel terrible."

"Well, don't. I wouldn't have done it if I didn't want to. And anyway, I give them enough of my time; they owe me." She takes a sip of her tea. "So, what's going on?"

I sigh. I don't really know where to start.

What I want to tell her is this: that Ed is dead, and that, for some bizarre, impossible-to-explain reason, I'm reliving my life, and desperately trying to do things differently so that he doesn't die; that I'll never forgive myself for our marriage having become hollow and about nothing more than making a baby; that I get an empty feeling in the pit of my stomach every time I think about never becoming a mum; that I feel sick at the thought that, even after all of this, I might still not be able to stop Ed dying.

But I can't tell her any of this.

So instead I tell her about how the fertility treatment makes me feel as though my body is being used for some kind of medical experiment; how the hormones race round me and I'm consumed by hot flushes; how I burst into tears at anything and blame Ed for everything; how I feel as though my life has become about nothing more than creating another life. About how I haven't spoken to anyone about it, and I feel as though I'm going to explode.

By the time I've finished my face is wet with tears and I'm surprised by what a relief it feels even to say this, after all this time. Jane looks shocked, her eyes wide.

"Fuck, what a nightmare."

It's so Jane, and so not what I would have said, that I laugh. The hysteria builds inside me and I can't stop, and soon I'm wiping tears of laughter rather than sadness from my face and holding my aching jaw. Jane starts to laugh too and for a few minutes neither of us can speak. It takes a while but slowly we begin to calm down. I try to speak.

"I —" *gulp* — "I'm sorry, it's just . . ."

"I know." Jane manages to get herself under control. "And sorry, I didn't mean to sound blunt. But Zo, I don't really know what else to say. It does sound like a bloody nightmare."

I nod, finally able to breathe again as the laughter subsides. "It is. But the thing is, what am I going to do about it?"

She shrugs. "Fuck knows."

"God."

I wish there was someone to come and tell me what to do: to tell me whether I was doing this thing right, whether I was doing enough to change things or whether I was just wasting my time even trying. Whether, if I just told Ed I wanted to stop all this right now, it would stop us falling apart, and things would be much better.

Or whether refusing to keep trying for a baby after everything we'd already been through would tear us apart anyway. What a decision to have to make.

"I do still want a baby. I do. I want Ed to have the baby he wants, and I want it too. I just don't know if I can go through all this and still end up not being a mother, and our marriage in tatters." A sob rises in my chest and I choke it back down.

"You don't know it's going to ruin things between you, Zo. It might still be OK."

"It already is ruined, Jane. I just want to fix it."

"Oh sweetheart, I know." She puts her arm round my shoulders. "And I know it doesn't make you feel any better, but there are other people going through it as well. Just because you see people with children all the time, it doesn't mean they've had it easy. Listen, there's a woman at work, she was going through IVF for years. We all knew every time she was going through a new cycle because she hardly spoke to anyone, and was really sad and teary, so we knew to leave her alone. It went on for a long time and most people wondered why she didn't just give up. But she didn't, and now she has twins. I'm not saying that it's going to take you years, but I just mean — well, other people have problems too, and maybe you should find some people to talk to about it, people who have been through it themselves. It might help."

I study my nails and chew roughly on the ends.

"Maybe. But I really don't think other people's stories of woe will make me feel any better. I just want to *do* something, to try and change things myself. Take action."

"Like what?

"That's just it. I don't know."

Jane sits for a minute, thinking. "Have you tried acupuncture, or, I don't know, reflexology or something?"

I stare at her. "Seriously? The most cynical woman in the world is suggesting alternative therapies?"

She shrugs, looking sheepish. "Yeah, well, just because I think something's a load of old bollocks, doesn't mean it actually is. What the hell do I know?"

I think about it. I didn't try anything like that last time. But last time I didn't get pregnant. Maybe Jane's right, even though she doesn't believe it herself. Maybe it is worth a go.

"Good point. Maybe you're right."

"Well, let's face it, Zo, it can't make you feel any worse. I mean, look at you." Jane gestures towards me, a snivelling wreck on her sofa.

I smile weakly. "I know. And thanks, Jane. I needed this."

"Any time, Zoe. Really. I'm always here."

I'm so grateful for her friendship. I don't know why I ever thought it would be easier to do this without her.

I take a deep breath. "Anyway, that's enough about me. What's the score with you? How's . . ." I trail off, realizing I can't remember who she's with, if anyone, at the moment.

248

Jane grins. "Joe is no more. I can't be arsed with someone who spends all his time in the gym and would rather go for a run than a pint. Great six-pack, but *man*, he was boring."

I smile, relieved to be talking about something else.

"So, anyone else interesting?"

Jane signed up for online dating some time around now. I hope I've got the timing right.

"Weeeell, I did have a thought," she says, a sly smile on her face.

"What are you up to, young lady?"

"Listen. I've had no luck choosing someone from the website myself, so I thought I might find someone better if you chose for me."

"Me?"

"Well, only if you feel up to it."

"Yeah, OK. I'd love to. And let's face it, I can't do a worse job than you've been doing."

"Good point well made, my friend."

Jane always chooses someone gorgeous, but they usually turn out to be boring or self-obsessed or skint, or all three. I know I can find her someone better. And if nothing else, it feels great to be thinking about something other than me and my weird second life.

Jane grabs her laptop from the kitchen counter and plonks herself back next to me on the sofa. The dating website loads and she clicks on the new messages. We read them together, rolling our eyes and giggling. Then she passes the computer to me and lets me scroll through some of the men on here. I read their profiles in amazement.

I love taxidermy, I hope you do too. He was surrounded by stuffed animals. Ew.

I'm in prison for fraud. A real catch.

I'm a naturist and spend most of my time naked. If you also prefer to be unencumbered by clothes then you're the girl for me! I laugh out loud.

"What? Let me see." Jane's trying to see the screen but I hold it away from her.

"No, I'm choosing, you have to be patient."

"But you're taking *ages*."

"Do you want me to find you the man of your dreams, or not?"

"Yes, but quickly."

I giggle, and carry on reading.

A few minutes later I stop. "Got it. *This* is the man for you."

Jane peers at the picture and wrinkles her nose. "But . . . he's skinny."

"He is *not* skinny, he's just not built like a brick shithouse — and you have to read his profile before you decide you don't like him. Anyway," I add, "you said I could pick someone for you to go on a date with, so you have to at least give it a go."

Sighing dramatically, Jane grabs the laptop and reads the profile of "Jamie, thirty-eight, from London." He's slim, and is wearing glasses. But he looks sweet, and he sounds fun.

When she's finished reading she looks at me. "OK, I'll ask him for a date," she says. "But I'm not promising to fall in love with him."

I roll my eyes. "Give the guy a chance," I say, and grab the laptop back and type out a message to Jamie, then press Send. "Right, done," I announce, clicking the mouse with a flourish. "No backing out now."

"OK, OK. Bloody nag. Wish I'd never suggested it."

"Want to make a bet that not only do you like him, but that you go on a second date?"

"You're on," she says, and we shake hands firmly. I hope I get to find out how it goes.

And as I say my goodbyes a few minutes later and get ready to head back to see Ed and face the music at the fertility clinic, I realize how happy I am for the first time in ages. It feels so good to have spent some time with Jane, talking about something other than babies. It's made me feel normal, and it's felt great to be so close to my best friend again.

I vow to do it more often.

Ed clutches my hand tightly as we sit side by side on the bus on the way to the fertility clinic that afternoon, in silence. My whole body is rigid, tense, as I stare blindly out of the window; the sky is dark grey and getting darker, threatening snow. I hope it's not a sign.

There's a low chatter around me, people getting on with their everyday lives. I envy them the normality. But I'm willing to bet there are people on this bus who would swap with me in a heartbeat if it meant they got the chance to see a lost loved one again. I tighten my grip on Ed's hand even more, and he squeezes back.

I don't know whether the results we get today will be the same as last time. Last time we were left heartbroken when we were told the treatment hadn't worked.

And while my head is telling me that today won't be any different, my heart is telling me something else entirely: that maybe, just maybe, I've made a difference. Maybe, this time, I might be pregnant.

I shiver suddenly and am almost flung from my seat as the bus comes to a sudden stop with a squeal of brakes.

"Shit." Ed clutches the pole next to him, his knuckles white. "Come on, this is our stop anyway." He stands and grabs my hand and I follow him from the bus, into the freezing air and on into the warmth of the hospital.

Five minutes later we're perched on hard plastic chairs, waiting to see the consultant. The days and weeks and months of pain and heartache have all led up to this moment, this brief appointment in this faceless brick building in the middle of London. It's all about what happens in that room in a few moments' time. That's what will decide our fate, decide what is to come.

And it's no easier the second time around.

I squeeze Ed's hand and he turns to look at me and smiles thinly. He looks as terrified as I am, and my heart surges with pain for him.

"You OK?"

He nods briefly. "Scared."

"Me too."

252

We fall into silence again. The clock on the wall opposite ticks on endlessly and the silence stretches until the only thing it can do is break.

And then it does.

The wooden door is flung open and a familiar face — familiar to me, at least; not yet to Ed — peers round it.

"Edward and Zoe Williams?" he says, smiling warmly as we stand and follow him through the door. My legs feel wobbly as we walk into the room where I've spent many tense hours discussing options, shouting and crying, and I have to struggle to blink back the tears. The warm-yellow walls, the pot plants on the desk, the comfortable faux-leather armchairs in front of the wooden desk: it's all in complete contrast to the rest of the sterile clinic, and the first time I saw it I was filled with hope. How could anything bad possibly happen here?

I shiver and sit on the chair and turn to face the consultant, Mr Sherringham. He's already sitting down, papers spread out on the desk in front of him, wiggling a pen between his thumb and fingertip. He smiles again, and I return it with a stiff, unconvincing smile. Ed's face stays blank. Mr Sherringham leans forward and peers at the papers in front of him.

"Hello, I'm Mr Sherringham." He coughs then holds out his hand and shakes ours warmly, one by one. We're both quivering. Mr Sherringham glances back down at the papers in front of him, then looks at me, then at Ed. "OK, I'm not going to keep you in suspense any longer because I know how important this is to you. I have your results here and I'm afraid it's not good news. You're not pregnant."

He stops speaking and the silence that fills the room presses down on me until it feels as though my head is going to explode. I want to scream but it won't come out. I hold my hand gently against my belly.

Nothing has changed. So why does it hurt even more this time?

I can't do this any more. All the pain of the last few years comes flooding out; the pain of Ed dying, of the endless rows, of losing my friends and family to the all-consuming nightmare of fertility treatment. Of losing myself. The tears feel as though they'll never stop.

Ed kneels down and wraps his arms around me, and for a few minutes it's as though we're the only two people in the room. He's crying too and our tears mingle and fall onto my lap, soaking through my jeans. The consultant stays quiet, letting us have these few moments to take in the news.

Finally, though, he coughs gently and Ed pulls away. The sobs have subsided but my breathing is ragged, a sudden shaking of my chest taking me by surprise every few breaths. We both sit and look at Mr Sherringham.

"I know how hard this is for you both," he says. His voice is soft, kind, which somehow makes it harder. "But it's not the end of the road. There are still plenty more things we can try. We still have plenty of time."

His words are meant well but I feel angry. Because I know there isn't plenty of time, not for us.

254

"It *is* the end of the road. We're never going to have a baby, it's going to ruin my life. It's going to ruin both our lives. I —" I stop, overwhelmed by tears again. Mr Sherringham hands me a box of tissues from his desk and I pull some out gratefully, pressing them to my swollen eyes. I daren't look at Ed.

"I'm sorry. I just — was hoping for more positive news." I wipe my nose and scrunch the tissue up in my fist.

"I know, and so was I. We all were. I'm so sorry this hasn't worked out for you this time. But I promise you I will do everything in my power to make sure that we get you the baby you long for."

"But . . . why has this happened?" I ask.

He shrugs. "I really can't say for sure. We all knew, starting this, that there was only a small chance of success. I know that doesn't make it any easier, but it doesn't mean it can't happen next time, or the time after that. We just have to take it a day at a time and find the best solution for you. And that's what I'm here for."

He pauses, then starts again, a little uncomfortable this time.

"You do know that any treatment you choose to have from this point you will have to pay for?"

I glance at Ed and he nods tightly.

"We'll pay for whatever we need to."

I think about the thousands of pounds we'll spend in the following few years and the problems it causes, and I want to shout out, "No, let's save our money and forget it." Instead I just nod in agreement.

"OK, so shall we talk about what happens next?" Mr Sherringham says.

"Yes please," Ed says. He looks at me and I give a small nod.

But my mind is racing, wondering. Nothing has changed so far, at least not as far as I can see. But perhaps *this* could be my moment to do something; my chance to save years of heartache, to save our marriage. What if — and I can hardly believe I'm thinking this after everything we've been through — I put my foot down right now and say I've had enough; that I don't want to keep trying for a baby any more? Would it make a difference?

I have no idea.

I feel dizzy and I focus on the clock above Mr Sherringham's head, on the second hand, ticking steadily on and on. Ed and Mr Sherringham are discussing our options but I'm hardly listening to a word. All I can think about is that time is running out. That this could be my last chance.

"No!" It comes out as a shout, and I surprise even myself. Ed and Mr Sherringham stop dead, the hum of their conversation replaced by a tense, heavy silence. I can't look at either of them so I continue to stare at the clock, the seconds ticking by monotonously.

"What do you mean, no?" Ed's voice is sharp, shriller than usual.

"I —" What *do* I mean? "I just mean — I don't think I can do this any more."

"Do what, Zoe?" His voice has softened a little and I turn to face him, to look into his eyes, a paler, weaker blue than normal.

256

"I don't think I can go through endless rounds of this, Ed. It's too much. It's too painful, and it's probably never going to work. I just think maybe we should stop."

He looks at me, silent for a moment. "But you promised, Zoe. This has been all you've wanted, we've wanted, for months now. You can't give up after just one try." He looks at Mr Sherringham pleadingly, almost begging him for help.

"Ed's right, Zoe. This is just a blip. It doesn't mean you won't have a baby, it just means we've got to try a bit harder. It's totally up to you, of course, but I suggest you two go away and have a chat about it, and we'll talk again. How does that sound?"

"Thank you. That sounds perfect. Zoe?" Ed's voice is cold again and I shiver.

I don't know what else to do. I've tried to stop this, to make a difference, but unless there's a way of telling them that I know it's never going to work, that this is going to tear us apart, how can I possibly explain what I mean? I can't.

The room starts to spin and I close my eyes, trying to shut it out. I lean forward, clutch my head between my hands and tip slowly forward. Then everything goes black.

I get ready to open my eyes, expecting to see the doctor's room with its dark, warm furniture, and Ed and Mr Sherringham staring at me, still waiting for my decision. I don't want to do this.

Finally, I flip my eyelids up, prepared.

257

What I see takes me by surprise. I'm lying on a hard couch, staring at a white ceiling. There's nothing remarkable about the ceiling. There's a crack running from the small chandelier towards the door which peters out halfway between the two. It's been painted over but I can still make it out through the layers of white emulsion. I flick my eyes towards the door and over the dark wood, down towards the floor, turning my head to take in more of the room.

I don't recognize it at all. I frown and turn my head slowly the other way; I almost fall off the couch. There's a woman with her back to me in front of a window with its blind drawn, writing something on a piece of paper. She hasn't seen me yet so I take the chance to study her more closely. Her curly, almost frizzy blonde hair spreads like a halo around her head, and every now and then her head bobs down towards the desk, making her hair sway gently. She's wearing a starched white coat, and a pair of glasses are pushed onto the top of her head. Thick black tights and a pair of sturdy, chunky black shoes peek out from under her coat. I wonder who she is. I'm sure I've never seen her before and for a moment I wonder whether I'm back in the present and not reliving a day at all. But I shake that thought off before it even properly forms. I can't be. I'm sure I'm in hospital in the present, and this definitely isn't a hospital.

So where the hell *am* I?

I shift a little, trying to work out whether I should sit up. There's a scratching feeling in my tummy, just above my belly button, and I wince. Hearing my intake of breath the woman turns round, pulling her glasses back down as she does so. She smiles.

"How are you doing?" she says, her voice soft.

"Um, OK." My voice comes out thick and slurred, my tongue dry.

She smiles again, revealing a slightly crooked front tooth. "You fell asleep so I was just writing some of your notes up." She indicates the pad in front of her, black pen scrawled across it in different columns. I can't make any of it out.

"The needles will be coming out in about —" she glances at her wrist — "five, six minutes. Are you still OK?"

I nod, as realization dawns. I'm having acupuncture.

She turns back to her desk and I let my head fall back into place again, staring at the crack in the ceiling, trying to get my thoughts under control.

Everything is so confusing: this is something new, a day I've never experienced before. I've never had acupuncture; did I take Jane's advice and give it a try? Very possibly. Which means something has changed! My heart soars.

I can't explain why I'm here and not back in the consultant's room, but I don't care any more, because this is proof that I'm doing the right thing; that changing things can make a difference.

Which means I can still save Ed.

"Right, let's get these out of you." The woman — I wish I knew her name — walks to the foot of the couch and I feel a pinch in my ankle. Then she leans forward slightly and I feel another pinch in my tummy, followed by three or four more in quick succession. Each time I flinch, expecting pain but not knowing where it will be, and she smiles and apologizes in a whisper.

"Right, that's the lot," she says, gathering the needles together and covering me with a blanket. "How do you feel?" She clasps her hands under her chin as she waits for me to answer, and I stare at her neat nails as I try to work out how I feel.

"I'm OK, I think."

She nods briefly. "You'll probably feel a bit strange for a few hours. But make sure you drink plenty of water to help your body in the healing process." She turns to her desk and picks up a piece of paper, glances at it briefly then replaces it. "Get up slowly and then come and take a seat here." She gestures to the padded chair next to hers.

I sit up carefully, feeling a dull ache in my tummy where the needles have been, and blood rushes to my head. I grab the edge of the bed and swing my legs round, reach for the floor and perch on the chair she indicated. She sits down next to me and as she shuffles through her paperwork I glance at the walls, where framed certificates hang, gathering dust. "Elizabeth Penfold," says one. Her name is completely unfamiliar.

At the sound of her voice I turn to face her. Her glasses have slipped to the end of her nose and she pushes them up, screwing up her nose a little as she does.

"Right, well, firstly, well done on your first session." She smiles again and I smile back nervously. "From what I've seen this time your fallopian tubes were quite

260

blocked. I'm hoping that what I've done today will have helped to clear them a little but you will need to come back regularly for it to make any real difference. How does that sound?"

"Yes, great."

We arrange another appointment. I scribble the date in my diary wondering, briefly, whether I'll actually go through with it; then we say our goodbyes and I leave.

As I make my way home I glance at my phone to see what the date is. 19 December 2010. It's nine days after the appointment with the consultant.

Back home, I turn the key in the lock and seconds later Ed's at the lounge door like an expectant puppy.

"How did it go?" He's obviously desperate for good news and it almost breaks my heart.

I drop my bag on the floor and shake myself out of my coat, hanging it carefully on the peg.

"Fine. It was fine."

Ed waits, hoping for more. I sigh and look him in the eye.

"Ed, it was fine, honestly. She said I need to keep going back for more treatments, and now I feel relaxed. And I need a coffee."

There's nothing more I can tell him but I know he's disappointed. He follows me into the kitchen and watches as I spoon coffee beans into the grinder. I press the button down and for a few seconds the room is filled with the sound of the beans churning round the machine. I release it and tip the coffee granules into the cafetière, breathing in the scent as I do.

There's a few seconds' silence, then I can hear Ed moving towards me. He stops just behind me and I spin round, a question on my face. He's frowning and I can see the hurt in his eyes.

"Is that it, then?" His voice is accusing, hurt. But I don't know what else to tell him.

"Is what it?"

"Oh, come on, Zoe, you know exactly what I mean. You promised to give this a go, and you know how much it means to me. I don't want to see you go through any more pain, but you can't shut me out like this. I just want to know if there's any point doing this, if there's any hope at all."

I look down at the mug in my hand and spin it round mindlessly. Even though I'm not exactly sure what's happened I can take a good guess. I've obviously agreed to give acupuncture a go before we try another round of IVF. And while this is good, from the evidence so far it doesn't seem as though it's making things any easier between the two of us. Just here, in this kitchen, in this moment, I can feel the distance between us opening up like a chasm. Ed clearly thinks the treatment will be the bridge that brings us back together, but I'm really not so sure. I'd love it to be, but I can see that things are not much different from the way they were before, when we went straight into another round of IVF. Are we already too far apart for things ever to be mended?

I take a deep breath and step towards him.

"I'm sorry, sweetheart," I say, wrapping my arms around his waist, and I feel his body soften beneath my

262

touch. "It's just so much to take in. Let's see how it goes, shall we, and not get our hopes up too much?" I glance up and see the set of his jaw. Then he looks down at me and I see the tears in his eyes.

"I'm sorry," he whispers. "I didn't mean to put you under any more pressure. I'm just so sick of it all . . ." His voice breaks and he takes a deep breath. "I just want this over with and for us to have a baby and live happily ever after, and it seems so bloody unfair that we can't have what we want." His arms tighten round me and we stand in the kitchen while the boiling kettle fills the room with steam and hold each other as though we're never going to let go. And right then, I wish I never had to.

It's late when we go to bed that night, partly because we spent the evening talking, and partly because I'm worried about what will come next once I go to sleep — after all, waking up on a day I'd never actually experienced before was out of the routine I'd become used to.

But there is a positive thing that's come out of tonight, and that's that Ed and I are actually, properly talking about things, and even what we'll do if this never does work — and that is a huge improvement on how we were before. Before, we were like robots, getting on with our lives while all around us the whir of IVF just happened, taking away us, and who we were, and replacing us with baby machines.

Tonight, though, we really talked.

So when at last we drop into bed, exhausted, I fall asleep for the first time in ages feeling as though maybe, finally, things have started to change. Maybe this time I've done enough. I can only hope.

CHAPTER
SIXTEEN

13 January 2012

God, I'm uncomfortable. Something is digging into my back and my arm is bent at a strange angle beneath me. I stretch my legs out and they stop dead, hitting something hard at the end of the bed.

I frown and open my eyes. It takes me a few seconds to work out where I am, but then it dawns on me and I want to cry. I'm in the lounge, on the couch. I have a spare duvet without a cover draped over me, and my head's resting on one of the cushions instead of a pillow. The sofa's not quite long enough for me so my feet have hit the arm at the other end, and the hard thing in my back is the wooden slat beneath the cushions jabbing into my spine.

But what makes me want to cry isn't the discomfort. It's the fact that there can only be one reason I'm here and not in bed with Ed — and that's that we've had another huge row.

Sometimes it was me, and sometimes it was Ed on the sofa, but many times over these months we'd found ourselves waking up in different rooms. And every time it happened I felt the bond keeping us together loosen a little bit more, until by the end it was hardly there at all.

I shiver in the cold blue light of the morning. I can hear the rumble of cars passing outside, and the clip-clop of high heels on the pavement, receding slowly into the distance. A car door bangs and an engine revs, and the usual muffled scrapes and bumps seep through the wall from next door, but other than that, the flat's quiet.

I stand and, with the duvet wrapped round me, I pad out into the hallway and down to the bathroom to start a bath running. My head feels fuzzy and my eyes sting, which is probably from lots of crying and not enough sleep.

As I walk back I see the bedroom door is slightly ajar, so I push it open quietly and peer round, watching Ed sleeping peacefully. I turn to leave but he stirs and looks up at me and I gasp at the look on his face. He looks so sad.

"Hey," I say, my voice quiet.

He grunts something and turns away. I feel as though I've been punched in the gut. He hates me. I grab the door frame to steady myself. I don't know what to do next so I stand there for a few more seconds, hoping he'll turn round and speak to me again. But he doesn't, so I walk shakily back towards the bathroom, turn the taps off and climb into the scalding hot bath.

As I lie there I listen, waiting to see whether Ed will come and find me, to talk to me, shout at me, anything. But the minutes tick past and I hear him pulling things from drawers, running the water in the kitchen and walking past the bathroom door several times. I'm about to call his name but then I hear the sound of the front door slamming, and I've lost my chance. He's gone without saying goodbye.

Things must be bad. Tears slip down my face and mingle with the bath water, my breath coming in painful, heaving sobs. I don't want to be reminded of the dark times.

When I get myself under control the bath is cool and I'm shivering. I step out of the water quickly and wrap myself in a towel and wander through to the kitchen. The absence of Ed hangs heavy over the flat. I'm about to turn away when I notice something on the table. It's a piece of white paper, tucked under a used coffee cup. It's folded in half and my name is written on the outside. I unfold it and see Ed's handwriting scrawled across the page.

I can't talk to you today, it's too hard. I'll come back about 5, when you've gone.

Just remember, I still love you.

Ed

That's it. But his note has brought back to me with terrible, blinding clarity where and when I am. This is January 2012, and it's the day I move out. The day we realized that our marriage was broken, and we didn't know how to mend it.

It had been coming for a while. The arguments, the tension, the nights sleeping separately, unable to face each other. Finally, things had reached a head.

"I think we need some time apart."

"What?" I'd been reading the paper and Ed had just stood next to me and let the words come out, without preamble.

He sat opposite me at the table and stared down at it, unable to meet my eyes. His hands were clenched in front of him, his knuckles white. "I think we need some time apart, get our heads straight. We can't keep doing this. It's making me — us — totally miserable."

I stared at him, at his gentle hands, at the frown creasing his forehead, his soft, full lips, and I felt my heart break in two.

"You want us to split up?" My voice cracked on the last words and Ed finally looked up at me.

"No, Zoe, that's not what I'm saying. I love you, but I can't keep having these rows. Sometimes — it feels as though you hate me, and I'm not sure I can cope with it any more. I think we need some time — just — away." He paused. "I don't mind moving out for a bit. Or — or you could go and stay with your mum and dad for a while . . ."

"Wow. You've actually given this some proper thought, haven't you? Talk about a stab in the back."

"Oh, come on, Zoe, for God's sake. Are you really happy?" His tone was hard, brittle.

"I love you."

"That's not what I asked. Are you happy at the moment? With this —" he gestured between us — "with us?"

I shook my head miserably. "No."

"Well, then." He sat back in his chair and looked at me expectantly. "So what do you suggest?"

"Me? I don't suggest anything, Ed. It seems to be you who's doing all the suggesting."

"Don't be like that, Zoe."

"I'm not being like anything." My face was hot and my shoulders hunched. I was terrified of losing him but I felt furious that he was trying to dismiss me. That he thought being apart was the best way to pull ourselves closer together. But then again, nothing else seemed to be working. My shoulders collapsed and I let out a big whoosh of air. "You're right. I know you are. It's just — hearing those words. I feel like I'll never be happy again, Ed."

"We can be. We can. We just need to do this right."

I sat and thought for a minute. I couldn't go and stay with Jane; she didn't have enough room. Ed could go and stay with his mum, but it felt as though he was always running away to her and, much as I loved Susan, I didn't want to admit to her how badly the pair of us had fucked up. Becky had two kids; there was no room there, and I wasn't sure being with two young children would help.

"I'll ring Mum and Dad, see if I can stay with them for a bit."

"Are you sure? What about work?"

"I'll sort something out. They'll probably let me do some from home for a couple of weeks."

Ed leaned over and reached his hands out to grab mine. I stiffened as he did. "Thank you, Zoe. It will all be OK, I know it will."

And now here I was, back on the day when I'd been moving out. I drop the piece of paper on the floor and stand there, rigid, my heart hammering. I don't want to relive this day; it was terrible the first time round. But worse than that, much worse: if it's January 2012, that means it's only seventeen months until Ed dies.

I'm running out of time.

I don't know what to do. Should I just leave without trying to change anything, knowing that we'll sort it out in the end? Or should I try to do something, anything, to make it different, better?

I sit at the table and pull my phone out of my dressing-gown pocket. There's no missed call. I make a decision. I'm going to call him.

I dial the familiar number and wait for the connection, running my thumbnail mindlessly along the scratches on the wooden table. Ed's phone starts to ring and my heart rate picks up speed. I don't know what I'm going to say if he answers, but I can't do nothing. The ringing sound goes on and on, and then Ed's voice, mechanical and tinny, comes on the line.

Sorry I can't take your call at the moment, please leave a message after the beep.

"Ed, it's me. Zoe. I — I love you. I'll ring you later, OK?" My voice sounds pleading, desperate, but I don't care. I am. I don't want to waste a day without Ed. I need to see him.

I end the call and stand. Ed's note is on the floor where I dropped it, and I stoop to pick it up. I open it and reread it, over and over again. The words sound so cold, so uncaring, that my heart hardens slightly as I read them. Maybe I do want to see him today, but what if I try to change too much and then never get a day with him again? At least this way I know we sort things out in the end — and then there's at least a possibility that I'll wake up to another day with him.

I'm going to have to go.

I walk back to the bedroom, where I get dressed and start shoving clothes into a suitcase I find under the bed. Ready to go, I wheel it out to the front door, go back to pick up my handbag with my mobile and purse, then turn to leave. But at the front door I pause. Should I write Ed a note?

I grab a piece of paper from the notebook Ed has clearly used and scribble a few words.

I love you. Remember our promise. Please don't give up on me. Zoe x

Adding a kiss at the end, I fold it in half, write Ed's name on the outside, and leave it in the same place I'd found my note. Then I pick up my suitcase and leave for the walk to the Tube station, and the start of what, before, was a terrible day.

I hardly remember the journey, but before I know it the train's pulling into Doncaster station and I'm stepping onto the platform. A man behind me helps me lift my suitcase down and I want to cry at the small kindness. I let my hair fall across my eyes to hide my tears.

I walk along the platform, down the stairs and back up, out into the sunlight, and suddenly there's Mum walking towards me, a look of concern on her face.

She stops in front of me and I drop the handle of my suitcase and we hug in the middle of the station concourse.

"Oh Mum," I say, hardly able to get the words out through my tears.

"Ssshhh," she says, rubbing my back like she used to when I was little. She holds me a few minutes longer then pulls away and peers at my face. She pushes my hair away and tucks it behind my ear tenderly and wipes a tear away with her thumb.

"Right, let's get you home."

I nod and pick up my suitcase and follow her to the car. As we drive along the motorway, rain gently patters the windscreen and the rhythm of the wipers sends me into a daze. Mum doesn't ask me anything, and I'm grateful for the silence.

We pull up outside the familiar house and for the first time since I woke this morning I feel a smile touch my face. As we pull into the driveway Dad's out of the front door and waiting by the car, desperate to help.

I climb out of the passenger seat.

"Hi, Dad."

"Hello, love. Want me to take your bags?"

I nod and as he busies himself dragging my suitcase from the boot I step inside and take a deep breath. The pictures of me and Becky along the wall, the little table with a phone and a green, rubbery plant on, a shelf with keys hanging from it and a few ornaments of cats, birds, a rabbit; it's all so familiar I feel a huge weight lift from my shoulders just standing there.

I'm safe.

272

I walk into the kitchen and find Mum rummaging in a cupboard.

"I've got some of those teabags you like," she says, reaching too high and almost toppling over. "But I think your dad has put them right up here." She admits defeat and slumps down.

"I'll get them." I walk to the cupboard and reach up, feeling around for a box of teabags. I find them and pull them out: a box of the decaf I used to love but don't have the heart to tell her I don't really drink any more. I pass them to her.

"Zoe." She stops. I know she's desperate to ask what's wrong.

"Mum, let's have a cup of tea and I'll tell you all about it."

"OK, love." She finishes making the tea and brings it over to the table, carefully putting a coaster down first. It seems a bit pointless, with the number of stains and scratches this ancient table already has, but I accept the drink gratefully.

Mum sits opposite me and sips her tea carefully, waiting. I stare beyond her, out of the patio window and into the already-darkening sky, wondering where on earth to start. The truth is, I haven't spoken to Mum as much recently as I should have done. Like Jane and Becky and anyone else I cared about, I'd shut her and Dad out when the bad times started, not wanting them to see my pain.

But this is the perfect chance to change all that. I think about the first time I was here; I'd refused to talk to either of them, hardly told them anything. I knew

Mum was desperate to help but I just couldn't bring myself to admit I'd failed.

This time, though, was going to be different. This time, I was going to tell her everything, let her help me. I needed her.

At the sound of footsteps I turn and see Dad picking up his mug and moving towards the table. Mum looks at him and shakes her head, almost imperceptibly, a warning to stay away. His eyes flit from me to Mum and back again.

"Oh, right. I'm just getting my drink . . ." He holds the cup up as if to prove it and some tea sloshes over the side and splashes onto the lino floor. Mum rolls her eyes but before she can grab a cloth Dad's wiped the spill with his slipper.

"Oh John."

Dad shrugs. "I'll just be off to watch the snooker, then." And with a look of relief he scuttles out, closing the door firmly behind him.

I turn back to Mum, who's looking cross.

"He never changes, does he?" I say.

"He gets worse, love."

There's a beat of silence, but I know I can't leave her waiting any longer. I take a deep breath and start.

"I can't have a baby and Ed hates me for it." I hadn't expected those words to come out and they surprise even me. Was that really what I thought, that Ed blamed me for all this?

But Mum takes it all in her stride. "Oh love, of course he doesn't hate you. Why do you even think that?"

274

And so I tell her everything; everything I hadn't been able to tell her last time, that I'd bottled up for years until it became too much.

I tell her about not being sure I wanted a baby but Ed wanting the perfect family; I tell her about how I'd become obsessed with having one since I started trying and realized I couldn't; I talk about the IVF, the physical pain and the terrible waiting game, knowing our future was out of my hands. About the pain of seeing other people with babies, of feeling robbed, of hating them, or not them exactly but the idea of them, for being able to have what I so desperately wanted and couldn't have; about the endless hope and heartbreak, desperation and disappointment, the rows, the blame, the silences and, of course, the final row.

When I stop talking I feel about a stone lighter. Mum's looking at me across the table. Her mug is empty now, mine still half full of cold tea. I look down at it and see the reflection of the kitchen light in the murky brown liquid.

"I can't believe you've been through all this by yourself," Mum says at last, her voice barely more than a whisper, and I snap my head back up at her words. "Why on earth have you kept it to yourself?"

"I don't know."

Mum gets up and crouches in front of me and wraps her arms around me, holding me tightly to her. And then I can't hold it in any more; my whole body shakes with sobs, letting out the pain of everything I've lost before and since this day, and it feels as though I'm never going to stop.

Slowly, though, I calm down, until just an occasional shuddering sob judders through my body like an aftershock. And when I stop, Mum's still in front of me, kneeling now, holding me and waiting for me to be calm. And I'm so grateful.

"Thank you, Mum."

"Oh sweetheart. It's what I'm here for."

She sits on the chair next to me and leans over and cups her hands round mine, as though she can hold all the pain in there for me.

Neither of us speaks for a few minutes; we just sit in silence, letting the clock tick on, and the words that have filled the room settle, take their rightful place. Then Mum says: "I can't believe you blame yourself." I look at her and she smiles, apologetically. "It's true. How can you possibly think any of this is your fault?"

"I just feel like we've failed. Like I've failed. Me and Ed — well, you can see. It's all falling apart and that has to be my fault. Who else's is it?"

Mum pauses for a moment. "When things like this happen, Zoe, it's natural to let it be something that pulls you apart rather than something that holds you together. That's the only thing that's gone wrong here, but it doesn't mean you've failed."

She pauses, as if she wants to say something more but isn't sure whether to. Then she takes a deep breath. "Zoe, you know, nothing is ever as simple as it seems, and things always go wrong. But you can always get through them. Before you were born me and your dad — well, we had a few problems having you, let's just say. Back then there weren't so many treatments and

276

things you could do about it, but that doesn't mean it didn't take its toll on us as a couple. We fought, we bickered, and yes, it started to become bigger than us. The truth is, darling, we have no idea what would have happened to us if it had gone on any longer. But then, luckily for us, I fell pregnant and you came along, and me and your dad were OK again.

"But nobody's perfect, and nobody would expect you to be happy and sunny and the best wife in the world when you're going through so much. So you have to stop beating yourself up about it, and realize that what you and Ed are going through is perfectly normal and that you will, and can, get through it. I know you can. You love each other and that's all that matters."

"I can't believe you've never told me any of this before."

Mum shakes her head. "It didn't seem to matter, really — not until now. But I want you to realize that, well, that you and Ed have to sort things out and fight for you. Listen, even if you never end up having a baby — which I'm sure won't happen — you'll still have each other and you have to be stronger than me and your dad and make sure this doesn't ruin everything. It's too important."

I know she's right. But it doesn't mean I have the slightest idea what to do about it. How on earth do I even start getting back from here? Ed and I have hardly spoken for the last few months, and when we have it's been to argue or snap.

There's nothing I want more than to have the old us back, the us that loved each other unconditionally. It's up to me to work out how to get back there. I've got to keep giving it my best shot.

For the rest of the evening I feel like such a fraud. Mum's being so kind and even Dad isn't being as annoying as usual. I've opened up so much, it now feels wrong to hide from them the even bigger thing that's going on — that I'm reliving this for the second time, and that they're probably by my bedside in a hospital, waiting for me to wake up from a coma. If that's where I actually am.

But when I imagine saying the words I know I can't do it.

This might sound strange, Mum, but I've already lived this day once and I'm just reliving it again. I've relived lots of other days too. Oh, and by the way, Ed dies soon so I think I've come back to try and save him.

No. Those words can never leave my mouth, not to anyone.

Instead, over shepherd's pie and red wine, we talk about Becky and the kids.

"Have you seen them much recently?" Mum says. Then her mouth drops open in horror. "Oh God, sorry, love, I didn't mean —" She trails off, mortified. "Sorry, that was really insensitive."

"Don't be daft, Mum. It's fine. I do see them, but not as often as I should. But I am going to do something about that."

"Good. Might stop Becky moaning every time she rings about how she never sees you any more." Dad scoops another forkful of mashed potato into his mouth.

"John!"

"What?" Dad looks up, confused. "I was only saying."

"Why do you have to be so — so rude!"

I can't help smiling. "It's all right. I know what Dad means."

"See? I didn't mean anything by it. Zoe knows." He takes a slurp of red wine and carries on eating, oblivious.

"Sorry about your dad, love." Mum shoots him a look but he ignores her.

"It doesn't matter. Anyway, how are you?"

"Oh, you know, love, same as always. Your dad's driving me mad, always getting under my feet since he retired, but, you know. It's nice to have him about. Most of the time."

Dad grins and as the conversation returns to safer ground, Mum relaxes.

I try to as well but I'm struggling, because there's something on my mind that's niggling at me, like a stone in a shoe that just won't go away. I know I have to ring Ed before I go to bed, and I'm scared. I'm scared about what I'm going to say, and how to speak to him without crying. Because this could be the last day I get to relive, and he hasn't even been in it.

Finally, about 10.30, Mum stands, yawning. "Right, I'm off to bed. Do you want to use the home phone to ring Ed, love?"

"No, it's fine, thanks, Mum, I'll use my mobile."

"OK. Well, night then."

Dad stays where he is, drinking the dregs of his wine. "John."

He looks up at her sharp tone. "Oh, right. Night then, love." He drains the rest of the glass and puts it in the sink. "Good luck."

"Thanks, Dad."

And then they've gone and I'm left alone with my mobile and my thoughts. I listen to Mum and Dad's footsteps as they climb slowly up the stairs, then hear them pottering around, their voices subdued as they go about their night-time routine. The toilet flushes, the boiler fires as hot water runs, there's a clatter of a toothbrush being thrown into its holder, and then the floorboards creak a few more times. Then it's silent and I know I can't put it off any longer.

My heart starts thumping wildly in my chest and for a minute I think I can't do it.

Don't be ridiculous, this is Ed. Your Ed, the man you love, who you've known since you were eighteen. This is not a scary phone call.

I breathe deeply a few times then pick up the phone. I press the green button, put the phone to my ear and wait for it to ring.

"Zoe?" Ed's voice, so familiar, answers before the phone has even rung, and I'm taken by surprise. The sound of his voice makes me want to throw my arms around him and never let go. But he's 200 miles away and even further away from me emotionally.

I feel my voice catch in my throat as I answer him.

"Hi." My voice sounds small.

"Thank God. I didn't know whether to ring you but I was desperate to speak to you before I went to bed." His voice sounds sad, lonely.

"How — how are you?"

The line hums for a second before Ed answers.

"I'm . . . not great. Not great at all."

"Me neither."

Another pause.

"Zoe, I'm sorry for leaving like that this morning. I just didn't know what to say. I thought it might be too hard, seeing you before you left."

"I know. I just — I missed you."

"Yes. Me too." A pause. "I went to see Mum. She told me off."

"What for?"

"Being a dick and letting you leave. She didn't say dick, though, obviously."

"No." I smile at the thought of Susan talking to Ed like that. It was so unlikely. "And what did you say?"

"Well, I agreed with her, of course. I just — I'm not really sure how we ended up here."

Part of me wants to say it was his idea, but I know he doesn't mean that.

"I don't know. I really don't."

Ed lets out a rush of air and the sound buzzes in my ear. "God, this is horrible," he says, his voice cracking. "Have you — have you told your parents?"

"Yes. Well, I told Mum. I'm sure she'll be telling Dad even as we speak."

"God, they must hate me."

"Course they don't. They just want us to sort it out. For us. For me."

"Me too. We will, won't we, Zo?"

"Yes, we will. Trust me, this is only temporary." Another pause. "So what now?"

"I don't know. I suppose I ought to stay here a bit longer. I've got some work with me. If I come back now, won't we be back at square one again?"

"Yes, I suppose we will. But I think I already know what I want."

"Do you?"

"Yes. I don't want to lose you."

"Good. I don't want to lose you either."

"So — when will you come back? Next week?"

"Perhaps. Probably. Let's make the most of this time, really think about things. Let's make it worth the pain. And Ed?"

"Yes?"

"Don't forget to feed George."

"I won't. He's here now. He misses you."

"I miss him too."

Silence crackles down the phone again, and I wonder what Ed's thinking. Then he speaks.

"OK, sweetheart, let's get some sleep. Can I ring you tomorrow?"

"Yes, definitely."

"OK, night then."

"Night."

And then I end the call, and the screen goes black.

I wipe my face, and am surprised to find I've been crying. It feels awful hearing Ed so desolate and sad on the other end of the phone, and for a split second I consider taking the train home right now and throwing myself into his arms. But I'm too exhausted so instead I stand, take myself up the stairs, climb gratefully under the covers and slip off into sleep, hoping that when I wake up I'll see Ed again.

CHAPTER
SEVENTEEN

9 June 2012

They say that when you lose a sense, your other senses kick in stronger than before to compensate. Which could be why, before I even open my eyes, I know that someone is looking at me. It's not scary, but my heart is hammering anyway at the anticipation that it might be Ed again, and at the disappointment I know will flood through me if it turns out not to be. If it turns out that yesterday was my last second-chance day, and I'm back in the present.

I can hear a gentle, rhythmic breathing, but I can't tell whether it's mine or someone else's. There's also a tap, tap, tap sound, which stops every few beats and then starts again. A radiator? Footsteps outside, but no squeaks or loud voices or rumbling trolleys to indicate I'm in a hospital. In fact, I'm fairly sure I'm at home, at my flat, in my bed. The sounds are so familiar it's as though they're part of me.

I open my eyes and squint slightly in the bright sunshine streaming through the open blind. There's a silhouette which, as my eyes adjust to the light, slowly comes into focus.

"Ed!" I throw my arms around him and he falls backwards.

"Who did you expect to see in bed with you, Father Christmas?" he laughs. I laugh too with sheer relief. I've got another day with Ed, and this time it seems we don't hate each other. Thank God. I can only hope today will be a good day.

"Why were you staring at me like that?" I say, flopping my head back down on the pillow.

"I was just looking. I'm allowed; you are my wife." Ed grins. He seems overexcited, like a small puppy.

"What are you so happy about?"

A frown crosses his face briefly and he sticks out his bottom lip. "You mean you've already forgotten?" He pretends to sulk.

"Um, no. Forget? How could I forget?" Forget what? Come on, brain!

"Are you excited? It'll be so nice, after everything we've been through."

"Yes, it will." Oh God, this is excruciating.

"So are you going to show me what you're wearing now, then? It's not our actual wedding, you don't have to be so superstitious about it."

And then it dawns on me. It's 9 June 2012. The day we renewed our wedding vows.

Ed had suggested it after we'd had our time apart.

"It's been horrible, the last couple of years," he'd said. "I just want to show you, and everyone else, that we're as strong as ever. What do you think?"

"I think, Edward Williams, that you're the loveliest man in the world. And a soppy old git."

"Does that mean yes, then?"

"Yes."

"Brilliant. And not so much of the old next time, thanks."

Which was why, almost seven years after we'd married, we were renewing our vows in front of a few friends and family. It wasn't a huge affair, but it meant so much.

I can't believe that, by the time he died a year later, we were so far away from this moment again. But for now, I shake the thought from my head. I don't want to spoil it, not yet.

"Good point," I say. Then I stand and walk to the wardrobe where my little blue dress is hanging.

"Ta-da!" I hold it up for Ed to see and a smirk crosses his face.

"Nice. You going to model it for me, then?"

I shake my head. "Not yet. You'll have to wait."

"Oh, come on, get your kit off."

I swat him round the head.

"Oi, what was that for?!"

"Being a lecherous old perv."

He grins. "Fair enough."

Giggling, I lift a pillow high in the air and before he knows what's going on I smash it down on the top of his head. The look on his face as he falls sideways onto the bed makes me laugh out loud. Then before he can react I grab the other pillow and hold it like a shield in front of me.

"You little bugger." He picks up the first pillow from the floor and swipes it wildly round in front of him. But

I turn and run into the living room, giggling like a child. I can hear Ed hot on my heels and I throw myself onto the sofa, kicking my legs in the air like an overturned woodlouse, trying to block Ed's pillow smacks. "Get off!" I laugh, gasping for air, and finally, defeated and exhausted, he stops whacking me with the pillow. I sit up, out of breath, and suddenly I'm flat on my back again and Ed's pinning me down, my arms above my head. I can't move. I look at Ed's face and it's suddenly serious. He's watching me, a slight frown creasing his forehead.

"What's the matter?"

"I just can't believe I nearly let you go." Ed's voice is almost a whisper. "I love you so much, Zoe."

I pull my arm out from his grasp and stroke his cheek softly. "God, Ed, I love you too. I wish you knew how much." I stop for a minute and we stay like that, watching each other.

"Can we promise never to be apart again?" Ed's voice is pleading.

"You don't know how much I want that to happen, I don't think I could bear to be without you again." My voice cracks and he kisses me, then drops his head onto my chest. I breathe in the smell of his hair deeply, and the memory of his scent pulses through my body.

The moment's interrupted by a buzzing sound and Ed lifts his head.

"Sorry," he says, and reaches into his pocket for his mobile. He glances at the display and whispers "Mum," before standing and walking into the kitchen to answer the call.

I take a moment to watch him through the glass panel of the door. He nods every now and then, the muscles in his neck bulging with the movement. He's standing at the sink, looking out of the window at the houses and tiny gardens beyond, his phone pressed to his ear. Every now and then he grunts his agreement, but he doesn't seem to be having much of a say in whatever his mum is discussing. I walk towards him and slip my arms around his waist, press my cheek into his warm back and breathe deeply.

Now the excitement has passed I feel a knot of anxiety twisting inside me. I loved this day the first time round but this time I'm not sure how to do it. I can't imagine standing in front of all those people, the people who love me, and lying to them. Pretending I'm something that I'm not, pretending to believe that everything will be OK. I'm sure I'm going to give myself away.

The taxi's waiting outside and I'm running around the house like a headless chicken, trying to find my mobile, my lip gloss, and get my shoes on. Ed's ready, waiting impatiently by the front door.

"Two minutes," he shouts out of the door, holding up two fingers to the taxi driver. "Sorry."

"Sorry, Ed, I thought we had plenty of time. I just can't seem to find anything." Or remember where I put things more than a year ago. Nothing's quite where I expect it to be.

But finally, I'm ready. The day has clouded over a bit but it's still warm and I feel comfortable in my blue dress and heels. Ed looks gorgeous in his shirt, no tie, but cleanly shaven and hair tied back in a ponytail at the nape of his neck. I love his hair this length and I think of the photo of this day I've looked at endlessly since he died: us in these outfits, looking happy, and I have to blink back the tears.

I climb into the back of the cab and it sets off down the street. Ed clutches my hand and I relax back against the seat and stare out of the window, watching the world flash past. And before I know it we're there, at Islington Town Hall, and I'm climbing out of the cab and I see Jane holding a man's hand, and Becky and Greg with Gracie and Alfie and Mum and Dad, and Susan, and Rob.

Mum comes forward and hugs me, and then to my surprise so does Dad.

"Good luck, love," he says.

"Er, thanks, Dad." I look at Mum but she just shrugs, as confused as I am.

"Hey, gorgeous," Jane says, squeezing me then taking a drag on her cigarette.

"I thought you'd given up?" I indicate the fag hanging from her hand.

"I did. But then I gave up giving up." She grins. "I'm too weak, Zo, I just can't do it. Anyway —" she tugs the hand of the man she's standing with, and he falls forward awkwardly, pulling his tie straight — "doesn't Jamie scrub up well?"

"Oh!" I gasp. "It's Jamie, thirty-eight, from London!"

"Sorry?"

Jane shoots me an odd look and too late I realize my mistake. This is Jamie from the dating website, but of course the real me — not the impostor here right now — will know Jamie well. I laugh nervously.

"Sorry, it's just what I sometimes call you, to Ed. You know, after the dating website . . ." I trail off and squeeze Ed's hand, hoping for support, but he stares at me as though I've gone mad.

"Are you all right, Zoe?" Jane looks concerned. "Have you been drinking?"

"No, no, sorry, I'm just nervous. Don't know what I'm on about. Ignore me." I smooth my hands down the front of my skirt and turn to Becky, hoping my mistake will soon be forgotten. She's clutching Gracie and Alfie's hands.

"Aunty Zoe!" calls Gracie, and runs towards me, her ribboned plaits flying behind her. I bend down and open my arms and she runs right into them.

"Hello, pretty girl," I say, hugging her.

"You look really pretty too, Aunty Zoe," she says. "I like your dress. Do you like mine?" She twirls round.

"I think it's absolutely beautiful." She beams broadly. I look down to see Alfie clinging shyly to Becky's leg.

"Aren't you going to say hello to Aunty Zoe?" she says, bending down.

"Hello," he says, quietly.

I crouch down to his level. "Hey, sweetheart, you look very handsome today. Can I have a cuddle?"

He looks at Becky for approval, then steps forward and lets me envelop him. Feeling his little body in my arms, I can't help but feel a pang. I know he loves me,

290

but he's terribly shy and is always like this when we first see each other. I try not to take it personally.

When I stand up I see Ed being almost bowled over by Gracie. She adores her uncle Ed. He scoops her up and tips her upside down, the tulle layers of her dress flying everywhere, and she screams in delight. I smile at him, and he smiles back, the skin round his eyes crinkling softly as he brings Gracie back down to earth. I know he's imagining what it would be like if we had our own child, and I try not to think about it as Gracie shouts "Again!"

"No, come on, Gracie, leave Uncle Ed alone." Becky takes her daughter by the hand and leads her away, Gracie protesting all the way.

Ed walks towards me and holds out his hand. Everyone has filed into the hall and they're waiting for us to start.

"Ready?" he says.

"Couldn't be more ready." I grab his hand and clutch it tightly, and then we walk into the room to tell everyone how much we love each other.

Later, at the pub nearby, the atmosphere is happy. The kids are running around the tiny garden, and I sit with Ed, Becky, Greg, Mum, Dad and Jane sinking a bottle of wine. It's been a lovely day and I feel sad it's already coming to an end. It's starting to get chilly and I wrap Ed's jacket round my shoulders, and he looks at me and smiles.

"You OK?" he mouths, and I nod.

He looks happier than I've seen him in a long time, and certainly happier than the day he died, and it makes me want to freeze time and stay in this day forever. I'm trying not to think too much about the fact that time's running out, that we're nearly back at the day Ed died, but it's almost impossible to ignore, like an insistent fly buzzing round my head.

I sit back and listen to the chatter around me and watch the children playing. They're huddled round some Lego bricks and seem completely immersed in whatever game they've made up. I try to imagine what it would be like if Ed and I had a child here too, joining in the fun and playing with their friends, but I just can't seem to conjure up the image. I'm not sure I ever did truly believe I was going to become a mum, even the first time round.

I look away and back at the table. Dad's telling everyone a story about when I was a baby. I roll my eyes, pick up my glass and take a huge swig and try not to get cross. He's just having fun.

Soon it's time for the younger children to go to bed, so Becky and Greg start to make a move. I wonder, as they gather their things, whether this is the last time I'll see them again in this strange situation. Whether next time we meet I'll be living the day for the first time — without Ed. I'm not sure I can even bear to think about it, not today.

"Right sweetheart, we're off," Becky says, leaning in to hug me with one arm, holding Alfie in the other. Her eyes twinkle with affection and drunkenness. "Thanks for a lovely day. I'm glad you're happy." She hugs me again, stumbling as she bends to pick up her bag.

"Oops, maybe Greg should take Alfie." She giggles as she hands him over, and shrugs her bag back onto her shoulder.

"Bye, Becky, have a safe journey home," I grin. "Ring me tomorrow?"

She gives the thumbs up and as they walk away Gracie yells, "Bye, Aunty Zoe," her arms waving like a windmill as they move through the pub and towards the door. I blow a kiss and she pretends to catch it and rubs it in her hair, and then they're gone.

I turn to the others.

"Right, another round?" I indicate their empty glasses.

Dad stands unsteadily. "I'll get these," he says. "Same again?" He sweeps his arm over the table.

"White wine, please," I say, lifting my glass up.

"Me too." Mum.

"Red wine, please." Ed.

"Anything wet." Jane, sniggering.

"Bottle of red and a bottle of white it is, then," Dad says, and makes his way through the thickening crowd towards the bar. It's getting louder in here and we're having almost to shout to make ourselves heard, but despite the terror I feel at knowing I'll soon be without Ed, I'm actually having fun. I've missed my friends and family.

Finally, Dad returns from the bar. He's carrying two bottles of wine, and behind him a barman carries a tray holding champagne glasses and a silver bucket with a bottle resting in it.

"It wouldn't be a proper celebration without a bottle of champagne, would it?" he says with a grin, setting the wine on the table. The barman carefully puts the tray down and Dad picks up the champagne bottle and starts to open it. The cork comes out with a huge pop and flies into the air, hitting the ceiling and narrowly missing a blonde woman standing nearby.

"Oops," Dad says, and gives the woman a wink. "Sorry."

"No worries," she says, and turns away. Dad pours the champagne sloppily into the waiting glasses, spilling more than he serves. It froths over the top and spreads across the wooden table top and he laughs.

"Dad, shall I do it?"

"Er, that might be a good idea." He hands the bottle over and I pick up each glass, pouring the wine at an angle into each one.

"Get a lot of practice pouring champagne, do you?" Dad says, watching me intently.

"Yeah. Every night." I grin and hand Dad a glass. "That's what us London types do."

"Course," he says, wrapping a fist round the stem of the glass.

When everyone has one, Dad raises his voice. "Right, I want to say something." We all look at him, and for the first time this evening he looks serious.

"I'm not one for speeches, as you know," he says. "But I just wanted to say that Zoe, Ed —" he raises his glass to each of us in turn — "we're so glad you've sorted everything out, me and your mum. We hated seeing you so sad." He pauses, looks at his glass for a moment. "And anyway, we were glad to get rid of her, she was making a right mess of the place."

Everyone laughs, and Dad raises his glass. "To Zoe and Ed. Cheers."

"Cheers!" everyone yells, and we chink glasses and drink the bubbles. Tears well in my eyes and I feel stupid. Because I know that this happiness can't last much longer. I know that, whatever happens, something is about to change.

I just wish I knew what.

Back at home later that evening, my head's spinning from the excitement and the champagne. Mum and Dad are staying the night in our tiny spare bedroom, and I can hear Mum crashing about in the bathroom. Soft snores come from the bedroom and when I poke my head round Dad's already fast asleep, taking up most of the sofa bed.

I stumble into the kitchen and fill a glass with water, and down the whole lot. I'm just refilling it when I feel Ed's arms wrap round me.

"Oh!" I jump and nearly spill the water all over the floor. "You scared me!"

"Why, who did you think I was?" he says, nuzzling into my neck.

"Mmm, that feels nice."

He plants soft kisses down my neck and along my shoulder, and my whole body tingles.

"Ed, not here." It takes all my willpower to say it. "Mum and Dad are in there."

I turn to face him and he carries on, moving his lips softly down towards my right breast. I groan, overcome with desire.

I hardly have time to think about it, but the decision is almost instant anyway. Last time, I'd pushed him away, worried Mum and Dad would walk in on us. This time, I don't care. I want him and this might be my last chance to feel his body against mine, to hold him and know he loves me. So I cup my hands around his face and kiss him deeply, then grab his hand and walk quickly towards our bedroom, shutting the door firmly behind us. His lips are instantly on me again, on my neck, my breast, down towards my stomach, and my whole body is filled with desire. I grab him tightly, pull him so close he's almost part of me, and we fall onto the bed as one. And then I let go, and give in to him entirely, as though this is the last thing I'll ever do.

I want this night to go on forever, terrified that when I wake up, it will all be over. But finally, we're done. We lie for a moment, staring at each other. Then, at last, I feel ready to let go. I lean towards him and whisper, "I love you. Please never leave me."

But his eyes are already closed, and he hasn't heard me.

There's nothing else to do but sleep.

CHAPTER
EIGHTEEN

25 December 2012

Usually, the sound of Christmas music — even Cliff Richard singing "Mistletoe and Wine" — makes me feel happy. I love Christmas, and everything about it.

But when I wake up this morning and hear Ed singing along to the Christmas CD, I feel sick. It's nearly time. In six months' time, Ed will be dead.

I swallow and try to push the thought from my head, and instead think back to the things I've tried to change. I've tried to be kinder; I've tried to stop arguments; I've tried to confront problems, see people more, talk about the future; I've even had completely new experiences. But in the end, in the grand scheme of things, it doesn't seem as though anything has changed much at all.

Here we are still, for instance, on the Christmas before Ed died, and I can only assume he's as cross with me as he was the first time round. It had been awful.

Susan had been there; so had Mum and Dad, and Becky, Greg and the kids. The flat was too small for us all really, but we'd wanted to do it, so we'd squeezed everyone in.

Ed and I had tried another round of IVF but there was still no sign of a baby, and we just didn't seem capable of saying anything nice to each other. I'd been starting to wonder whether we should even be together any more. We'd sniped and snarked at each other all day, which meant that nobody had had fun, everyone chewing their roast potatoes in a strained silence. I shiver at the memory.

This time, I'm going to make sure things are different. Even if it doesn't change anything in the end, I can at least make today happy. And I can also have hope.

I climb out of bed, grab my dressing gown from the back of the door and walk down the hallway to the kitchen. Ed's dressed and is wearing the jumper I bought him with the snowman on the front, and my heart leaps at the sight of him. I sneak up behind him.

"Boo!" I yell, tweaking his sides as I jump up on him.

"Argh!" He drops the knife he's holding and it clatters to the floor, narrowly missing his foot. "Jesus Christ, what are you trying to do, kill me?"

I was right. He's furious with me. Instead of reacting, I take a deep breath, determined not to cause a fight.

"Sorry, sweetheart, I didn't realize you had a knife in your hand." I bend down and pick it up, then place it back on the worktop. I put my hands on his waist and peer round him, trying to see what he's up to.

"What's that? Something for me?"

His face still looks like thunder.

"Come on, show me." Silently, he moves across to let me see, his body stiff with rage. There on the worktop are some peeled potatoes and a pan of water.

"Aw, thanks, Eddie, you've started making dinner." I reach up and put my arms round his neck. "Come on, let's not be cross with each other. Give me a smile."

Finally unable to resist the onslaught of niceness, the corner of his mouth twitches and curls briefly upwards.

"Come on . . ." I tickle the back of his neck with my fingertips. "Let's try and make this a lovely day. Even if it's just one out of hundreds of awful days, let's try and be nice today. What do you say?"

He stands there, stiff as a board, watching me.

"Yeah, OK," he mumbles, and turns back to the worktop and picks up the knife to start peeling potatoes again. It's a small breakthrough, but it's a start.

I move into the lounge and switch the Christmas tree lights on, listening to Ed humming along to "Rockin' Around the Christmas Tree".

I shower and get dressed and when I come back through Ed is on the sofa, an open box of Cadbury Roses next to him, a pile of discarded wrappers on his other side. He looks up at me and his face softens.

"Fancy one?" He hands me a yellow toffee.

"Yeah, but not that." I lean over and snatch a purple one from the pile in his lap.

"Hey, that's my favourite!"

"Hoo hate, mine hoo," I say through a mouthful of chocolate.

"Meanie." He grabs a nut whirl and pops the whole thing in his mouth, and for a couple of minutes neither of us can speak. I think maybe that's for the best anyway. We don't want or need to spend today agonizing over what's gone wrong. We need to enjoy it for what it is.

Ed stands and walks to the fridge. "Do you want some Buck's Fizz?" He holds up a bottle of champagne and a carton of orange juice.

"Please."

Ed hands me a glass and holds his up to me. "To us. You're right. Let's make this Christmas special."

My shoulders sag with relief as we clink glasses and the cool liquid bubbles slide down my throat. "God, that's delicious."

"Hmm."

We sit quietly for a few minutes, listening to cheesy Christmas tunes and watching the lights twinkle on the tree. My heart is heavy with the knowledge of what's to come, but at the same time I can't help feeling a sense of contentment that, even if I have failed to change the future, at least I have this memory now, rather than one of shouting and hate.

My thoughts are interrupted by the shrill tone of the doorbell. Ed leaps up.

"Right, party time."

I smile weakly. But I don't have time to dwell as moments later Becky, Greg and the kids are bursting into the room.

"Merry Christmas, Aunty Zoe!" Gracie flings herself at my legs and I lift her in the air and she giggles wildly.

"Happy Christmas, sweetheart."

"Aunty Zoe, guess what? Father Christmas has been and he brought me loads and loads of things. I did get a new doll's house and some Playmobil with a swimming pool what you can put water in and everything, and he did bring me a new bike and a helmet and a bell to put on the front which is all pink and sparkly and shiny."

She pauses for breath and I laugh. "Blimey, it sounds as though Father Christmas has been very generous this year."

Becky meets my eyes over the top of Gracie's head and rolls her own skyward. "You have no idea."

The doorbell rings again and before we know it the place is full, with Mum and Dad and Susan all piled into our too-small living room, squashed onto sofas, spread out on the floor and filling every available space. And it's bliss. It's helped take away the anxiety, having everyone here and feeling happy, and as I look around the room at all the people I love, I'm glad they don't know what's to come. I'm glad they can have this moment of happiness to hold in their hearts forever.

And I can't help thinking, in a small corner of my mind, that maybe, just maybe, the fact that this day has turned out differently means there's still a small chance that things might turn out differently in the end.

"Merry Christmas," Ed says, and raises his glass in the air.

"Merry Christmas," everyone choruses back.

"Cheers!" Gracie shouts, and everyone laughs. Christmas Day has begun.

It's dark outside and Ed and I are lying in bed, watching the moon through the open curtains. His breathing has slowed and I know he'll be asleep soon. But I'm not ready to leave him yet and I'm trying to stay awake, to stay with him a few moments longer. My mind drifts back to earlier that day, just after we finished eating dinner. Ed had taken his last mouthful of Christmas pudding, then sat back, rubbing his belly and puffing his cheeks out. "Well, that's that for another year then," he said, suppressing a burp. "I'm bloody stuffed."

"Ed, don't swear in front of the kids," Susan hissed, nodding at Gracie and Alfie.

"Oh, don't worry, they hear much worse from Greg, believe me," Becky said, giving her husband a wry smile. Greg had shrugged. "Yep, total potty mouth, that's me."

But I was hardly listening, because Ed's words were echoing around my head. *That's that for another year*.

Even now I can't stop thinking about those words, and my heart aches for him, for me, for the future that we might not have. For the fact that, if nothing changes, this will be the last Christmas he ever has.

The room spins and I hold my head in my hands and groan.

"What's the matter?" Ed's stirred and is looking at me, a frown on his face, and I realize I have tears in my eyes. I wipe them away with the back of my hand and shake my head.

"Nothing, nothing. Sorry. Just the stress of the last few weeks. I'm just so glad you're here and . . ." My voice catches in my throat and I stop. "I just love you, that's all."

"Hey, I know you do, sweetheart. But it's all right, we're all right, aren't we? For today, anyway?"

"Yes. Yes, we are. At least we have today."

Ed frowns and I look away, unable to explain what I mean and hoping he doesn't ask. And then he drifts off and I watch as sleep takes him away from me again. And as I let my eyes close, as I finally give in to the darkness, I pray that I get to see him again, just one last time.

CHAPTER
NINETEEN

19 June 2013

It's the day.

The second I wake up this morning and see where I am, I just know. Today is the day Ed is going to die. It's also the day I might lose him for a second time if I don't try and do something about it.

My heart seems to stop at the thought of the massive responsibility ahead of me, and I think I'm going to throw up. I've been lucky, I know, seeing Ed again, having the chance to see him, hold him, be with him, talk to him. But the thought of him dying has been hanging over me the whole time, like a huge black rain cloud. What if I haven't done enough to save him? What if I can't do it today?

What if I've failed him?

I lie still and try to steady my breathing, but it keeps coming in short, ragged bursts. Beside me Ed continues to sleep peacefully and I prop myself up on my elbow to look at him properly. He's lying facing me; his long lashes are stretched across his cheeks, his skin is deeply tanned, his chin sprinkled with stubble. His mouth is slightly open and he whistles lightly on each out-breath. It's hard to believe he has no idea what today is going to bring; and yet how could he?

Ed stirs and I gently press my mouth to his. His breath smells stale but I don't care. I need to touch him, to be close to him. He opens one eye and looks at me blearily.

"Huh? What time is it?" His voice is still thick with sleep.

I glance at the clock. "6.30."

"Hnggg. Why am I being woken up?" He rolls onto his back and closes his eyes again, his arm slung above his head.

I shuffle my body closer to him and snuggle into the crook of his arm, leaning my head on his chest. I stretch my other arm across his belly. His skin feels warm and the familiar scent is a mixture of shower gel, washing powder and sleep. A sudden memory flashes into my mind, piercing it like a lightning bolt of pain: me, lying on this bed after Ed had died. Instead of Ed wrapped in my arms I held the pillow he has his head on right now. I'd lain there for hours, still, numb; in too much pain even for any tears to come, and pressed my face further into the pillow, trying to breathe in this very smell, the faint, lingering smell of Ed on the pillowcase.

I push my face further into his chest.

"Ow, Zoe, get off, you're hurting me." He pulls away and rubs his chest.

"Sorry. I just wanted a cuddle."

"You can have a cuddle when I'm awake. Let me sleep, I'm knackered."

Reluctantly I pull away, and slip out from under the covers. I don't want to cause a fight today. Forget what's come before, I want today to be perfect. I want Ed to know how much I love him, whatever happens.

I move into the kitchen and pull open the cupboards mindlessly. My heart feels heavy at the thought of the day ahead. I want to enjoy this time with Ed but all I can think about is the moment he left the house last time. That moment, when he strapped on his cycling helmet and pedalled off into the traffic; that's the thing I need to change today. I need to stop Ed leaving for work on his bike, whatever it takes. And I mustn't be angry with him.

Decision made, I start pulling together breakfast. Toast and tea in bed is a good start to the day. I scrape butter and jam onto toast, pour tea and milk into mugs and assemble them on a tray from the back of the cupboard. Then I glance out of the window and see Ed's beloved garden. I open the back door and pad outside in my pyjamas and pick a rose from the pot on the patio; back in the kitchen I stick it in a glass of water and add it to the tray. Better.

I pick up the tray and head back to the bedroom. It's 7 a.m. now; Ed should be getting up soon anyway. I can't wait any longer. I place the tray on the duvet and sit next to it, leaning over to kiss Ed's exposed neck. He jumps and his eyes snap open as he rolls over to look at me.

"Have I overslept?" He rubs his eyes and peers at the clock.

"No, it's OK. It's still early. I just brought you this."

306

He glances at the tray on the bed and then back at me. "What's this for?"

I shrug. "I don't know. I just thought it would be nice to have breakfast in bed together."

"Oh, right. Thanks." He looks at me quizzically, and who can blame him? We don't really like each other right now. "I'll have to be quick, though, I've got to get to work."

"I know." I climb under the duvet and wait while Ed shifts into a sitting position, then place the tray across our knees. It wobbles slightly and the mugs slide towards Ed.

He grabs them. "Careful, you'll spill it."

I take my tea from him and take a sip. Then I put it down on the side and take a bite of toast. We sit in silence for a few minutes, chewing and drinking. I can see some of the garden from here and a tiny patch of sky above the house behind. It's bright blue, just a few wispy clouds, hardly enough to bother the already hot sun. The sunflowers Ed planted a few weeks ago are starting to poke their heads above the windowsill, swaying in a very gentle breeze. I sigh.

"Big sigh. Everything OK?"

If only he knew. "Yes, fine. I was just thinking."

"Careful."

"Ha ha." I pause, unsure how to say it. "It would be nice if we didn't have to go to work today."

"Yeah, it would. It looks like it's going to be boiling." He squints out of the window.

"We could always stay here."

"What do you mean? We've both got work."

I turn to face him. "I know, but — don't you think it would be nice to have a naughty day off? Call in sick and spend the day here, in bed, in the garden, just — being together. We haven't done enough of it recently."

I'm trying not to let the desperation show in my voice but I'm aware of my words speeding up, running away with me, the tone rising gradually. Ed's noticed it too and gives me a strange look.

"We can't just take the day off. I'm in the middle of a huge job and I've told you what a total pain the guy's being about his decking. If we don't finish it today we'll be out on our ears. And you — well, Zoe, you just don't skive. It's not in your nature. First breakfast in bed and now this. What's come over you this morning?"

I just need to keep you here, safe, with me, and not let you go anywhere, not until today is over, because then I'll know you're alive and you haven't left me. These are the words I long to say. Instead, I say, "I just want to be with you, Ed. That's all. I'm tired and I need a rest and I want you to stay here with me. Please?"

He looks at me for a minute, and lifts my chin gently with his finger so I have to force my neck into an uncomfortable position.

"You know we can't do that, right?"

"But why not?" My voice has become whiny and I stop. "It's no big deal. Other people do it all the time."

"Yes, but not us. At least, not you."

"I am today."

"No, Zoe. Sorry, but I need to get going. I'm going to be late as it is."

308

I watch desperately as he places his mug deliberately on the floor, moves the tray to one side and swings his legs out of the bed. He leans over, gives me a peck on the nose and stands and stalks off to the bathroom. It's clear the conversation has finished. I wish I was strong enough to grab him, pin him to the bed and hold him captive all morning. But I'll need to think of something else.

I clear the dirty cups and plates away and walk into the bathroom where Ed's taking a shower. The shower screen is clouded over and all I can make out is the blurry outline of his naked body. I pop my head round and watch him for a few seconds before he notices me.

"Oi, get out!" He sprays me with water and I pull my head away and wipe soapy water from my eyes.

"Can't I come in with you?"

The water stops and Ed's head appears round the screen. "I'm done, it's all yours. Seriously, what is wrong with you today?" He steps out of the shower shaking his head, and wraps a towel round his waist. My heart races at the sight of his naked body.

"Thanks."

As I stand under the cool water I let it pound my face and head, run down my neck and body, cooling me down. Ed seems to be resisting every effort I make to keep him here, and now he thinks I'm being weird. I don't know what to do.

I step out of the shower and drip water slowly onto the mat, shivering in the cool air of the bathroom. Wrapping a towel round me, I walk back to the bedroom where Ed is already dressed in shorts and a

T-shirt. His damp hair is tousled; I step towards him until we're just an inch apart and run my fingers through it and drop my towel onto the floor, pressing myself against him. I can feel his body stiffen and he takes a quick in-breath of air as I plant my lips full on his. I can feel his resistance; he's trying to pull away before it's too late, but I can't let him leave so I lift my leg and wrap it round him and pull his face to mine to deepen the kiss. He responds and his body relaxes; then his arms are round my waist, his fingertips caressing my back, and I arch in pleasure. I bring my hand round and start unbuckling his belt and then he stops and pulls back.

"Zoe, stop. I haven't got time for this."

I ignore him and kiss him again, but he's stronger than me and pushes me away, his hands firm on my upper arms.

"Zoe, stop, please. I have to go. I can't do this, not now. God, you pick your moments, don't you?"

"Oh, come on, Ed, it's been months. I know you want me; please come to bed with me."

"No, Zoe, I can't. I don't know what's happened to you today, but I have to get to work and so do you."

"But I love you, Ed."

He gives me a strange look. "I know, but — Look, I'd love to spend the day with you and know that it could change the way things have been between us recently, or make things better. But it won't and, well, I've got work to do, and so have you. We'll work things out, Zo, we will, just not right now."

310

"We have to." The words are out before I can think about them.

He frowns. "What?"

"Well, why not today, why not right now? Why can't today be the day we change things between us forever? Why can't you just admit it's worth a go and trust me that this is the day we need so we can be happy together for the rest of our lives? I . . ." I pause, aware from the puzzled expression on Ed's face that he has no idea what I'm talking about and that I've already started to say too much. "I just don't see why we can't do it today, that's all." I shrug and sit down on the bed, deflated. Ed stays standing, watching me.

"But why does it have to be today, of all days?" He sits next to me, his body angled slightly towards mine. "Zoe, what is going on here? Is there something I should know?"

I long to tell him; I imagine telling him I've been living my life again, that I've been trying to change things to try and stop him dying; that this is the day he died and that I need to stop him going anywhere, to keep him safe. To save him.

But there's no way to explain it.

As he waits for me to answer all I can see is Ed's furious face as he stormed out of the house last time on this day. The last time I'd seen him he was angry with me and we'd almost hated each other. I can't let that happen again.

"No, there's nothing you should know. I just —" I pause. "I just don't want us to be like this any more. I want us to love each other again, the way we used to."

311

He sits and watches me for a minute, then takes my hand. "Zoe, I do love you. I always have and always will. But this isn't the time to try and sort out everything that's gone wrong between us. I promise I do want to, of course I do, and we can. But right this minute we're both very busy at work and there's a weekend coming up and we could spend a day together then when we don't have anything else on, instead of today, when we both have to get to work." He takes a breath and sighs. "I just don't see the urgency, to be honest. Let's face it, it's been going on so long now, I don't see what difference a couple of days is going to make."

"But it might. I dunno, I just have a feeling that today needs to be the day." I don't expect him to listen — why would he? I wouldn't. But it's worth one last shot.

Ed shakes his head. "I'm sorry, Zoe. I've got to get to work. But listen, why don't we both come home early and have a special evening — nice meal, candles, the works? I'll even cook . . ."

"OK," I say reluctantly.

"Great."

He turns his back and my heart sinks to the floor. Nothing seems to be working. As he walks out of the room I wrack my brains trying to think of another way to stop him getting on that bloody bike and leaving me.

And then it hits me.

I listen carefully as Ed clatters round the kitchen making another cup of coffee. I pick up my bag off the floor and rummage around until I find what I'm looking for. Then, quietly, I creep from our bedroom and down the hallway to the front door. I open it, hoping it doesn't squeak. It doesn't, and I let out a rush of breath I hadn't even realized I was holding. I turn to the left and there's Ed's bike, chained up to the fence between us and next door. The street is unusually quiet and I work quickly before anyone comes: I crouch down, lift my arm up high, then plunge it down quickly until the sharp nail file pierces the rubber of the tyre and I can hear the gentle hiss of air. I do the same to the other one, my heart hammering, sure I'm about to get caught. I make sure enough air has left them so he sees they're flat, then stand and creep back into the house, closing the door silently behind me.

He won't listen to me. But that will stop him.

Ed's head pokes round the bathroom door. "Zoe? Was that someone at the door?"

Heat flushes my face but I shake my head. "No, I didn't hear anything."

He shrugs. "OK."

He walks towards me. He's cleaning his teeth now; there's toothpaste dripping from his mouth and I watch as it slowly falls from his chin onto the wooden floor.

We both stare at the patch of white paste by his feet. I can't help remembering how angry this made me last time and now I have no idea why: I don't even feel like the same person any more.

"Whoops." Ed grins as more toothpaste sprays from his lips into the air. A few spots hit my face and I wipe them away.

"You're gross."

"Sorry." He walks into the kitchen, grabs a handful of kitchen towel and mops the toothpaste from the floor. As he does, a drop of white paste falls from his mouth onto his shorts.

"Go and spit your toothpaste out before you drop it anywhere else, you messy bugger," I say, pushing him towards the bathroom, laughing.

Ed trots off looking sheepish.

I put on a show of packing my bag, of brushing my hair, applying some make-up. But I'm waiting for Ed, to make sure he doesn't leave. At least, not on his bike.

"Right, I'm off." He gives me a peck on the cheek. He smells of mint, and there's still a tiny smudge in the corner of his lip. I wipe it gently with my thumb.

"OK, love, see you later."

He straps on his helmet, shrugs his rucksack onto his back and steps out of the front door, shutting it loudly behind him. I stand, holding my breath, waiting. I don't have to wait long. A few seconds later I hear his key scrape in the lock and Ed walks back in, muttering to himself.

"Some little bastard has let the air out of my tyres."

"Oh no, that's terrible. What are you going to do?"

"I don't know. Get the Tube, I guess. But it's a right ballache, all the way down to South Norwood. Little shits."

He's really cross but I don't care. I had no choice.

"I could give you a lift if you like?"

"A lift? Aren't you meant to be at work?"

"Yeah, but — well, it would make it easier, wouldn't it?"

314

"Not for you."

"No. But. Go on, let me take you. I fancy a drive; I haven't driven for ages."

Ed looks at me for a minute, unsure. Then he nods. "OK, if you really want to. That would be great, thanks."

"I'll just get my keys."

My heart's hammering as we climb into my battered old Beetle, the car I bought months ago but rarely got the chance to drive. I've done it, I've stopped him getting on his bike! I can hardly believe it worked.

I wind down the windows and get the fans blowing but it's pretty ineffectual against the already intense heat of the day. We drive in silence for a while. I feel so elated that he's no longer on the journey that took him away from me that I don't know what I could possibly say anyway.

We crawl through the north London traffic, the heat in the car building at each set of traffic lights, each set of roadworks. But I don't care. I'm here, with Ed, and he's alive. I feel as though I'm floating.

"What are you grinning about?"

"Oh, nothing. Just — well, it's a lovely day, isn't it?"

"Yes. Lovely." Ed gives me a quizzical look, then turns and stares out of the window some more.

It takes more than an hour to do the fifteen-mile journey with the odd shouted direction from Ed, but finally we're there. "This is it, just here on the right." Ed points at a white truck that's already parked half on the pavement and I squeeze into a space behind it and switch off the engine.

"Thanks for the lift. Hope you're not too late for work."

"You're still coming home early though, aren't you?" My voice wavers at the thought of leaving him here.

"Yes, I'll get out somehow. I'll get the train home, though, OK?"

I nod. I can feel tears building and I don't want Ed to see them. "OK."

"See you later, then." And he's out of the car and walking up the garden path. He's gone.

The tears are falling down my cheeks now but I need to get away so I pull out into the road. A horn blares loudly and there's a screech of brakes, then a car pulls past, its driver shouting through the open window.

"Sorry," I say, weakly, holding my hand up.

I drive home, hardly noticing the traffic, the people, the heat. I park the car back outside the house, grab my bag from the passenger seat and walk to the Tube station.

And standing on the Tube on the way to work that sticky June morning, I stare mindlessly at the adverts above people's heads as I swing to the rhythm of the train.

I can only hope I've done enough to stop Ed dying.

When I get to my desk — two hours late — my boss, Olive, is waiting for me. She taps her watch and points to the meeting room on the other side of the open-plan office. "Zoe, you're needed," she says. "Sorry," I mumble, throwing her a half-smile and grabbing a notebook and biro and practically running across the room.

316

Finally, the meeting's over. I haven't heard a word; all I can think about is last time I sat through this meeting, and what happened afterwards. The police officers, the silence, the hospital . . .

I race to the kitchen and switch the kettle on, staring out of the window at the street several storeys below as I wait for it to boil. I watch people scuttling about in the heat of the day and I think about Ed, outside in the sunshine on the other side of the city, working up a sweat, and thinking about leaving work early to come and see me.

Hopefully.

The kettle boils and snaps off and I splash the steaming water into the cup of instant coffee powder. I give it a perfunctory stir, tap the teaspoon on the edge of the cup and turn to walk back into the office. But when I get back to my desk I stop. Olive is standing there, her face serious, and my heart crashes to the floor.

Oh God, it's happening all over again.

"Nooo," I groan, sinking to my knees, hot coffee splashing all over the worn carpet. I can't hear anything, I can't think about anything else and, even though I knew this day had to come, I realize that there was always a part of me that had a spark of hope.

Now that spark has gone out.

Through the white noise rushing in my ears I hear Olive's voice, coming to me as though from miles away.

"Zoe, Zoe, what's the matter?"

She's shaking my shoulder roughly and I lift my head to look at her. She's frowning, her face filled with concern, but I can't speak. I don't want to hear the words she has to say.

"Don't," I whisper, holding my hands over my ears.

"Zoe," she says, more urgently this time. "Are you ill? What's happened?"

I say nothing. But as I crouch in the middle of the floor, Olive's words start to seep into my consciousness and I look up again. She keeps asking me if I'm ill, over and over again. And if — I hardly dare think this — but *if* she doesn't have the news for me that I think she does, then my behaviour would make it look as though I were ill.

I stop sobbing and take my hands from my ears and for the first time I properly listen to her words.

"Zoe, come with me," she says, slowly pulling me to my feet again. She guides me to the meeting room I've just come from and closes the door firmly behind her.

"Sit down," she says, gesturing to the chair next to her, taking one herself. "Please."

I pull the chair out and perch nervously on the edge of it. My hands have started to shake and I try to hold them still in my lap.

"Zoe," she says, her voice serious. I hold my breath, waiting for her next words. But the expected words don't come.

"I'm worried about you. What on earth was all that about? You looked as though you'd seen a ghost and then you just collapsed."

I look down at my hands. What can I say? That I thought she was going to tell me Ed was dead because that's what happened last time, and I couldn't bear to hear her say the words? Of course not. So instead I just shrug.

A gentle knock on the door breaks the silence and someone pops their head round it. I don't see who it is but Olive shakes her head almost imperceptibly and the door shuts again, leaving us in silence. It's my turn to speak.

"I . . ." I stammer, unsure what to say. "I'm OK, honestly. I'm really sorry about that, I just . . . I don't know, you looked as though you had bad news." It sounds lame but it's the best I can do. Olive frowns.

"Far from it," she says.

I look at her, surprised.

"I was actually coming to tell you something really exciting," she continues. For the first time I notice she has a pink folder in her hands, the one I handed in a few days before with ideas for a pitch. I watch as she gently places the folder on the table and opens it.

"It's about this." I wait expectantly. "The client loves it and they want to use your ideas — which means you'll be heading up the campaign."

She's watching me, waiting for a response. I know I should be thrilled that this has been successful; I've worked hard on it, been working late most nights to get it right. I should be dancing round the office. But the only thing I'm really interested in hearing is that Ed is OK; that he's still alive, and that I've saved him. By comparison, this seems unimportant and irrelevant.

"Oh, that's great!" I say, painting a smile on my face. Olive frowns.

"You don't seem quite as excited as I thought you'd be. Are you absolutely sure everything's OK?"

I nod. "Really, I'm fine. Everything's fine. I just had a funny five minutes, that's all. Bloody hormones." I attempt another smile but it falls flat.

"Okaaay." Olive's not convinced but she leaves it for now and I'm relieved. Instead she turns back to the folder.

"Obviously we'll need to talk it through in some detail, but basically they love your idea and want to run with it with almost immediate effect. Will that be OK with — you know, everything?"

I've had so much time off for treatment I've had to tell her some of what's been going on, and I nod, grateful for her concern.

"Yes, no problem."

"Great. Well, let's get together first thing tomorrow and go over the details. How does that sound?"

"Perfect."

Olive stands, shuffles the papers back into the folder and walks to the door. As she leaves she turns. "Zoe? Take care of yourself, promise?"

I nod, trying not to cry. "I will." It comes out as a whisper and I cough to cover it.

The door closes behind her and I sit there for a few minutes, part of me desperately wanting to ring Ed and find out if he's OK, the other part of me not wanting to know, and to stay in this moment, where, as far as I know, he's alive and safe.

I take a deep breath and walk out of the room and across the office back to my desk, ignoring the curious

320

looks shooting my way. I check my mobile but there are no messages. I don't know whether this is good or bad. I compose a message to Ed but don't send it. Waiting for him to reply would be worse than not having sent the message at all.

Suddenly Olive is at my shoulder again and my heart lurches. I'm not sure how much more of this I can take today. She crouches down.

"I think you should take the rest of the day off. You've been working so hard recently, and things are going to get even more hectic. I think you just need a rest. Go on, go home."

I don't need to be told twice. I stand, shove my phone in my bag and grab my cardigan from the back of the chair.

"Thanks, Olive." I kiss her on the cheek and she blushes.

"Just make sure you do rest and come in bright and early and ready to go tomorrow morning," she says, smiling.

"Will do, promise."

I almost race out of the office, retracing my steps towards home. On the Tube I think about the horror I felt when I saw Olive standing there, and my skin prickles. I can't let it happen again. I just can't.

I exit the Tube station and hurry along the road to our flat. The pavements are hot and sticky and the sun beats down on my head, making me sweat. I grab my hair in a handful and shove it roughly into a ponytail and the air on the back of my neck feels like a sweet relief. At this time of day, just before lunch on a

Wednesday, it's peaceful here, and I savour the moment, listening to the rumble of cars and the flap, flap, flap of my sandals as I walk.

Suddenly the silence is shattered by a loud ringing and it takes me a few seconds to realize it's my phone. I dip my hand into my bag to find it and squint at the display.

"Ed!"

"Hey," he says, and I have to sit on a wall to stop myself falling over with relief.

"Where are you?"

"I'm at work, but I'm just ringing to say I can get off early and I'll be leaving in about an hour — so we'll have all afternoon together."

"Brilliant."

"When can you get off?"

"I'm nearly home. I got some good news about work and Olive gave me the rest of the day off."

"Great. Tell me all about it when I get home. See you soon, OK?"

"OK. And Ed?"

"Yes?"

"How are you getting home?"

"Train, I suppose. The buses are rubbish from here."

"I'll come and get you." The words are out before I've really even given them any thought, but I know as soon as I've said them that it's the right thing to do; if I have to drive across London in the blistering heat to keep Ed safe, then that's what I'll do.

"What? Don't be silly, it'll be quicker on the train."

"Maybe, but let me. I want to. Please?"

322

"Well, OK, then." I can hear the uncertainty in his voice but I don't care if he thinks I've gone mad.

"I'll be there as soon as I can. And Ed?"

"Yes?"

"I love you more than anything."

"I love you too. See you soon."

The phone goes dead and I stand and hurry home to get the car. By the time I climb in I'm sweaty and out of breath but I don't care. I just need to get there, and bring him home. I could tell from Ed's voice that he was wondering what was wrong with me today, that he didn't have a clue why it was so important to me to come and get him. But it doesn't matter. All that matters is keeping him safe. And who knows, maybe one day, if I can get him through this day alive, I'll be able to explain some of this to him. But for now, he's just going to have to trust me.

The traffic's heavy and it's almost ninety minutes later that I pull up outside the house where I dropped Ed off this morning. I'd been expecting to see him waiting for me, but there's no sign of him. The knot in my chest has tightened and is creeping up into my throat so that I feel as though I'm choking.

"Don't be silly, he's probably still in the garden," I tell myself. But I can't seem to block out the nagging voice, so I almost abandon the car on a yellow line and run up the path, my eyes swivelling wildly from left to right. But I still can't see him anywhere and I can feel my heart beating too fast in my chest; combined with the heat it's making me feel panicky and dizzy and I have to stop and rest my hands on my thighs.

"Zoe?"

It's only one word but it makes me gasp as I stand and whip my head round. And there he is, my Ed, his familiar shape loping down the path in his cut-off shorts and T-shirt. He looks tanned and healthy, just the same as he did this morning, and my heart soars. It's hard to believe that this was how he looked when he was knocked down and killed the first time round. He seems so — alive.

And this time, he is.

I watch with shaking legs as he gets closer; then he smiles at me and I run at him, almost knocking him over with the impact. I throw my arms around his neck and cling to him, my tears mingling with his sweat as I swear never ever to let go.

"Hey, what's this? What's wrong?" His voice is muffled in my hair but I don't loosen my grip. I hold on tightly and breathe in his scent, feel the warmth of his skin on mine, feel his heart beating in his chest. I can't believe that, after everything that's happened over the last few days, weeks, years, however long I've lived through, I've done it.

I've saved him.

Finally, I pull away. Ed's face is serious, confused. I wipe my face with the back of my hand and sniff. I must look a state.

"Sorry."

Ed tips his head quizzically. "What's going on, Zo? You didn't want me to leave this morning. I've only been gone a few hours and now you're behaving as though you haven't seen me for years. I'm confused."

I shrug.

"I just missed you." It's pathetically inadequate, but it's all I have.

"Are you sure?"

I nod mutely, sniffing again.

He stays silent for a moment, studying me, and my face burns under his gaze. Finally he seems satisfied, and walks towards the car.

"I'm sweating like a pig. Let's get home." He walks towards the car and as he passes me he takes my chin gently in his hand. My whole body shivers. "Are you sure you're OK?"

"I'm fine. Really." My voice is a squeak, but I hope he doesn't notice. "Come on, let's go."

The drive home is quiet, the hum of the radio in the background taking up the space between us. There's so much I want to say to Ed that it's overwhelming me and I don't know where to start. Instead I think back through the days I've relived, through the things I've tried to change. Nothing had seemed to work up to now, but I can only think it was all leading up to this day. This was the day I needed to change.

I glance at the clock. Three o'clock. Last time, Ed was dead by now.

This was my chance to save Ed's life. And I've done it.

A shiver runs through me and I will my heart to slow down. The sun beats through the windscreen, making me sweat, and I try to still my shaking hands.

Finally, we pull up outside our flat. As we let ourselves into the cool hallway, I try to behave like everything's normal and take a deep breath.

"I need a shower. Want to go first?"

Ed nods. "If you don't mind. I'm filthy." He shows me his hands which are covered with dust, mud packed tightly under his nails.

I nod.

"Thanks, sweetheart. See you in a bit." Then he pecks me on the nose and heads to the bathroom, shedding his clothes as he goes. Moments later I hear the gush of water as Ed starts the shower, and I finally allow the tension to drain from my body. I feel as though I'm going to pass out, so I sit on the sofa, letting my head tilt back, and sigh deeply.

I blink back tears and close my eyes, exhaustion suddenly overwhelming me.

"Hey." Ed's voice beside me makes me jump and I sit up quickly. He's dressed, his hair still wet from the shower, droplets of water sliding down his neck and gathering at his collarbone. I imagine licking them off.

He kisses me and smiles. "I'm glad to be home."

"Me too."

A moment of silence. "So what was your good news?"

"What?"

"Your good news, at work?"

I'd forgotten all about it. "Oh, yes. I got a new contract, the one I've been working on. Olive wants me to head it up and — well, it'll mean a lot more work."

"That's great news. I knew you could do it. You're such a clever girl."

I smile weakly.

"You don't seem very happy about it."

"I am. I'm just — sorry, I've got a lot on my mind."

"Care to share it?"

I shake my head. "No, it's fine. It's just work stuff."

"OK." Ed shrugs and moves to stand. Then I have a sudden flash of inspiration. Something that feels worth talking about, now I know it could make a difference. I blurt it out without preamble.

"I think we should stop the IVF."

Ed stops, sits back. "What?"

"I think we should stop. It's ruined enough of our lives. I'd rather be with you, with no baby, than be without you. It's time to stop."

"Wow." Ed looks at me then down at the floorboards. "I didn't see this coming."

"I've been thinking about it for a while."

Ed nods. "I see. So this is why you've been so weird today." I'm happy to let him think that. He turns to face me. "I have to say I'm pretty shocked, Zo. I mean — this is what you've wanted for the last — I don't know, few years."

I shrug. "I know. It was. But it's ruined everything, Ed, and I just think it's time we stopped. I've had enough."

"Wow," he says again. He stares at the fireplace for a few minutes and I wonder whether he's going to say anything else. Then he turns to me. "Zoe, I have to be honest: I'm so glad you've said that. I mean, I'd love to have a baby with you and the thought of us never having one makes my heart hurt. But you're right, this can't go on. It's tearing us apart and I can't lose you. But are you absolutely sure? I mean, I know you are right now, but do you really think this is a decision you're going to be happy with for the rest of your life, just being the two of us?"

I nod. "I know you're worried I'll blame you, or feel resentment every time I see someone with a child, and maybe I will to some extent. I'll always wish I had a child. But if we keep trying and failing I'll always wish I'd stopped and hadn't lost you. I . . ." I stop to wipe the tears from my cheeks. "I can't lose you again, Ed."

He doesn't realize the significance of this but it hardly matters.

Ed shakes his head and looks at me in wonder. "Zoe, I'm so relieved."

"Me too."

He reaches out a hand and wipes my face. I realize my dress is soaked with tears, making it stick to my thighs.

"Come on, sweetheart, don't cry. This is a good decision."

"I know," I say, sniffing. "I know it's good. I just . . ." I stop, leaving it for him to fill in the blanks. But the tears are as much about saving Ed as about losing the baby I never had. And they're tears of relief at suddenly being released from the horror that baby-making has become.

I feel, for the first time in years, free.

I have no idea how much time passes but finally the tears subside and Ed and I are left here, side by side on the sofa. He grabs my hand and lifts my chin so we're facing each other.

"This might not be the right time but I don't care. Shall we go to bed?"

We haven't slept together for months and desire makes my body tremble. I realize I'm gripping his hand as if for dear life.

"Yes please," I whisper.

Silently, Ed stands and I follow, and he leads me by the hand to the bedroom. The bed stands, like a symbol of our mended relationship, waiting for us. Gently, Ed peels my dress from my body, leaving me in just my pants and bra. He lifts his T-shirt over his head, pushes his shorts to the floor then holds his arms out for me to walk into. I almost fall into his embrace and his hands gently stroke my back, my shoulders, my neck and my face. It's passionate but so, so gentle. I tighten my grip on him and lift my head to kiss him.

As we sink onto the bed, a tangle of hot, sweaty limbs, I lose myself totally in the moment. Ed's on top of me, kissing me, then he's inside me, and everything is right with the world.

Later, as we lie on the bed, wrapped in each other's arms, I can't help thinking about how much things have changed. Last time I lived this day it was the worst day of my life and I ended up at Ed's bedside, and he was dead. This time I'm here with his arms around me, and I feel like the luckiest woman in the world.

Next to me, Ed sits up and props himself on his elbow and looks back down at me.

"I reckon this calls for a celebration," he says. His eyes twinkle.

"You're right."

"We should celebrate, tonight."

I roll my eyes and smile. "Any excuse for a drink."

"Yep." He hauls himself into a sitting position.

"Well, if you're so desperate, why don't we go to that cute wine bar in Muswell Hill?"

"Wine bar? Wine won't cut it, Zo. We need champagne!"

"Do we, now? Well, if you insist . . ."

"I do insist."

"OK. But just a few more minutes here. Please?"

"Go on, then."

He grins and lies back down beside me. I watch a shaft of light move slowly across the ceiling as the late afternoon sun burns through the window, still as fierce as it was earlier. Minutes tick by, the day moves on.

"I need a shower."

Ed sniffs. "Yep, I'd say you do."

I slap his arm. "Rude."

He grins. "Maybe. But you do honk."

Laughing, I throw my legs over the side of the bed. I'm starting to feel giddy with the excitement of having saved him, mixed with a knot of tension that's slowly diminishing as it gets later and later in the day. "Don't go anywhere."

"I won't." He throws his arms behind his head and closes his eyes. I turn and head towards the shower. As I stand under the cool water I feel the stress of the day seeping away, down the drain along with the dirty water.

I jump out and dry off, wrap myself in a towel and walk through to the bedroom. When I get to the door I stop. Ed's not there. I peer into the lounge. He's not in there either. I frown. He's probably just making a cuppa.

I throw a clean dress on then walk through to the kitchen to find Ed. He's not there either. Despite myself, I start to feel the knot of tension returning in my belly. Where the hell has he gone?

I grab a Diet Coke from the fridge and head to the back door. The heat hits me in the face as I step outside and I squint against the light. As my eyes adjust I look around the garden. It's only small and I can see instantly Ed's not there.

My heart starts to pound a little harder as I turn and go back into the kitchen. And then I see it. A piece of paper on the table, Ed's writing scrawled across it.

Bugger it. I want champagne now. Have popped to the shop, back in 10. Love you. E x

As I read the words I almost drop my drink, and my hands are shaking so much I have to put it down on the table. He went out!

I have no idea how long he's been gone, so there's no point going after him. I sit down, try to think it through rationally. The shop's only a few minutes away. He'll be back soon, and then everything will be fine.

It will be fine. It has to be.

I take a swig of my Coke, listening for Ed's key in the front door, trying to stay calm. Breathe in, out, in, out.

Ten minutes later there's still no sign of him.

Trying not to panic, I walk to the front window and peer through it. The sun blazes through the glass, making beads of sweat appear on my face and chest again, but still there's no Ed.

I head back into the kitchen and sit down at the table, my breath coming quickly now, my pulse quickening and reaching to the ends of my fingers, into my toes, until my whole body thumps in rhythm. Condensation has gathered on my Coke can and is dripping onto the table. I pick the can up and hold it to my forehead. It feels good on my overheated skin. I hold my head in my hands and stare down at the wooden tabletop, following the lines in the wood with my eyes. The silence in the flat fills my ears and I'm aware I'm holding my breath, listening for the door to open. I sit like that for a while before glancing up at the clock. 5.05. Ed's been gone for fifty minutes now. The blood rushes to my head with a roar, making me dizzy. Why did he have to go? What was he thinking?

I stand on wobbly legs and walk into the living room; I flip the TV on, blindly watching the pictures flicker past. But it's not taking my mind off Ed not being here. Nothing will.

I grab my phone from the table. There are no messages so I press the green button and call the last person I spoke to. Ed. My heart thumps wildly as I listen to the ringing tone and I feel sure that if Ed answers now he'll be able to hear it.

But he doesn't answer.

A wave of nausea washes over me as the voicemail service clicks in and I hear Ed's voice saying, *Sorry I can't take your call at the moment, please leave a message after the beep.*

I click the phone off. I take a deep breath, trying to fill my lungs with air, but I feel faint. I sit on the sofa and tap out a text.

Where are you?

I press Send and then all I can do is wait and hope that it's him that sees it . . .

I lie back on the sofa and try not to let my mind wander to what might or might not have happened to Ed. I reassure myself: *it's only an hour, he's on his way home. Any minute now he'll walk through the door and you'll laugh about this and wonder what on earth you were worried about.*

But the nagging voice I'm trying to subdue is getting louder and I can't ignore it any more.

Did you really think you could change history? it's saying. *Did you really think you could stop Ed dying? Silly girl.*

Tears are running down my cheeks and dripping onto the cushion under my head, and I can't do anything to stop them. I stare at the ceiling, at the patterns the light's forming on it, and the lampshade swims before my eyes. I pull my knees up and twist onto my side so I'm facing the front door. Just in case he comes. Then I'll see him there.

I don't know how long I sit like that, but I watch the sunlight move slowly across the floor and onto the wall so I know some time is passing. And still the flat is filled with silence, so much silence I can hardly bear it, until it presses down on me and I can hardly breathe. I pick my phone up but there's no message, no returned call. I place it gently back on the table again with a shaking hand.

I should ring someone: Jane, Mum, Becky, anyone. But what could they say? They wouldn't understand my terror. They couldn't. Because they don't know what I know. They don't know what happened last time.

So I sit alone, and wait.

The heat of the sun is fading slightly when the ringing of the phone shatters the silence. My heart almost stops and I stand up and snatch the phone from the table, almost dropping it. It's Ed's number.

"Hello," I say, out of breath even though I haven't moved for hours.

There's a beat of silence, and in that moment I know. I know.

"Hello, is this Zoe Williams?" says a deep, unfamiliar voice.

I want to scream; I want to throw the phone across the room and refuse to hear a word this man has to say. But instead I say, "Yes." My voice breaks and I cough to clear my throat which feels dry and sore.

"I'm so sorry but there's been an accident. It's your husband, Edward . . ."

He keeps talking but I don't hear any more. My knees give way beneath me and I perch on the edge of

334

the sofa, tensely. Then I realize there's silence at the other end of the phone.

"Mrs Williams, are you there?" says the voice again.

I know I have to speak, to let them know I can hear them, but somehow the words just won't form in my throat and make their way through my dry, arid mouth. Instead I let out a strangled gargle and the phone drops to the floor, clattering on the wooden floorboards. Seconds pass, minutes, hours, weeks, and I sit there, still as stone. My heart is stone, my body is stone, my mind is stone. Yet I can hear a banging, gentle at first, and then louder, more insistent, like a drummer reaching a crescendo. I move my head slightly towards the front door and I can see two figures silhouetted behind the stained-glass panel, outlined faintly against the dying light. I know I have to open the door and let them in but I can't do it. I can't. It will only be bad news.

But they're not going away, and so I stand and move, zombie-like, towards the front door. The door swings open and two people are standing on my doorstep; sombre faces, dark uniforms. They step into my house and I let them, moving aside numbly as they enter, and leading them into the living room. We sit, the three of us, and I wait for them to speak, not wanting to hear their words but knowing I have to.

"I'm so sorry, Mrs Williams," the female police officer says. "But your husband was hit by a car while he was crossing the road. The car — was travelling too fast and I'm — I'm afraid he didn't make it . . ."

335

I find myself staring at the shiny floorboards, not knowing what to say or how to react. I stare at the police officer's shoes. They're polished to such a shine that the fading sunlight outside is reflected back from their toes. Instead of thinking about Ed dying all over again, I think about this woman getting ready for work this morning, standing in her kitchen, buffing her shoes to a shine, thinking about the day ahead. Had she imagined she'd have to tell someone their husband had died? Had she imagined what that would be like?

I continue to say nothing. My eyes move across the carpet, taking in the scratches on the wooden floor where we'd moved the sofa a few weeks before. I try and work out how I feel, what I want to do, but I don't know, even this time around, what's expected of me. So I just sit there, looking at the floor.

"Mrs Williams?" a voice says.

I look up. Two faces are watching me, waiting for me to say something.

"I . . . I . . ." The words won't come out. "Where is he?" I finally croak.

Relieved finally to have something to say, the male police officer clears his throat. "He was taken to the Royal Free," he says. "We can take you there if you like?"

I nod and stand up, pick my phone off the floor and follow them as they lead me out of the flat and to the waiting police car. The street is oddly quiet, and it feels fitting somehow. In the back of my mind I know I have to ring Mum, Jane, Ed's mum, so as the car rumbles quietly towards the hospital I call the familiar numbers.

I ring Jane first. She's closest and I need someone here with me, right now.

"Hey," she says, her voice light and bright, and it sounds so incongruous I gasp. "Zo, what's wrong?"

"Ed . . ." My voice cracks and I struggle to get the words out. "It's Ed. He's . . . there's been an accident and . . ." I can't finish. I can't say the word.

"Fuck, Zo, where are you?"

"Royal Free." My voice is barely more than a whisper.

"I'm on my way."

As I end the call we're pulling up outside the hospital. There's no time to ring anyone else. The sun is low behind the brown brick building, giving it a strangely Gothic feel silhouetted against the bright sky. I climb out of the car. My legs are shaking and I stumble and the female police officer — I wish I could remember her name — takes my elbow to steady me. We walk together towards the doors and as I walk through them I feel as though I'm being swallowed into hell.

They lead me to a bank of chairs in a small room tucked away in the depths of the hospital. As I wait I stare blindly at the posters on the wall opposite me for bereavement counselling and depression. I read the words but I don't take them in. And then I hear a familiar voice and I look up and there's Jane. She runs towards me across the tiny room and then her arms are wrapped tightly round me and I'm sobbing: huge, jerking, body-wracking sobs that make me feel as though I'm going to break in two.

"He — he's dead," I gulp through thick, snotty tears.

"Oh Zoe, Zoe, Zoe." Jane holds me and rubs my back until my sobs subside and then we sit, holding hands.

"Things have been so bad — between me and Ed — but — but today was different. Today he didn't hate me . . ."

"Zoe, Ed would never hate you. He's always adored you, and he knew you loved him. Please, please don't think like that, my darling friend."

"But we've been so angry with each other and — he only went to get champagne and — I told him not to go but he went anyway and now it's all too late and I didn't even get to say goodbye. What the hell am I going to do?"

Before Jane can answer, the doctor is there and we're being led to where Ed is, to identify his body. The doctor explains that he was hit by a car as he was crossing the road, that he stood no chance, that he was dead on arrival at hospital. The words "massive brain trauma" drift in and out of my head but I can't think about Ed in pain, hurting. All I can think is why. Why did I let him leave the house? He'd got home safely, we were on the home run, we'd almost got through the day with him alive, and had possibly even changed things forever. And then I'd let him leave.

A part of me knows that maybe this was always going to happen anyway, that maybe there was no way I was ever going to be allowed to change the course of history. But I can't stop thinking about the moment I left him, lying in bed. About how alive he looked, how happy and content.

I'm led to Ed's bedside. And despite the injuries — they've cleaned him up as best they can but there are still traces of blood on his face and down his chest — I can see my Ed lying there, and the urge to reach out and touch him, hold him and tell him everything's going to be OK, is overwhelming. But I can't do it.

Instead I nod. "Yes, that's him." Then I turn and walk away numbly, Jane holding me up by the shoulders.

The next few hours are a blur. People bring tea, give me hugs; there's the whoosh of trolleys passing by the relatives" room. Then Susan arrives and we hold each other, united in a grief that threatens to overwhelm us both.

And through it all, I feel angry too. Angry that I've been made, for whatever reason, to live through losing the love of my life all over again. Once was hard enough; once was almost enough to break me. But twice — twice was just cruel when, in the end, nothing changed. In the end, Ed still died.

How can I live the rest of my life knowing that I let him down?

CHAPTER
TWENTY

10 September 2013

My eyes are still closed but I can already tell that today is different. It could be something about the light, about the brightness of it seeping through my eyelids; or it could be the noises filtering into my consciousness. Instead of the gentle sounds of everyday life — kettles boiling, socked feet padding softly on carpet, radios playing gently in the background — everything here is louder and more abrasive. Heels clack on hard tiles, voices shout loudly, bangs and beeps and scrapes and bumps pound into my head, like a woodpecker trying to bore a hole in wood. The sounds of a hospital.

And with a crashing certainty I know where I am. I'm back in the present — whenever the present actually is. What I don't know is how I'm going to be and who's going to be here when I open my eyes.

I listen more carefully, trying to tune my ears to any softer, more subtle sounds. Can I hear someone breathing? I'm not sure. Wait, what was that? A rustle and a soft pat. A page turning? Someone reading next to my bedside? Or is it just someone looking at my notes, checking up on me?

340

I inhale deeply, readying myself to open my eyes. One, two, three . . . *open*.

But they won't move. They feel as though they've been closed forever. I long to lift my hands and rub them, as though just waking from a good night's sleep, but my limbs don't seem to want to work either so I try my eyes again. Slowly I feel my left lid moving and a tiny slit opens, letting sunlight pour in, filling my head with white. I snap it shut again and wait for the light to stop dancing in the dark of my mind.

Right, I can do this. I can open my eyes. I have to do this.

I force them open again and this time my left eye opens almost all the way and my right eye opens a little. It feels as though a 1,000-watt bulb is being shone into my eyes, but I don't close them; I keep them open, blinking and watering against the pain. I blink the tears away and feel them running down my cheeks towards my ears and dropping onto the pillow, and slowly, slowly, the world starts to swim into focus. A light fixture on a white ceiling. A ceiling divided into squares. An ugly light fixture, switched off. I flick my eyes to the right. A window with ribbons of light pouring through the dusty grey blinds, making the room feel more cheerful than it should. And then there's a movement next to me and a face appears above me. There's a gasp and an, "Oh my God, she's opened her eyes," and a cold hand grabs mine and squeezes, and I squeeze back as hard as I can.

"Zoe, can you hear me? Zoe, it's Mum."

"Nnnggngng."

"Wait, don't try to speak, let me get someone." Footsteps running off and then getting closer again. "I'll be back, will you be OK?"

"Nnngg."

Footsteps retreating once more and excited voices in the corridor outside. Lots of footsteps coming back towards me, and then there are figures silhouetted against the sunlight surrounding my bed. I feel like an animal in a zoo as they stand over me, fussing and discussing me as though I'm not there. Only two voices stand out against the murmur.

"Mum . . . Dad," I manage through a dry throat.

"Oh Zoe, thank God you're awake." Mum throws herself against me, trying to be gentle but squeezing me as tightly as she dares. I long to throw my arms around her too but my muscles don't want to work.

"Hi, Mum," I say instead.

I want to know what's happened to me. Where I am, why, and most of all, whether anything has changed. Is Ed still dead or did I dream it all? I can't work out what's fact from fiction any more. But I know they'll tell me and for now I just need to adjust to being awake again.

Mum takes my hand and holds it tenderly as the doctors fly around me. There are wires and leads attaching me to various monitors, and printouts covered in lines and graphs and numbers are being waved around the room. It's all about me but I don't want to know any of that now. It doesn't matter.

"Mum," I whisper, and she leans down towards me to hear me better. "Can you sit me up?"

Nodding, Mum presses a button and slowly the bed tilts me into a sitting position so I can see what's going on.

"That's enough, Mrs Morgan," says the doctor. "We need to do some tests first; try not to disturb her too much, please. And try not to tire her out." Then the room empties and the room is quiet.

Mum perches on the edge of the bed, nervously. "We thought we'd lost you, love," she says. Her voice cracks and there are tears shining in her eyes. She pauses, looks at Dad, then back at me. Her eyes are dark with worry. "Do — do you remember anything at all . . .?" She trails off, unsure.

I nod, my neck stiff. "You mean Ed, don't you?"

"Yes, love."

"Yes, Mum. I remember. Ed's dead."

Silence fills the room as the words settle round us, as my mind takes in the certainty that he's still gone. I groan, the pain too much to bear.

"Oh love, I'm so sorry. Try not to get too upset, you've only just woken up." Mum's stroking my hair down, her skin soft against my cheek. "Do you remember anything about your accident?"

Do I? I remember being soaked to the skin, wet leaves, a pain in my head, bright lights, shouting. And then I'd woken up in the past. I shake my head. "Not really."

"You banged your head, love. You were — doing some gardening and it was raining and you must have slipped and hit your head. Jane found you, when she called in after work. She was worried about you. And thank God she did or we could have lost you . . . we didn't know what you might have done to yourself, with the grief." She stops, a sob escaping her lips.

"Sandra." Dad's voice is firm and she looks up, shocked. He shakes his head. "Don't."

"No. Sorry, love. I just mean — you were still so sad. We've all been so worried about you since —" She stops, but I know what she was going to say. Since Ed died. She sits up straight, smooths the blanket under her hand. "Anyway, you knocked yourself out and you've been here ever since."

"How long have I been here?"

Mum looks down again, then back at me. "Almost a month, love."

A month? I've just relived the last twenty years of my life in less than four weeks? It doesn't seem possible.

"Oh." There's so much I want to say but can't; it's all I manage.

Mum glances at Dad again and I can tell there's something else.

"What? What is it?"

"What do you mean?" But Mum's a terrible liar and she knows it.

There's a moment of silence as we sit there looking at each other, each waiting for the other to speak. What are they going to say? Is it about Ed? Is it about me? Has something terrible happened since I've been in hospital? I can't bear it any longer.

"Come on, just tell me!" I shout and they both jump, shocked.

Dad speaks first.

"Well, there is something." He waits a beat and it stretches into a lifetime. "It's about the baby."

The room seems to tilt as he says these words and I grip the bed tightly, afraid I'm going to fall out.

"Baby?"

"Yes," Mum says. "Your baby is OK, it's going to be OK."

I think I'm going to be sick and I clutch my hand to my mouth to stop it.

"Oh God, Zoe, what's wrong?" Mum leaps up from her seat, grabs a cardboard bowl and sticks it under my chin, scraping my hair back from my face. My stomach heaves and I retch but there's nothing to come out, and after a few minutes the heaving stops and I settle back onto the pillow, totally drained.

"I didn't know there was a baby," I whisper.

Mum gasps and claps her hand to her mouth. "But . . ." She stops. "Oh God, Zoe, we assumed you knew and would be worried about it," she says. Her words fall out of her mouth like a torrent of water. "I mean, after everything you two went through to have a baby, we just thought you must know and . . ."

The silence between us is enormous as what I've just found out hits us all.

I'm pregnant.

"How . . . how many weeks?" I say.

"The doctors think about twelve . . ."

Oh my God. Twelve weeks. My mind races back, trying to work out what that means. When I collapsed Ed had been dead for two months. Plus another four or five weeks since then, and that means the day I fell pregnant must have been the last day we had together, the day we were never meant to have . . .

"Oh my God. I changed it." The words are barely a whisper but Mum hears them anyway.

"What do you mean, love?"

"Nothing, Mum, sorry. I'm all over the place." I give her a weak smile and she smiles back, unsure. She looks as though she wants to say something else, then changes her mind.

I have a sudden need to be alone, to take in the enormity of what's just happened.

So I close my eyes and lie still for a few minutes until I hear Mum and Dad standing up and opening the door. They slip outside and the door closes behind them and then there's just peace and quiet, and time to think . . .

I think back to that last day. I'd been so sure Ed was going to live: that saving him had been the reason I'd been taken back to live the whole thing all over again. Then when he'd died anyway I'd been utterly distraught, thinking I'd failed him. I hadn't had time to think about the possibility that maybe, just maybe, the last day we'd had together *was* the thing that I'd changed, the one thing that I'd managed to make different from the first time. We'd loved each other that day, and been together in a way we hadn't been for a long time before that.

But even if I had thought about it, then of course it would never have occurred to me that I might be pregnant. I'd never managed to fall pregnant before, even with all the help we'd been given. We'd been

346

through hell and back to have a baby and we'd been left heartbroken time and time again.

And now, after all that, this.

A baby.

Ed had left me, but he'd given me the greatest gift of all. He'd left a part of him behind.

I open my eyes and push the covers off me and place my hands gently on my belly. If you didn't know you wouldn't know there was anything in there, but I can see a slight swell through the hospital gown and I rub my palms gently across my tummy, back and forth. It feels warm to my touch.

"Thank you," I whisper, and for a moment I can almost imagine that Ed is there with me, watching this moment.

And then, with my hands placed across my tummy and the gentle hum of the hospital behind me, I fall asleep. And this time, for the first time in months, it's a proper, deep, dreamless sleep.

I snap my eyes open and my heart is pounding. My eyes flick round the room desperately, and I try to lift my head but it feels too heavy and drops silently back down onto the pillow. I take some deep breaths and try to calm myself down. I'm in the hospital, it's OK, it's finished. It's not happening all over again.

My heart rate is gradually slowing, the seconds between each beat increasing, stretching out, the rushing in my ears diminishing.

And then I remember.

I lift my hands from the bed and slowly bring them to rest on my tummy. The tiny swelling I'd noticed yesterday doesn't seem as obvious now and I'm worried I might have dreamt it all. After all, it's not as though the last few weeks have been exactly normal. But I know it's true. Somehow I feel different. I feel as though this is what is meant to be.

I lie like that for a few moments, believing that I'm bringing myself closer to the baby I knew nothing about until only a few hours before. It's been growing for twelve weeks without any help from me, and I try to picture what it must look like now. Will it have any features, or will it still be a round blob of matter? Will it have any resemblances to Ed that will take my breath away when I see them for the first time? Will it have his eyes, his nose, his mouth?

Tears roll down my cheeks, soaking the pillow beneath me, but I don't wipe them away. I want to keep my hands where they are, for now.

Minutes pass and the room is filled with peace. There are no machines whirring, beeping or humming, and there's no one else here. Just me and my baby, and the sounds of the hospital rumbling away outside the door. Then I notice a creaking sound and I glance over to the door, which is very slowly inching open.

"Hello?"

A familiar face peeps round the door and I smile.

"Hi, Mum. What are you doing creeping around like that?"

"Sorry, love, I didn't know whether you were asleep or not. I didn't want to wake you." Mum comes fully

348

into the room and sits down gently on the edge of my bed. The mattress sags under her weight and I roll slightly towards her. "How are you feeling?"

I think about it for a minute before answering. How am I feeling? Happy, sad, relieved, frightened, excited, confused . . . all of those things and more.

"I'm scared, Mum."

She squeezes my hand. "Oh sweetheart."

"I just wish — I just wish Ed could be here to see this. To meet our baby."

She nods silently.

"What if I can't do this on my own?"

"What do you mean?"

"Well, I've never been a mum before, and I always thought if I did have a baby me and Ed would look after it together, both feed it, cuddle it, change its nappies. I never once pictured doing this alone, I —" My voice catches in my throat and I stop.

"I know, I know. But you know your dad and I will do everything we can to help you, don't you? And Becky too."

"Thank you." My voice is a whisper. But I haven't said half of what I'm really feeling. I feel empty, like a shell, and I'm terrified I won't have enough love left in me to give to my baby; I'm scared that the grief and the pain will be too much for me to ignore and that I'll let my baby down. Like I let Ed down. I should have been able to save him, so he could be here with us right now.

But I don't say any of this. Instead I just sink slowly into my pillow and close my eyes and pretend to be asleep until I hear Mum get up and leave.

Epilogue

19 June 2015

It's a cloudy day and a gentle breeze blows my hair across my face. I'm out of breath as I push the buggy in front of me up the steep path to the top of the hill and I pause for a second to catch my breath before carrying on.

At the top we stop and look at the scene below us. London stretches out for as far as the eye can see. A dark thundercloud looms in the distance somewhere over Canary Wharf, and I shiver.

I place my bag on the bench and glance around. The weather means there are not as many people about as usual, and I'm grateful. It makes this a little easier.

"Mummy ba-bim," Edward says, pointing in the air and grinning.

"Yes, sweetheart, Mummy's got the balloons," I say, and I untie them from the handle of the buggy and bring them down level with his gaze. He reaches out a chubby hand and pushes one and giggles as it bounces straight back up in the air again.

"'Gen!" he shouts and does it again, giggling hysterically.

"OK, sweetheart, shall we get you out of the buggy?"

"Yeah!"

Careful not to let go of the balloons that are bouncing about wildly in the breeze, I unclip Edward's straps and he climbs cautiously out. I sit down on the bench and he plops himself down next to me.

"Right, we're going to let these balloons go into the sky and see Daddy," I explain slowly.

He nods solemnly.

"Hopefully Daddy will catch one and keep it with him forever and know it's from us and know we love him."

He nods again.

"Shall we do it?"

"Yeah!"

I hand him a balloon and he grips it tightly. "OK, when I say go, let it go. One, two, three, *go!*"

"Go!" he shouts, and throws the balloon up into the air. It catches the breeze and floats sharply to the left before taking flight. We sit and stare after it, then I let another one go, and another, and another, until all eight of them have lifted into the sky.

"Dada," Edward says, pointing at the sky with a chubby finger.

I smile and pull him onto my lap and hold him tightly.

"Yes, exactly, Daddy," I agree.

We sit like that for a few minutes until the last balloon has floated out of sight. Then I notice the temperature has dropped and I shiver.

"OK, let's go home."

I scoop Edward up and clip him back into his buggy and walk slowly back down the hill, lost in thought. I'd been desperate to do this alone, to mark the two-year anniversary of Ed's death, just me and our son. But now it feels a little lonely and I wish I'd asked Mum and Dad or Ed's mum to come along.

But at least I'll see them later. Last year had been awful — Edward had been three months old and we'd tried to hold a memorial service for Ed. But I was a bundle of emotion and I couldn't stop crying. This year, determined to make it special for my precious son, I'd brought him to Alexandra Palace, where Ed and I had spent so many happy times, to release some balloons in memory of the daddy he never knew. He was too young to understand, but the joy in his face as he watched them rise up into the sky and disappear into the clouds made it worthwhile.

Later, we're having a memorial service with close friends and family. Jane has helped me organize it and I'm so grateful. She's been there through everything since Ed died and I'm not sure I could have done it without her.

Now, as Edward and I make our way back home to get ready, I smile. It's been a long time coming, but I finally feel ready to face life without Ed.

After all, he left me the most precious gift of all.

Acknowledgements

Writing a thank you section for the back of my very own book makes me feel how an actor must feel writing an Oscar acceptance speech: it's something you dream about, but never really believe you'll need. So forgive me if I ramble, or if I forget anyone. It must be all the excitement.

First, I need to thank my lovely, lovely first readers, Serena and Zoe (whose only resemblance to fictional Zoe is the name!), whose enthusiasm for the story helped me carry on and make it to the end. Thank you also to the very talented Katy Regan, who helped me see the wood for the trees, and, of course, to my very tolerant friends for listening to me endlessly going on about it, especially Sarah G, Rachel and Viks, who undoubtedly bore the brunt.

This book would have lingered in my virtual bottom drawer, however, had it not been for Judith Murray, who is not only a brilliant agent, but also one of the nicest people I've ever met. She saw potential in me, Zoe and Ed, and helped me shape the book into what it's become. So thank you Judith, you made my dream come true. There are of course many other people at

Greene and Heaton to thank, in particular the indomitable Kate Rizzo for her amazing tenacity and hard work.

A massive thank you also goes out to the wonderful team at Pan Macmillan — everyone who enthused about the book and how much it made them cry (sorry!) gave me a huge boost; but most of all thank you to Victoria Hughes-Williams, my brilliant editor, who knows a thing or two about making people cry herself, and helped me bring out the best in the final drafts.

Some very kind people gave up their time to talk to me about various subjects in the course of my research, including Andrew Taylor from the charity Headway and Sophie Franklin from Zita West Clinics. A special thank you goes to my friend Jo Littlejohn for sharing her story with me. It helped enormously with understanding Zoe's heartache about infertility.

There are no doubt many many more people I should be thanking, including my lovely Mum and Dad, who always encouraged me to follow my dreams. But I can't finish without saying a huge thank you to my husband, Tom, whose patience and kindness helped me find the time to finally get the book finished. I couldn't have done it without you, even if you still haven't read it . . .

And thank you, Jack and Harry, for always being my inspiration.